# CHARLIE FORD MEETS THE MOLE

# Charlie Ford Meets The Mole
## by
## J. D. Tynan

A-Argus Better Book Publishers, LLC
North Carolina***New Jersey

# Charlie Ford Meets The Mole

A-Argus Better Book Publishers, LLC
For Information:
Argus Enterprises International, Inc.
P O Box 914
Kernersville, NC 27284
www.a-argusbooks.com

ISBN:  0-9801555-8-4
ISBN:  978-0-9801555-8-7

Book Cover designed by Dubya

Printed in the United States of America

# ~~Dedication~~

To Jim, James and Shea. You are my life, my loves, my best friends and all I could ever ask for.

# ~~Thank You~~

To Tisha Woodard, for being lifetime friend and excellent editor. Thanks for catching my mistakes and helping me with the daunting task of getting this novel ready for publication. I love you.

To Debo, from J.A. for the good times past and the ones still yet to come. Thanks for your unconditional friendship.

To Maggie and Bill for their guidance, patience and perseverance

To my friends Linda and Terri. You mean the world to me and life wouldn't be the same without friends like you.

To John P. for listening.

Thanks to all the staff at Blackstone in Vancouver who stand beside me in the toughest of times. To Tony for believing in me even when I was in a horrible December funk...and thanks for inventing the Pink Pear Martini. To Cherica, Wendy and Joy for being the best coworkers ever. Tara, thanks for your laughter and witty sarcasm that kept me smiling on a daily basis. Shawn...you know why I love you! Thanks for coming into my life and making it a more 'sparkly' place. Melissa for putting up with all my nuttiness, sometimes when things aren't even that funny. Christina, thanks for the hugs. Nicole—for your smile and enthusiasm. And to

Dennis who has opened my eyes to the world of wine.

# Prologue

"You're a very difficult woman to find, Charlie Ford." His deep voice was husky and tattered. Thank God, he sounded American. My heart flip-flopped again, but in a good way that time. I saw his lean arm ease toward the lamp, and then he clicked it on and sent me the sexiest, most confident smile I had ever seen. He eased forward and leaned so his elbows rested on his knees. He seemed completely relaxed and damned sure of himself. The man definitely had cajones.

I, on the other hand, was expressionless and bamboozled and so far from relaxed it wasn't funny.

He looked so much different from the last time I set eyes on him. His black hair was extremely short, and he'd grown a goatee. His face had healed nicely except for a small scar across his left cheek that was clearly visible in the dim light. I'd never been fond of Hawaiian shirts, but he managed to make it look sexy as hell.

I opened my mouth to speak, but no words would come. It was as if someone had sucked my brains out through my ears and all that remained was undecipherable gibberish.

He just stared at me, willing me to speak and then tried to speed it along by raising one eyebrow and giving me a wink.

"You," I finally shouted because I was that mad he scared me, and that happy to see him. I moved toward him swiftly, unsure if I was going to fall into his arms or smack him in the face.

He jumped up and caught my fist in his hand before it connected with his chin. This man kept me on my toes. He twisted my right arm behind my back and held it tightly against my bare skin.

"Aren't you happy to see me?" he asked.

I whimpered in his grasp. I was so fucking happy to see him, I couldn't see straight, but that didn't change the fact that he deserved a good pop in the mouth. It had been six weeks. Six weeks without a phone call or a post card to apologize for the interrogation room. Nothing.

His hot mouth closed tightly over mine when I didn't respond to his question. I think at that time my body language told him exactly what he wanted to know. I couldn't get enough of him and when I felt the warmth of his tongue touch mine, I crawled up his body and wrapped my thighs around his hips. I'd never felt so much raw desire for a man before. It was as if I was being sucked into a vortex of sexual need and nothing short of death was going to stop me from crawling into his shorts. Besides, it was very cool to be kissing Secret Agent Man again.

Then again...

I pulled back abruptly and gave him a glare, dropped my bare feet to the tile floor and moved away from the hand that had just clamped onto my erect nipple. I had so many questions.

"Why were you there? Why did you sit there and pretend that you didn't know me? Why?"

"Do we have to do this now?" he asked breathlessly, and moved closer, so close that I felt every hard part of him and he felt good. He began kissing down my neck, across my throat, up to the soft flesh of my ear. He whispered some things that he wanted to do to me.

My knees buckled, my toes curled. I let out a throaty whimper and then pushed him away.

"I don't even know you. I don't know your name. I don't know if you have brothers or sisters, or where you were born." I did slap him this time--in the chest, because he was too cute to slap in the face. He grabbed my hand and pulled me closer; so close that his lips touched mine when he smiled.

"Can we play twenty questions later? I've waited a long time for you, Charlie Ford."

Well hell, if that's not a good line -- I don't know what is.

I kissed him this time and wrapped my arms around his neck to bring him even closer. I kissed him with passion and tenderness, ran my fingers up and down his neck, into his stubbly hair, around his ears, and finally cradled his face in the palms of my hands before coming up for air and then starting all over again. I moaned and shifted against his body before breaking from the kiss again. I brushed his lips with mine and stared into his dark sultry eyes.

"No." I pushed him away playfully and ran from his grasp. I moved to the other side of the bed. "We do this now." Looking over at the bedside table, I let out a giggle. That stack of Belgium chocolate bars wasn't there when I left for dinner. My laughter prodded him to move closer to the bed.

I reached up and held the button of my red sundress between my fingers, teasing him into telling me the truth. "What's your name?" I asked sternly, and tried to keep the smile from spreading across my flushed cheeks. "Real name this time."

This action on my part induced a salacious grin to tug at his lips and then he popped the top button on his denim shorts. "Jack."

"Jack what?" I asked.

He smiled and took two more steps towards the bed. "Jack Edward Sullivan."

I undid one button and let the first strap hang over my chest, exposing the top half of one bare breast. I could see the change in his eyes. He'd seen my breasts before, but not quite like this. I watched his eyes narrow, his brows crease together and his chest rise and fall quicker than normal.

I had him right where I wanted him.

"Where were you born?" I held on tight to the button on the other side, rolling my fingers along the button before slipping it half way through its loop.

He licked his lips. "San Diego."

I let the other strap fall, but my breasts held the dress in place.

I looked down, then back into his eyes, and smiled.

He smiled. "Here's my driver's license." He grabbed for his wallet and tossed it onto the bed.

I opened it, found his driver's license that had the name Jack Sullivan on it. The address read Baltimore, Maryland. His age was thirty-six. That surprised me, I figured him for about thirty-three. Height: six feet, weight: one hundred and eighty five pounds. I flipped through the credit cards. They all read Jack E. Sullivan too.

I looked up and caught him taking off his Hawaiian-print shirt. My jaw dropped. I swear his pectorals had grown over the last six weeks. I think I licked my lips and moaned.

"This doesn't mean anything. You could have forged these." I flipped through his money. A couple of twenties, three fives and four ones and then I found…. "What's this for?" I held up the condom and grinned. I suppose I was doing a good job at pretending to be demure, that is until I giggled. "What? Only one?" That didn't last long. Now I was doing a good impression of an insatiable hussy. Oh well.

He smiled and kicked off his shoes.

~~~

When I once said he was quick, I only meant on his feet. In bed, he moved like a sloth. Every minute counted. Each stroke of his hand against my bare skin felt perfectly orchestrated. Every precisely planted kiss meant something special and there was not one damn thing about it that I took for granted. I made love with him as if it was the only time in my life I was going to be lucky enough to do so.

When the intense breathing stopped and I was appreciating my afterglow, Jack rolled onto his side and smiled. "I heard about Bella from my sources at Interpol and I knew you had to be with her." He offered out of nowhere then laid his cheek on my bare breast.

I wasn't even thinking about Armenia. I was thinking how magnificent he was in bed. The past was the past. Okay, so I did appreciate the confession at that point. Hell, I'd just slept with the man. It was nice that he was finally opening up to me.

"How did you find me?"

"I have my ways." Once a Secret Agent Man, always a Secret Agent Man.

"So, it was you who orchestrated my rescue from The Rat?" I asked as I snuggled my arms tighter around the man who had saved my life. More than once, I might add. I inhaled deeply and closed my eyes.

"Uh huh." He nodded and kissed me again with tenderness. I appreciated his caresses because I knew he came for me. He was so much more than Secret Agent Man. "I also heard everything about what happened to you and I'm sorry that you got caught up in that mess that had nothing to do with you. DuLucere taped your statement and sent it to me." He actually looked sympathetic to my pain. "I also know that you were paid a visit from one of ours.... Doug Lyons."

I popped my head off the pillow. Doug Lyons was the man who had threatened to erase my memory in that damp little room in Armenia. He was also the nice man who gave me a makeshift passport and paid my airfare home. "He's one of yours?"

"Sort of," he said, and began kissing me again with that same lustful yearning.

I knew I'd never get a straight answer out of him, but I was willing to bribe him with sex, repeatedly, until he spills his guts.

~~~

We ended up doing it four more times before cuddling under the covers and finally talking about his family.

"I have two sisters, Robin and Kristina. My parents Edward and Megan are still married. They live in Sacramento." He licked his lips slowly. "If I tell you anymore than that I'll have to kill you." He kissed me again and licked down my stomach to find where he had left that last piece of chocolate.

When he returned, I still couldn't catch my breath, but I was smiling and I felt fine with the fact that I wasn't receiving oxygen.

"Come to work with me, Charlie," he said, then quickly kissed me before my eyes popped out of my skull.

"Uhhhh." I was still recovering from the tongue bath I had just received. "What do you mean?"

"We'd be good together, Charlie."

Okay, so his mind had melted into mush by all the hot sex. He couldn't be serious.

"Are you serious?" I propped up onto my elbow and looked directly into his satisfied dark eyes. I do have to say that it did sound appealing in a weird and freakish kind of way.

"Think about it." He rolled off the bed and left me alone and naked to think about going to work with Secret Agent Man. This sort of thing doesn't happen every day, not to people like me.

"I'm not finished with my masters," I yelled toward the kitchenette. He came back to me with a bottle of champagne and no glasses. "I'm going to be a police detective, I was going to buy a place in the country, with acres and acres of

8

jackrabbits and I already bought my dream SUV...."

His kiss was warm and inviting. As was his hand on the back of my neck. "A police woman, Charlie?" His head shook in disapproval. "Come on, honey. You have skills. You have instincts. Your moves need a little bit of work..." he chuckled playfully, and dodged my hand. "...but other than that, you're pretty much a shoo in."

I blinked once or twice and scrunched my brows together. My moves need a little work? If I weren't naked, I would flip his ass onto the ground and show him a thing or two. Oh. Maybe that would be fun with no clothes on.

The cork bounced off the ceiling.

"I don't even know who you work for." I took the bottle of Dom Perignon that he offered me and sipped carefully, never taking my eyes off his.

One of his brows cocked and bounced up and down dramatically. "I think you know."

"Okay," I scoffed. "So I have an idea."

He bent and nibbled my ear, whispered something intriguing and crawled back into my bed.

I was right. He works for the _ _ _.

# Chapter One

When I was a little girl, I had dreams of becoming a doctor. My father was a surgeon, and to me, he was Godlike. We lived in Bend, Oregon and he was on staff at St. Charles Medical Center, where he spent the majority of his time. He wasn't the most doting father, but he looked like an angel in his long white overcoat. After a few visits to the hospital at the tender age of twelve, I soon found out I had a slight adverse reaction to the sight of blood. To be completely honest, it wasn't all that slight. My eyes would roll back into my skull. My fingertips and toes would tingle, and then I'd see millions of tiny white specks right before my head would hit the cold Linoleum. Yep, that pretty much sealed my fate as a pansy-ass girl. I spent more time on a gurney than I did walking around behind my father. Pathetic, aren't I?

Well, I eventually grew up. Now I'm a nanny. It's a pretty fair assumption to say that blood usually doesn't come into play much in my occupation. Just sometimes, when a toddler falls off his tricycle, or scrapes his knee while playing

Duck, Duck, Goose. I've been in the 'domestic technician' line of work for over four years now. Before that, I spent eight years in the Army learning all sorts of new and valuable, yet deadly, skills.

Currently, I live in a small cottage out behind the main house of the most impressive mansion that I've ever seen. My employer's name is Roald Munson. Never heard of him? Then you must not go to the movies. Roald Munson happens to be the hottest and most sought after action hero of our time. He's a legend in Europe from his earlier days of really bad B movies, but ever since Hollywood's top producer discovered him, it's been champagne wishes and caviar dreams for the Fabio look alike. And I live with the man. How lucky am I?

That's subjective of course. Not too long ago, I accompanied his daughter, Bella to Africa and well -- let's just say -- No, I'm not lucky. Our plane ended up being hi-jacked; we were shanghaied by a secret agent man and nearly died on several occasions. I was forced to eat burnt peacock and barbecued figs and had to see a lot of blood, some of which I had a hand in spilling. The one good thing that came out of it was it strengthened my relationships with those I love-- one in particular.

"Bella!" I shouted from the bottom of the stairs, nearing a glass-breaking-caliber shriek. Bella and I have been through a lot together. At first, she hated me, much like any other kid I've ever babysat for. Then we grew much closer during our adventure abroad last summer and now I love her like a friend or even a sister, but she's just so darn…well, she's a teenager! "Bella, get down here, now!" I screamed.

The living room looked as if it had been hit by a tornado. Pizza boxes were stacked in the corner by the stereo. Pop cans and empty bags of chips were crammed between the black leather couch cushions. Every CD was lying on the table, some of them broken. A bra was dangling from the crystal chandelier and the television had been slimed by… "Gross." I wiped my finger across the gunk and gave it a whiff. "Chocolate pudding and popcorn. Son of a bitch…"

"I heard that. You owe me twenty-five cents," her voice shrilled from atop the long flight of stairs. Bella has long blonde hair that she pays good money to have highlighted with burgundy and brunette. After last fall's growing spurt, she's now my height; five-foot-eight, and she could easily pass for seventeen thanks to the clothes that her mother, famous actress Nicole Harrison, lets her buy. -- Most likely to dissuade her guilt for leaving Bella's father and bed-hopping her way through Hollywood's A-list. Nicole Harrison had been married three times before marrying Roald, and shortly after their divorce was final back in December, I heard a rumor that she was already secretly engaged to another action star who shall remain nameless.

"What do you want? ' Pimp my Ride' is on," Bella said with contempt.

Pimp my what?

Needless to say, I know nothing about the age of
MTV, teenagers, and what is cool in this day and
age. When I grew up, we listened to Duran
Duran, Tears for Fears and New Kids on the
Block. We had pictures of Michael J. Fox on our
walls. Izods were popular, along with Polo and
Esprit, and our Lawman and Guess jeans were
actually made to stay on our teenage butts. Bare-
midriffs were only visible on sluts, and our
parents would never permit us to watch
something with the word Pimp in the title. A lot
has changed since I was thirteen.
I blinked and wiped the pudding off my finger
and back onto the seventy-two inch high
definition plasma television where it apparently
belonged.        "Get down here and clean this up,
now!" I stomped my foot into the hardwood.
"And that bra had better not be yours." I glared
hard. I kept her in line most of the time because
she respects me and I tend to not take as much of
her bullshit as her parents do. I'm her one and
only link to the outside world when her father is
out of the country; so needless to say, I try to run
a tight ship. But right then, my pulse was in high
gear. I'd had a very good night's sleep after an
amazing bout of hot sex. I'd already had my V-8,
been to the gym, and taken my first final of the
week. I had three more to go before I was
officially finished with my master's degree in
Criminal Justice and Bella was not making it easy
on me. Finals are hellacious enough without
having to worry about a teenager on the rampage.
Her father was coincidentally out of town again,

re-shooting an entire battle scene in Greece for an upcoming Epic called Zeus and his Mistress.

"As if." Her fingers wrapped around the brass railing as she leaned over and shrugged, completely flippant about the mess she'd made. "Laura-Lee can do it. That's why Daddy pays her." Her long blonde hair flipped over her shoulder as she turned on her heel to leave me alone with the mess that she and her entourage had made the night before.

"Damn it, Bella, I'm not kidding. Get your ass down here, now!"

I could almost see the smoke seeping from her ears as she mentally counted up how much money I owed her for that one. Gregory had coerced me into giving up cussing, therefore Bella was on my ass about every obscenity that was uttered. Gregory Pike has been with Roald and Bella for over ten years. He takes care of the house, the pool and the seven acres that surround the house. He does it all, except for the cleaning, the gardening and the cooking.
Honestly, I don't really know why he gets paid.

"Thirty-five cents, please." She actually snickered at me and stuck out her hand.

I felt as if my eyeballs were going to pop from their sockets, then I heard the pitter-patter of Hamlet and Othello, followed closely by Gregory. His bedroom was to the right of where I was screaming and from the looks of his scowl, he wasn't happy that I woke him. Both Great Danes walked at attention by his side.

"Well, holy Hell!" He planted his hands on his hips and rotated his head to also look up at Bella.

She stared wide-eyed at me until I huffed and turned my venom on Greg. "Where the hell were you when all this was going on? Those earplugs I gave you can't work that good. This place is a national disaster area."

Gregory and I had traded nights watching Bella when Jack had suddenly become available last night because someone had leaked information about his whereabouts and thus his car had been blown to smithereens somewhere in East Los Angeles.

Jack's the secret agent who shanghaied us in Africa. He not only saved my life a couple of times, he also seduced me into bed, and more recently was still trying to coerce me into working with him. I'm still not quite sure about that last part, but I'll remain in his bed for as long as he'll have me. Jack is sexy!

Gregory was still contemplating his apparent brain-fart with a confused scowl. "Oh shit."

Both Bella and I spoke at once. "That's a quarter."

Gregory was also trying to clean up his own potty mouth, so it was a group venture. Even Bella had to fork over her change if she got caught. But come on, she's just thirteen. She still knows how to be sneaky.

"That was last night?" Gregory said and sank back against the couch, leaning right into a

big smear of something brown and shiny. More
pudding I presume. "I completely spaced it. There
was this vintage film festival downtown and Luke
and I just got to talking and the next thing I knew
we were holding hands and watching Breakfast at
Tiffany's." He sighed, clearly remembering his
intimate moment with Luke. "I love that movie!"
Or more like fantasizing about George Peppard.
Frankly, I think George was much hotter when he
was in charge of the A-Team, but that's just my
humble, female opinion.

 I stared in wonderment as his eyelashes
flittered. Greg doesn't look physically gay. Not
that I even know what that is really, but he's very
cute, has a great body that he takes care of and
he's very -- dare I say-- butch. He has shaggy
brown hair that hangs in his blue eyes. He wears
Levi's and doesn't use a lisp when he talks. But
he also likes lavender bubble baths and manicures
and he's probably the most anal-retentive man I
know, so I guess I can see it now.

 He must be livid inside, seeing a mess like
this in his space. It goes without saying that
Gregory spends more time here than Roald does.

 "I completely blew it. I'm so sorry,
Charlie." He gave me a warm hug and then
growled in a facetious manner. "How was last
night? I want details." He whispered in my ear
and gave me a wink. I think he's probably
pushing forty, but acts like a sixteen year-old girl
at times. "Bella, I'd really appreciate it if you'd
take a moment to clean this up. Laura-Lee is far

too busy to be picking up after you and your
friends, don't you think?"

I almost choked on my own tongue when
Bella smiled and galloped down the stairs.
Gregory must have some sort of magical powers
that I lack because I get attitude and I'm
supposedly her best friend.

I watched her with eagle-like precision
until most of it was cleaned up and then I heard
the chime of the gate.

The Munson household sits atop a hill in
West Greenwich, Connecticut. I'm guessing at
least two acres of pristine lawn are between the
house and Wisteria Street. There's a long
driveway that leads to a large wrought iron gate.
No one gets through that gate without Vinny's
approval. Right then, Vinny was in California
showing off his muscles at a Gold's Gym
championship, so Gregory and I were playing
gatekeeper. It was sort of fun being in the security
booth, eyeing prospective salesmen, and giving
the pizza delivery dudes a hard time.

We both heard the chime and went
running for the little room at the same time. I was
closer, so I got to the controls first.

"State your business," I said sternly,
pressing the intercom button and then turned to
watch Bella and Gregory snicker at me.

The car was black, tinted windows all
around. Mercedes S Class with California license
plates. No one spoke back to us, causing all three
of us to shudder and stare harder at the computer
screen. I moved the camera angle and repeated

myself. This time taking the edge off my voice and sounding a bit more like myself. "What the hell do you want?"

Again, nothing happened. The driver's side door opened and something was dropped to the asphalt. We watched the car pull slowly away and before I heard the screech of tires, I called the police.

"We'll have an officer out within minutes, Miss Ford. Don't try to retrieve the item, just leave it be and stay in the house." The kind dispatcher told me.

"Okay," I said and hung up. Both Bella and Gregory were huddled around me, staring in awe at the brown package beyond the front gate. I tried to narrow the camera angle and get a better look, but the security system wasn't that high-tech. "It's probably nothing. A gift maybe." I shivered and attempted a lame smile.

"A bomb sounds more like it." Bella scoffed.

"A snake. Probably poisonous." Gregory said and then looked down at me. "Who have you pissed off lately?"

"That's…" Bella tried to add more quarters onto his tab, but I cut her off.

"Me?" I shouted and swiveled the leather chair around to face him. "How about you? I'm nice! I'm the nanny for Christ sake. Everyone loves the nanny. You're the butler." I pointed my finger at him. "Everyone knows the butler did it."

His eyes rolled back in a pretentious fashion, much like Bella's often do, and his hands made it to his lean hips. He was still dressed in his silk black-and-white striped pajama bottoms and hadn't bothered to put on a shirt. He has a very nice chest. Hairless, so I assume he gets it waxed.

"I...am...not...a...BUTLER!"

"Whatever." I bit my tongue. Yes, he was so a butler, but we had bigger things to worry about.

"It was probably Jack," Bella said, then bit into her fingernail. I grabbed her hand and yanked it from her mouth. "Thanks." She clasped her hands around her back and smiled. We were all working hard to break nasty habits. "Jack probably sent it. He's always pulling stupid pranks on you."

"I agree," Gregory said. "Remember when he snuck into the house that night we were watching Scream? Scared the piss out of me." He shivered and lengthened his spine. I think Gregory might have a small crush on Jack. He'll never admit it and I'd never say anything to Jack, but he gets a sparkle in his eye when Jack enters the room. It's sort of cool that he's envious of me, in a completely sick, twisted way of course.

"I don't think he'd do this."

"Where is he now? Key Largo?" Gregory smirked.

"Very funny," I growled and stuck my tongue out at him. I'd once or twice confided in Gregory about Jack's sick habit of torturing me. The man most certainly keeps me on my toes. He'll tell me he's leaving for a secret mission

abroad –and I'll believe him -- and then he'll
sneak into my SUV or follow me to the mall just
so he can scare the crap out of me while I'm
sneaking cheesy fries at the food court. It was
humorous the first few times, but since we've
now been dating for nearly seven months, I don't
find it funny anymore. Now I just want to kick his
ass. "He's probably on his way back to
Baltimore. I didn't even bother to ask. He was
still asleep when I left him at the hotel." I know,
my love life sounds somewhat tawdry, but we
have no other choice. I refuse to do the nasty in
my cottage when Bella is in the main house and
Jack still resides in Baltimore. It's either sex in
my Ford Expedition or we get hotel rooms. We
rarely see each other anyway. Sometimes an
entire month will go by and when we do finally
get to see each other, we do more than just have
sex. We eat, we talk, and we watch TV… mostly
in bed, but… It's really not as explicit as it
sounds.

 "Case closed. Jack's in town and we've
just received a spooky present," Bella said.

 "I don't think so," I said, and just then we
saw the Greenwich police pull up. Two cars
approached first and three officers got out,
huddling around the package and probably
expecting a little drama. We watched them on the
screen. I pushed the intercom. "What is it?"

 The policeman looked into the camera and
frowned. "Are you Charlene Ignatius Ford?"

 "Yes," I said. My pulse skyrocketed.
Everyone I knew and loved understood just how

much I hated being called Charlene and I didn't
go around telling people my middle name. It just
didn't fit me, but thanks to my wonderfully
Catholic parents, I was doomed with a middle
name that often raised eyebrows. My mother
named me after St. Ignatius who died a martyr
and deemed himself Theophorus, meaning bearer
of God. I think my mother had indulged in a little
too much sacramental wine when she came up
with that middle name. What's wrong with
Marie? Or Denise for Christ's sake? Then again,
it was also the name of the church that my parents
had gotten married in.

   "It's addressed to you," the officer
replied.

   "Me?" I felt the blood rush to my face. "Is
it ticking?" I didn't know of anyone who wanted
me dead, but I did piss some people off last
summer during my time abroad. I doubt any of
them would come take their revenge on me, but
the thought did cross my mind every once in
awhile. I couldn't help it; I have a very active
imagination.

   The taller, younger policeman studied the
package, talked into the walkie-talkie that clung
to his shoulder and then stood back and shrugged.
"We'll just let the experts handle this one. It
doesn't have a return address and there's no
postage."

   Gregory left my side for a few minutes
and came back with a bowl of microwave
popcorn. Who knew my life was that interesting?
We shared the entire bowl and watched the bomb

squad do their thing. When it was deemed safe, the officers asked me to open the gate and we met them outside the sixth garage bay. (There are actually eight bays. Excessive? I think so!) Four squad cars pulled up and my pulse raced. I couldn't wait to be one of those guys. I pretty much went into giddy convulsions whenever I thought of myself in uniform. I'd worked hard to get my education, I had extensive military experience, and after living in other people's homes for the past four years, I was ready to grow up and move out on my own…I think!

I shielded my eyes from the sun and pulled my parka closed, zipping it to my chin. It was mid-March, the air was crisp, the sky was clear, but it was still extremely chilly out. My jeans seemed to freeze the minute I walked outside and I could see a fluffy white cloud of steam whenever I exhaled. Bella was by my side in her sweatpants, her father's leather bomber jacket and his big furry Ukrainian hat. Greg was still in his pajamas and wrapping his arms around his naked chest, waiting for the explanation from the cute cops.

"Seems okay. Want me to open it for you?" Officer Dan Triller asked, staring down at the parcel.

Normally, I wouldn't have feared a strange package, but I was apprehensive and extremely paranoid that my past would soon come back to haunt me. "Sure," I answered.

He ripped carefully along the edge and peeled back the brown paper. An athletic shoebox with European writing of some kind was underneath. I sucked in a quick breath and reminded myself to repeat the procedure as to not pass out and make a complete fool out of myself. The officer cautiously opened the box, then grinned and pulled out a pair of underpants. They were purple with tiny white flowers and I recognized them right away.

"They're very pretty. I bet they'd look good on you." His smile widened and he actually checked out me out from my running shoes all the way up to the tip of my Yankees cap.

Bella stood completely still, waiting for my reaction, so I knew I couldn't freak out about some strange European fascist sending my underwear back to me. I'd been wearing those underwear when I'd been abducted by a man I called The Rat somewhere in Armenia. The Rat, coincidentally still had my driver's license, passport, Blockbuster coupons and probably about thirty American dollars that he had taken from me on that fateful day last summer.

"Oh my God! How embarrassing!" I laughed and grabbed the underwear with a certain amount of false bravado. "I forgot I ordered these." I winked at the officer and crammed them into my pocket before Bella recognized them. She'd been with me when I had bought them and when I had put them on -- only because we had both been held captive together. Long story, but she was still in therapy about it, so I needed to keep my cool.

I don't think she bought it, but the color did return to her face when I laughed off the bizarre present and took Officer Triller aside.

When we were out of earshot, I explained that someone was just playing a sick joke on me.

He rammed his hands into his navy blue uniform pockets and smiled. "Want to have dinner tonight? Maybe go to a movie?"

I smiled. It was flattering, and Officer Dan was fairly cute in a little brother sort of way. He looked like a rookie, right out of the academy. I had recently celebrated my thirtieth birthday, so it was fun being the older woman for a moment, and then I snapped out of it and realized that it could have been Jack who sent the undies. After all, Jack had just been in California and his car had been blown up. Perhaps he bought a Mercedes while he was there.

"I'll have to take a rain check," I said sweetly. Perhaps after I carve Jack Sullivan a new rectum, I might be free to date. "Thanks for coming."

"Not a problem." He winked and was off without another word. The other three cruisers followed him out of the driveway and I closed the gate, staring out at the vast yard, wondering if Jack was out there watching.

"Sonovabit…" I stopped myself when Bella glanced in my direction. "Doesn't count," I said and took off through the house on a mission of seek and destroy. I slammed the door to my cottage, grabbed the cordless phone off my nightstand, and dialed Jack's cell phone.

"I'm not laughing!" I shouted before he
even finished his usual greeting, which was just,
'Sullivan' in his deep husky voice. "It's not
fucking funny, Jack Edward Sullivan!"

"Charlie?" he asked, probably trying to
identify my shrill voice.

"What?" I snapped in fury. I felt my toes
curl up when he started laughing at me. Him
laughing at me wasn't a new concept, he did it
often, but I was usually laughing right along with
him. Not this time!

"It's not funny, damn it! Bella was there.
She saw them and I've told you a hundred times I
don't want her involved in your little spy games.
Do you not listen to me?"

"Bella saw what?"

"The underwear, you prick."

"Bella saw your underwear? I'm
confused." He actually sounded sincere, but let
me tell you something about Jack Sullivan. When
I first met him, he said his name was Duane.
Then he told me it was actually Vince and then I
came to find out it was actually Ryan...and his
name is Jack. Do you get where I'm going with
this? He'd been trained by the best of the best to
lie, deceive, kill...seduce.

I huffed and sat down on my bed, glaring
at the picture of him that sat on my nightstand.
My father had taken the photo of Jack and I at a
Buffalo Bills game, it was snowing and we were
cuddled close together, wearing matching snow
hats. I felt warm and tingly all over remembering
that day fondly. Jack has amazing brown eyes,

the color of dark chocolate. His hair is black and extremely short and he has a body to die for, but he's just impossible sometimes. "I bet you're having a good time with this one, aren't you? I would bet money you were actually watching me through high-powered binoculars the whole time, weren't you? Well, did you get a good laugh out of it?"

"Babe, I'm on my way to Baltimore. I don't know what you're blabbering about."

My eye sockets throbbed and who knew that bit of information would have made my situation worse. "You didn't send me underwear?"

"Are they crotch-less -- or edible?"

"No."

"Then why would I send you underwear?" His voice deepened, and for a brief couple of seconds, all I heard was deep breathing. "I could drive back, you know. I don't really have to go home today." I think he was imagining me in said underwear. My nipples puckered slightly due to his slight vocal change.

"Jack, I'm serious," I droned. "This isn't funny anymore. I told you I needed time to decide what I want to do after I graduate and your little Cloak and Dagger pranks aren't swaying my choice in the matter. If anything, you're just driving me crazy. Just admit that you got my underwear back from The Rat and sent them to me as a joke…and please tell me that since you got my underwear back, you also got my purse and my driver's license."

He muttered something completely undecipherable, yet obscene, under his breath and I knew I had hit a nerve. "I'm an hour away. Don't leave the damn house." And then he hung up.

I stared at the phone and then ran for the main house. If Jack didn't do this and he was so concerned that he was turning his car around, then I was in big, big trouble.

# Chapter Two

It unnerved me slightly that Jack pulled into the driveway exactly forty-eight minutes later. Gregory punched in the code for the gate, while I nibbled on my fingernails and continually scuffed the hardwood with my Nike cross-trainers. I heard Gregory flirting over the intercom and then I told Bella to go to her room.

"I'm not done," she said from under the glass-covered, teak coffee table. Gregory was adamant that she scrape every last piece of chewed bubblegum off the underside of the antique table. The room was already a huge improvement, but the TV was going to need some more work. "What's the big deal? Why's Jack coming?"

I ignored her and repeated my plea. "Just go up and watch your Pimp show, I just need you to listen to me and don't ask questions."

"Whatever," she replied as she crawled out from under the table and stood up. "Hey Jack," she said sweetly when he sauntered into the room.

He was quite calm for someone who just drove sixty miles in forty-eight minutes.

"Bella." He nodded and gave her a quick kiss on the forehead, keeping his narrowed gaze on me. Hell, he looked pissed off to say the least. "How's life?" He sank down on the couch and pulled the copy of Sport's Illustrated off the table. He lifted one of his jean-clad legs onto the other, resting his ankle on his opposite knee. He was wearing the same shirt from last night, a red and blue rugby, sleeves pulled up over his slightly tanned forearms.

"Good," she grumbled and then retreated when I gave her a sinister look. "See ya."

Jack stared at me over the top of the magazine and waited for Gregory to sashay past us and into the kitchen. Gregory had showered, gelled his hair, and even shaved before putting on his favorite pair of tight jeans and a lime green bowling shirt. What did I tell you?

"What?" I grumbled at Jack and nearly broke into tears. I hated when he looked at me like that. I liked it better when we were in bed and he was staring at me with his dark bedroom eyes. You know, come to think of it, Jack always looks serious when we aren't in bed. "What do you want me to say?" I sat down next to him.

He isn't very good at consoling me in my times of duress. At best, he cocks his brow and gives me a wink when I'm upset. I nearly failed one of my classes not too long ago, and when I told him about it, he did the same damn thing. Sort of like he was doing right then, arms crossed in front of his chest. Narrowed eyes, brow cocked with a slight scowl. He shook his head at me and pinned me to the back of the couch with his strong hands. I thought for a second he was going to kiss me and give me a hug, but he didn't. The man actually frisked me. I giggled slightly when he grazed under my armpits, but his scowl remained on his face.

"Where's your gun?"

My jaw dropped. "I don't carry it with me all the time."

"Why the hell not?" He eased back and raked his thumb across my lower lip before kissing me. The room seemed to spin and I most certainly enjoyed having his tongue caress mine. Too bad he pulled back and creased his forehead at me. "Haven't I taught you anything?"

I tucked my chin to my chest and inhaled sharply. "I don't think it's necessary for me to be armed while I'm babysitting. That seems a bit excessive." I straightened my pale pink cardigan and stood up. "Why are you here? To give me shit or to help me?"

"You don't need help, Charlie. You're the most self-sufficient broad I know. I just wanted to see your underwear." He tried to yank me back onto the couch, but I was fast and I hated being called a broad.

He got serious when my face flushed with fury. "Sorry, Honey," he said while patting the couch cushion.

I remained where I was.

He stood up and raked his hand through his short black hair, his temples were slightly graying, most likely from stress because he's only thirty-seven. He continued that routine for a minute or two before pulling me into his arms and hugging me tightly. The man can hug. Albeit, it's rare, but it's nice when he does it.

"You're scaring me." I leaned back and watched his deep, brown eyes flicker with a mysterious glint. "Do you think it could really be The Rat? Is that why you're here?"

"The Rat is dead, and stop calling him that," he groused and helped himself to my Diet Pepsi.

"How do you know that?" Duh, the man's a secret agent and has all sorts of connections.

"I made a call." He narrowed his eyes at me. "Malcolm Rchevicha, a.k.a Your Rat died in an Armenian prison about three weeks ago."

"Wow." I was lucky to even get that much information. Usually Jack is one tight-lipped super-spy. "What happened?"

"Classified."

Damn!

I sat down and nibbled on what was left of my fingernail and then got busy on my lower lip. "Okay, then who else would have had access to my underwear?"

He didn't say anything, but I could see that I had almost made him smile. He was probably wondering the same thing...who else had access to my underwear...besides himself?

"You're a very strange man." I said, keeping the anger from my voice. "I think since it's my underwear and my ass we are talking about…you should include me in your theories. I'm a big girl, I can take it."

He still didn't say anything. The only sounds in the room were the whirring of the ceiling fan and the sound of Jack swallowing another gulp of my soda.

"You're coming to Baltimore with me. Go pack."

"Yeah right." I snorted. He knew it was finals week because that's why I had crawled out of bed at five A.M. and insisted that he keep it in his pants this morning. "I have finals."

I got the look again.

"Go pack, Charlie, or I'll do it for you -- and if I do it, just know that you'll be spending the next month in nothing but sexy lingerie and high heels."

I laughed and, by God, it felt good to do so. I don't even own any high heels and he can't be serious.

"Jack, I think you're over-reacting. It was just a prank…right?" I swallowed hard when he stood up and abruptly walked to my side. He looked as if he was ready to toss me over his shoulder. "Right?"

"Just go pack. I'll write a nice letter to your professors explaining the situation and you can make up your finals in a month. I'll even have the president sign the damn letter!"

I stomped my foot into the hardwood floor and felt my blood bubble in my veins. "No, damn it! I've worked eight long and exhausting years to get my masters. I'm not waiting another week, let alone a month. You're insane!"

I knew then that I was probably going to get the caveman treatment, only because he had that look in his eyes and he hated it when I called him insane. I think it might be that I hit a nerve with that one. Of course, he's insane. He's been trained by the Government to be that way.

I saw his nostrils flare just as he reached out to grab me. I jumped away and raced around the end of the couch to position myself out of arm's reach. "Let's not do anything rash." I held out my hand to dissuade him from coming at me. "I've been taking karate again and don't think I won't use it." My voice quivered slightly. Damn.

"Very funny, Charlie." He moved left and I moved right. "I'm not in the mood for this, Honey."

A ripple of panic raced up my back at the way he said Honey. He sounded possessed.

"Babe," I said, reining in my terror—and to be totally honest—my arousal. "I have three more finals. I'll be done on Thursday at two and then…sure, I'd love to come to Baltimore with you…but I'd probably have to bring Bella," I said and then creased my brow, staring at the ceiling thinking of all the things I had still promised to do with her. "We were going to go to…"

Did I happen to mention how fast Jack is? I was in mid-sentence when he hurdled the couch and tossed me over his shoulder.

"…go to Orlando when I graduated." I continued, resigning myself to the fact that Jack is taller, stronger, and more persistent than I am. My voice shook slightly as he swiftly began walking. His hand hot on my butt, groping me and making sure I couldn't squirm away. "And then I told her I'd take her to Oregon to see my folks. We were going to do some rafting on the Deschutes River and look at cute boys." I continued on from atop his shoulder.

We were already through the kitchen, en route to the back door. "That's nice, dear," he said, opening the back door and carrying me through the rose garden that led to my peaceful oasis out back.

I was still being jostled until he dropped me into the middle of the bed and jumped on me. His weight bearing down on me like a steamroller. I felt him from my toes all the way to the ends of my recently highlighted brown hair. Bella had introduced me to the wonderful world of highlights and now it's as if I'm addicted to getting my hair done. I usually add in a couple streaks of blonde, along with some golden brown, but last week, I also had Gigi add some dark brown. I feel like such a girl!

He nuzzled my ear, told me how disappointed he was that we couldn't do it this morning and then wiggled his hand down between my legs and attempted to unbutton my fly.

"Nooooo," I growled, but to be totally honest, my body was screaming yes in recollection of everything that he had done to me the night before. "Not…"

His forehead dropped to my chest when he groaned like an injured animal. "Not while Bella is home." His tone was tainted with sarcasm. "See," he said, then kissed me long and hard with lots of tongue. I could feel my cerebral cortex softening to the consistency of oatmeal. My muscles clenched as I had a fairly intense flash of heat roar through my unmentionable place. "You coming home with me is such a good idea on a multitude of levels. Just think of it, sex whenever we want. Think of the money we'll save on hotel rooms." He pressed another deep lingering kiss against my lips and grinned. I love his bedroom eyes. "Please. Do it for me."

"How about a compromise?" I loved that he cared and was also worried about strange Europeans getting even with me for foiling their assassination plans last summer. It was quite endearing and although he'd never uttered the words, I was sure it meant he loved me...or at least liked me enough to keep me alive.

His brow rose. "A compromise?"

"Yes," I squirmed under his weight until he rolled over onto his side and clamped his hand across my breast, wiggling his fingers along the buttons of my pink cardigan. "Strange concept for you, I know, but most people live with compromise everyday."

"How's this for compromise?" He actually smiled. "We'll pack your things together and I won't cuff you."

"That's not really what I had in mind," I whimpered when his hand found my bare nipple.

I was trying to think and come up with a solution and my damn body was betraying me. I slapped my hand around his wrist and lifted it off my boob. "You stay here with me, then on Thursday after my last final, Bella and I will come to Baltimore with you until you think it's safe for us to head to Orlando. Sound fair?"

He shut his eyes tightly, probably trying to dissuade obscenities from spewing from his suddenly taut lips. His head shook from side to side and I heard a stifled growl erupt. "That will never work. I'm knee deep in hell right now with...."

I love it when he almost slips up and tells me what missions of national security he's currently working on. I eased up on my elbow and grinned. "With what?"

"A new priority. I'm headed out of the country on Thursday night."

"So...what? You're going to lock me in your house and then leave me?"

"No, I was thinking you'd come with me. It's time you see exactly what you'll be getting yourself into if you come work with me."

I nearly peed my pants. I know he's mentioned me working with him several times in the past, but never, ever has he thought about including me on any of his cases. Oh my God! "Seriously, you want me to come?" I felt a familiar panic ripple up my spine when he smiled at me. I narrowed my eyes and I'm fairly sure I injured him when I dug my fingernail into the soft

37

flesh of his hand. "This is just your way of getting me to do what you want, isn't it?"

"No," he said, shaking the pain from his hand. "I want you to come. See how things run, meet the unit, and start seriously considering my offer. I don't offer to take just anyone onto my team. You have to earn it."

"But this is contingent on me leaving with you right now."

"Yes."

"That's extortion!" I sat up and slid away from him. Just being on a bed with Jack was enough to cloud my better judgment and this was the rest of my life we were talking about. Before I met Jack, I had high hopes of joining the police force, but ever since that night in Hawaii when he suggested I aim higher – that I had skills far beyond a normal law enforcer, I've been considering doing something more exciting. I know what three-letter national agency Jack works for and, yeah, sometimes I stand in front of my mirror and practice my super-spy monologue and pretend that I'm a big shot secret agent like Jack. I don't really know what I want and I want to keep my options open and take my time making the right decision.

"Charlie, give it up. I know you're completely freaked out by the fact that your long lost underwear was just delivered to your door, so just grab a bag and let's go."

"I can't, Jack. You know that I can't. What's a few more days?" I stammered and moved closer to him again. "Please? Vinny will be back tomorrow morning and I'll be extra careful. I'll carry my gun. I'll only go to school to take my finals and then I'll take the first flight to Baltimore when I'm done…I want to seriously consider your offer and I'd love nothing more than to go someplace fun and exotic with you and watch you work, but I have to take my finals."

I bent down and kissed him. "Please, Jack. I'll be careful."

"I'm not happy about this," he replied with a grimace.

"Then stay with me."

"I can't."

"Well, I can't come with you." I said, quite adamantly. So much for compromise. I have the most stubborn, headstrong, and arrogant boyfriend on the planet. There's no way to win this war.

Without another word said, he rolled over and stood up. "Call me if anything else strange happens."

"I will," I said. "Will you still consider me for your team?"

He nodded with an exaggerated groan of defeat and hugged me tightly, kissing the tip of my nose. "Think we could talk Gregory into taking Bella out for ice-cream?"

I grinned and felt my body soften with anticipation.

~~~

Tuesday morning I slid into my SUV and gripped the steering wheel with white knuckles. I'd kept my word to Jack and since he'd left the previous afternoon, I'd remained inside, armed and on my toes. I really didn't think anything else was going to happen, but I was still a wee bit apprehensive about leaving the house without Vinny, or even Gregory. My final in Professor Wilkins' class was the one I'd been dreading the most and I couldn't wait to get it over with.

"Want me to come with you?" Bella's voice brought me back out of my trance and into the present. She was standing beside my window, holding my purse and notebook that I had apparently left on the kitchen table. "You're not okay, are you?"

Bella and I had been through hell together. While in Africa and Armenia, she had shown me that she's one very brave, very mature teenager. She'd seen me in my direst hour and I'd seen her at her lowest of lows also. We both grew from our experience in Africa in very different ways. I grew in the sense that my love of excitement and adventure was re-ignited and I knew I wanted something more challenging out of life. I also grew in that I no longer blamed my father for my past failures and had decided to not take life for granted ever again…nor take anyone else for granted either.

I think Bella just grew up. That's the only thing that explains the amazing effect she has on my emotions. Sometimes I think she's the stronger one and I'm the kid who needs consoling. I wasn't about to fill her in on the spooky details, but she's a lot smarter than I give her credit for sometimes. "I'm fine. I just have a lot on my mind."

She rounded the front of my Ford Expedition and climbed in beside me. "Did Jack know how your underwear got here?"

"No," I said and turned the key. The engine roared and I let it warm up for a minute while I engaged Bella with my motherly scowl. "I want you to be extra careful for awhile. Don't go anywhere without Vinny and I think it would be best if you see if you can stay with your mom for awhile. Just until your dad gets back from Greece."

"Seriously?" she balked. "Why would she want me? Why can't I just stay with you?"

"Because," I growled and exited the eighth garage bay, punching the button for the gate while adjusting my black suede driving gloves. "I'm going to Jack's on Thursday and it looks like we have to postpone our trip…just for a little while."

"What?" Her eyes welled with imminent tears.

I hated that her relationship with her mother had taken a nosedive recently. I really had high hopes that Nicole would snap out of her selfish phase and take more of a mothering role in Bella's life. The last argument I had overheard was not a pretty one. Let's just say that Bella screamed a lot and told her mother to go to hell

41

before slamming down the phone. If there was any other solution to her staying safe while I was gone, I would have suggested it.

She sat quietly and almost nibbled her fingernail before realizing what she was doing and sliding her hands under her butt. "Why can't I come to Jack's with you?"

"I wish you could, sweetie, I really do, but Jack has a job out of town and he asked me to go with him." Both Jack and I are keeping up the illusion that he's an insurance adjustor. That's what he told my father when they first met, so we still use that as his cover. Bella, I'm sure, has her suspicions because of the things she saw Jack do in Africa, but it's our story and we stick to it.

She sniffled and stared out the window. "I hate her."

"You don't hate her. You're just angry that your parents got divorced. It's completely normal."

"No," she said with a venomous tone. "I hate her!"

"Fine," I grumbled and headed toward campus and then an idea of epic proportions bit me in the butt. "What about Gammy? Why don't you see if Gammy can come stay? It's been a couple of months since she was here. What do you think?"

Gammy is Roald's mother. She lives in Belgium with Bella's grandfather, Claude Munson. He's a very important diplomat and former director of Interpol in Eastern Europe. They were both an intricate part of having Bella and I rescued last summer. Well, at least Bella had been rescued. Me, not so much, but it was my own fault. I thought the good guys were the bad guys and ended up making my situation more difficult than it had to be. Nonetheless, I had been saved from The Rat and finally brought back home, thanks to a couple of French Interpol inspectors and, of course, Jack.

I couldn't believe that I was actually shirking my nanny obligations just to save my own ass. Shame on me.

She shrugged; clearly it wasn't the world's worst idea. "Promise me that we'll still go to Orlando…and your parents' house. I really, really want to."

"Absolutely."

Twenty minutes later, I pulled into the parking lot at the edge of campus and adjusted my holster after Bella got out. I had a sleek black nine-millimeter strapped across my kidneys, hidden under my UCONN sweatshirt. The only thing I needed now, was a couple of shots of espresso and a barf bag. I had no idea – well, that is until I got out of my SUV – that I was that freaking scared. My limbs were shaking and to be quite honest, I felt like I was going to pass out. I steadied my breath and inhaled a couple of times.

Why didn't I listen to Jack? I could be lying in his bed right now, getting a tongue bath, or a foot massage or both. Damn it to hell!

Bella remained by my side until we entered Covington Hall and I approached the professor, explaining that I was babysitting and

Bella would be camping out in the back of the lecture hall. The man glared at me and handed me an exam.

For a small fleeting moment, I fantasized about ramming my gun against his throat and telling him how much I hated coming to his class. How much I loathed that he talked with a lisp and that when he spoke I could smell whatever atrocity he'd eaten for lunch. I'd tell him how much I romanticized running him over in the parking lot and how I wouldn't miss him if he fell and broke his leg on the way downstairs after class. I guess in his expert opinion -- that would make me a closet psychotic. Psychology was never my strong suit, so I was looking forward to getting my usual C- and never looking back.

~~~

When we finally arrived back home, I took the liberty of getting the mail because Gregory wasn't home and since Vinny's car was back in garage bay number seven, I felt okay about walking to the mailbox and retrieving the contents. On any given day, the Munson/Squire household receives about three pounds of mail. None of which is fan mail. It's mostly catalogs; junk mail and solicitations for mortgage refinance companies and pretty much the usual crap. Every once in a while, I would get a letter from my parents or old Army buddies who wanted to update me on their weddings and the births of their children.

Today was no exception. I got a letter from my old friend Cory Welch. I slid open the envelop and paid close attention to where I was walking because Othello and Hamlet were out in the yard, sniffing around and trying to find a new place to do their business.

I laughed as I read the first line and then I read down the letter and learned all sorts of new and interesting things about my old unit and what they had been up to lately. Of course, most of it was in code and technical jargon that the normal person would never understand, but I understood. I used to be part of Sector 72G. A special unit of the Army Rangers. I was a sniper and a damn good one too -- thus Jack's interest in bringing me aboard his team. Well, at least I think that's why he wants me. He's never really said.

I finished up the letter and laughed a couple more times before cramming it into my purse and flipping through the rest of the mail. I stepped into the house, via the garage door and dropped the pile onto the granite countertop. Bella was already sipping a root beer and eating cold pizza. "Anything for me?"

I slid over about eight catalogs and a couple of CDs that she had recently ordered. She began thumbing through them just as I slid open another letter addressed to me. Wow, two in one day.

The fancy ivory paper was tri-folded yet there was no writing on it. When I flipped it all the way open, my old driver's license fell onto the countertop and seemed to bounce a couple of times as if in slow motion.

I felt the air in my lungs exit my body and I had to sit down to stop myself from falling onto the floor. Before Bella could see how white my cheeks were, I opened a J. Crew catalog in front of my face and pretended that I wasn't hyper-ventilating. I think I wheezed a couple of times, but she probably just thought I was excited about their spring sale.

I didn't want to touch it. My God, it was like seeing a ghost. I quickly got myself together for the sake of self-dignity and brushed it onto the piece of paper, quietly folding it and sliding it into my purse. At that particular point, I wished I had an ally. Someone who I could confide in – besides Jack. Jack would have me kidnapped, cuffed, and delivered to a safe-house in the country if he knew about the little present I had just received. I don't have sisters; no friends to speak of really and my brothers knew nothing about my life. Sure, I once confided in my older brother, Dave about what I really did in the Army during my eight-year enrollment, but my oldest brother Josh knows nothing. He thinks I eat bonbons all day while babysitting spoiled kids. My parents are oblivious also, but that's an entirely different can of worms.

I felt like my head was going to explode.

"What?" Bella said with a slight grimace. "What's wrong with you?"

I completely forgot that I was attempting to keep my cool, but in my haste, I had dropped my catalog and began chewing on my lower lip. My hands were trembling and I was staring at the ceiling muttering a silent prayer to God. "I'm good." I fumbled with my purse and hurried out the door, through the rose garden and finally landed in a heap in the middle of my bed. "Damn, shit, fuck, shit, damn hell motherfucker!" I shouted into my pillow a couple of times and then felt much better. "Crap!" One more for good measure.

Okay, so I had choices. Call Jack, tell him that my driver's license arrived and listen to him mutter obscenities much like I had just done, or I compose myself, take a few deep breaths, and remember that I, too, am trained to kill. Granted, I hate killing people. It makes my stomach ache, my palms sweat, and I really feel very remorseful afterwards and, really, no one had threatened me. I'd just received my belongings back. Why was I so dang upset about getting my driver's license back?

Because, it was spooky. That's why.

I bit into another nail and stared at the photo of Jack on my nightstand. Sometimes he looks like just an ordinary guy. Someone I could possibly imagine spending the rest of my life with. Other times, he just looked downright scary. Right then, I just wanted to see him, to hear his voice and get a hug.

The phone rang beside my head, sending a shiver across my skin. "Hello."

"So, how'd it go? Did you pass?" Jack asked as serious as ever. I felt my stomach roll a couple of times. I was either excited by hearing his voice, or I was afraid my voice would give away my fret. After all, Jack knew me pretty dang well. "Charlie, are you there?"

"How did what go?"

"You're final with Professor Bad Breath?" He chuckled. "I thought today was the toughest of your finals…the one you were dreading?"

I brushed the hair from my eyes and inhaled deeply to calm my nerves and squash the idea of telling Jack how I got my driver's license back. "Oh, it went well. I think I got a C, but that's all I need. Glad it's over. Everything's fine here, nothing strange going on and I'm fine. Really, I'm fine." My voice hit a high note. Crap!

"Charlie." Sometimes he sounds like my father. I heard deep breathing for a heartbeat or two, and then I heard a door slam and more heavy breathing. "Shit!" he shouted. "Now is not a very good time for some European prick to be messing with my life."

"Excuse me?" I said through clenched teeth. "Whose life is being messed with here? I said I'm fine and that means I'm fucking fine!"

"I thought you were cleaning up that potty mouth of yours."

"Well, I was, but hell if I'm just a bit on edge right now. Jesus, Jack. It's finals week. Give me a break."

"Babe, don't you know by now that I lo…"

My heart stopped for a moment, then he cussed up a storm and said, "I have to take this call. Are you really fine, or do I need to send for you?"

"I'm fine," I squealed.

Holy crap, he was going to say it. Oh God! What does this mean? I mean, I think I love him -- I mean, I know I love him, but he's a secret agent man. He lives dangerously and is out of the country more than he's here with me and I'm young. I'm barely thirty. I'm not ready for whatever that means. Oh my heck!

I deserved to be slapped in the face. I really did, but there was no one there to do it, so I splashed cold water on my face instead. I looked into the mirror and couldn't help the big cheesy grin that was spread across my face from ear to ear. He loves me. I've never had a man tell me he loved me before. My knees buckled and by golly for the next ten minutes, I completely forgot all about my driver's license. That is until I emptied my purse, looking for my last piece of gum. The ivory paper fell out onto my purple comforter and my smile faded.

There was a loud knock on my door and then Bella poked her head in. "Gammy can't come visit. Do I have to go to my mom's?" She looked heartbroken to say the least.

I patted the bed and she crossed the room to sit down with me. "No, you don't have to go to your mom's. I'll think of something, okay." I kissed her temple and gave her a warm smile.

~~~

Thursday morning, I went to take my history final, which just entailed dropping off my term project and thanking Dr. Schneider for being such an inspirational educator. She was my idol and I respected the fact that she too was a rebel like me. She had rebelled against her father who was a financial analyst and she ended up just like me; in the Army, attempting to find herself as an underdog in a man's world. We had a lot in common.

"I'm sure going to miss you, Charlie," she said, handing me a cup of coffee. Her office was tidy. On the walls, neatly framed in cherry wood, were her credentials and many accomplishments.

"Have you talked to your father yet?" She sat across from me, stretching back in her leather chair, carefully sipping from her mug.

I shook my head. "I want to see his face when I tell him. This isn't something that I want to do over the phone, you know. I mean, I really, really want to look in his eyes." I grinned. My relationship with my father used to be fairly rocky. I grew up in the shadow of my two perfect brothers who did nothing wrong. Dad wanted all of us to attend college, perhaps medical school and to basically follow in his footsteps. Dave and Josh both got into the University of Oregon with full-ride scholarships for football and academics. I barely finished high school with a three-point grade average because I spent so much of my time rebelling against my father. When I was seventeen, I told him I didn't want to go to college. His response to that was that I enter the military.

After graduation, I did just that. Only because I loved the shock factor. He was kidding when he suggested it, but I loved pushing his buttons so I joined and ended up staying eight years. Every so often my father would rag on me about getting an education, but little did he know that I'd been slowly getting my education during my stint in the Army, using my GI Bill to fund my bachelor's degree. He still harps on me about going to school and finally growing up, and I love that in a couple of weeks – barring any fascist freaks abducting me again –I will be able to sit across from him at the dinner table and tell him that I just received my master's degree. I was so excited. More so about having that discussion than I am actually about having done it. I know that sounds insane, but that's just how I am. My whole life, it's been about trying to make my dad see me.

I sipped from my coffee and felt my shoulders relax. "I'm taking Bella back home to meet them and then I'll hit him with it over a plate of Mom's Chicken Kiev."

"And how's everything with Jack? Will you be moving to Baltimore now that you're finished with school?"

I shook my head fervently. "No, of course not." Then I thought long and hard about that.

Now that I was going to be on my own, out of
school and thinking of my future in law
enforcement, I should be thinking of where I want
to live. I just hadn't thought things through. I'd
been so concerned about Bella and studying and
keeping focused that I sort of forgot about that.
Where was I going to put down roots?
Connecticut, so I could be near Bella, Oregon to
be near my family or Baltimore to be near Jack?
Obviously, if I go to work for Jack, I'll probably
live in Baltimore. But what if I don't want to
work for him. What if I just want to join the
force? Oh hell, I haven't thought any of this
through. "I guess I didn't think about that yet."

"Well, it's scary to move on and to make
big changes in one's life. You'll figure it out."

"What if I don't? What if I make the
wrong choice?"

"Charlie," she said, leaning forward onto
her desk. "I've known you for nearly four years.
I've seen you mature into this wonderful,
sensitive woman who isn't afraid of anything and
I couldn't be prouder. You're a strong, capable
woman and I know you'll make the right decision
for you. Just remember that. This is your time; a
time in which you have a multitude of options. If
you want a career with the FBI, then you go for it.
If you want to marry an insurance man and live in
the suburbs, then do it. You've had an amazing
life so far, you're wonderful with kids and you're
going to make a hell of cop. Don't worry so
much. It'll give you wrinkles." She winked at me
and smiled.

I felt tears well behind my eyes as I stood and hugged her tightly. "I'll never forget you." She was like the big sister I never had.

"Then come back and visit me often. I want to hear all about your life and find out where you end up." She pulled back and handed me a packet of papers, brochures, and a very important application. "Special Agent Dean Williams is the man you'll be meeting. He's the FBI's top recruiter and if I were you, I'd go in somewhat prepared as to what you might want. They've had their eye on you for quite some time and you've got some bargaining power. Keep an open mind, okay?"

"I will. Thanks again." I tucked my jacket under my arm and flipped through the packet of information. It's not the first time that the FBI had tried to recruit me. It was a little over a year ago, when I met with a different recruiter at the college and told him that I may be interested in hearing what they had to say. The only thing is, is that I hadn't mentioned this to Jack. It actually happened before I met Jack, so I didn't really feel the need to divulge that information when he approached me about working for him. Jack's organization is a bit higher on the food chain. It's on a broader scale and mostly handles international matters. Much like the CIA, but the organization that Jack is affiliated with outranks even them.

Dr. Schneider was so right. I have choices and, boyfriend or no boyfriend, I need to make the right choices... for me.

# Chapter Three

I'd been on campus much of the morning, had lunch with my only friend, and taken my last final with Dr. Manheim Strudelhoffer. That's not really his real name, but since I could never pronounce it correctly, it'll have to do. He's German and very demanding. I did well in his class, only because he reminds me of my father, and therefore I tried extra hard to get in his good graces from the get-go. I think I may have aced my final and that's why I was skipping to my car, without a care in my head. I had done it. I was finished, done, finito. I felt as if a huge weight had been lifted off my chest and I was free. All my hard work and sacrificing was over. The smile didn't leave my face all the way home.

The minute I returned to the Munson house, the bottom dropped out. I opened the door to my little guesthouse, tossed my purse onto my bed, and then screamed like a girl when I saw the pile of dead rats right where I had thrown my purse.

"Holy shit!" I screamed again and clutched my chest. I was way too young and physically fit to have a coronary, but I sure felt like I was having one at that very moment. It was hard to breathe and the room began spinning as I squealed and sidestepped my way toward the door.

Gregory was already out of the main house; on his way to me by the time I exited my tainted quarters. "Jesus, what's up with you?"

I felt the blood drain from my cheeks. "Rats," I squealed breathlessly. "Lots of rats!"

"Not possible." He planted his hands on his hips, highly miffed that I even suggested rats on the property. Needless to say, he takes his job very seriously. "The exterminator was here just last week. He said we were mouse free."

I didn't want to argue, but now that someone had breached security and tossed decaying rodents onto my bed, I thought he deserved the truth. "I need a martini, how about you?"

He slung his arm around my shoulder and gave me a squeeze. "How does it feel to be done? I know you've worked hard, you're probably overly exhausted and seeing things."

"I don't think so," I said, following his lead through the French doors that led into the kitchen. I stepped up to the countertop and watched him grab the Grey Goose vodka and Apple Schnapps from the liquor cabinet. He poured a couple of ounces into his tin shaker and then added ice, not saying anything, other than singing along to Bella's obnoxiously-loud Britney Spears CD. Despite the mess in my cabana,

watching Gregory sing, 'Oops, I did it again,'
while shaking up apple martinis made me giggle.

He winked, gave me a warm smile, and
poured me a double. "Cheers."

"Cheers," I said and downed the entire
drink in one gulp. "Hit me baby, one more time."
I chuckled and watched his eyes widen in
surprise. I'm not much of a drinker and he knows
it. A minute of silence ensued while he digested
the truth.

"Rats, really?" he said, sinking down on
the barstool next to me, realizing I wasn't
kidding. "Does this have anything to do with your
underwear and why you're trying to get rid of
Bella?"

I nodded and then prodded him to get me
another drink. "I don't know what to do. I can't
bring her with me and I don't want to leave her
here."

"Is it that bad? Should I leave too?" He
fanned his face and quickly got off his ass to
shake up another round of drinks. "By God, who
is doing this?"

Gregory knew bits and pieces of what
Bella and I had been through in Africa and
Armenia. He knew about the man I called The
Rat, so I felt okay in telling him of the imminent
danger.

"Remember how I told you that The Rat
had taken me from the ambulance after the
Interpol car had been overturned during the
crash." I had been in that Interpol car, with two
French inspectors, who had recently become my

pen pals. Inspector Russo is a kind, older gentleman who likes to tell me about his travels and three grandchildren and Inspector Bellavia is about my age and likes to tell me how much he wants to take me skiing in Switzerland. He has a slight crush on me and it's flattering, so I milk it for all it's worth.

> Gregory nodded and sat back down with another green martini en route to his lips. "Well, those underwear…" I started to explain further.

"Oh shit," he grumbled. "Those were yours…the ones they took from you in the hospital? But why rats?" He shivered and grabbed the phone, most likely dialing a cleaning service to revamp my room and probably re-decorate, fumigate and douse with antiseptic. I listened in on his conversation and then felt my toes begin to tingle from the alcohol. That was just fine because I had a plane to catch to Baltimore once I figured out where to put Bella for the time being. I sure as hell wasn't about to send her to Greece to see her father. I shivered thinking about the last time I had been in Greece, last summer with Bella. That's where we had been when all hell broke loose.

The sound of the phone slamming onto the counter brought me back to the present. "So," Gregory said after disconnecting. "The rats?"

I finished swallowing and held up my hand in front of his face. "I want one of those goose down comforters with a lavender cover, you know, one of the French ones that I never pronounce correctly…" As long as we were going to do some revamping, I wanted to make some changes, not that I would be living here that much longer. Damn!

"Duvet," Greg said with pride. "Done. Now why the rats?"

I shrugged. "I think The Rat is trying to make a point. I got my driver's license back the other day too, but…" It dawned on me that The Rat was dead – or was he? "I don't know why. Still, I think it's best if Bella is safe somewhere else for the time being."

"Hel-lo?" he griped. "What about me?"

"What about you?"

"I'm not staying here with a psycho Rat-man on the loose. Why don't I take Bella to Taos for a bit."

"Can't," I said, sipping the rest of my drink. "Nicole is there and Bella wants nothing to do with her." I sat with my chin in my palm, elbow planted on the granite countertop until another idea of epic proportions rattled my fuzzy brain. "My parents. I'll send Bella to my parents' place."

"And me too?"

I thought about that long and hard until I hiccupped and giggled hysterically, thinking of my conservative father and Gregory making toast in the same kitchen every morning. "No, you go on vacation. I'm sure Roald won't mind under the circumstances. I'll call the CIA to watch the house and that'll be that!" I slapped my hands together and gave Gregory a wink.

I don't think I amused him with that last part.

"C.I. Fucking A?" he gasped.

"It was a joke, Greg. Lighten up." I hiccupped again and stood up. "You owe me fifty-cents, by the way."

~~~

I waited three hours for the cleaning crew to arrive and get to work and when they did, they found my old purse under the dead rats, along with my Blockbuster coupons, money, and wallet, which I instructed them to burn along with most everything in my cabana. It needed a makeover anyway. I called my mom from the main house and begged her to help me out in a bind.

"I don't know what to do with a teenager, Charlene. What am I supposed to do? And how long will you be gone?" My mother asked after I explained my need for assistance.

"A week, possibly two."

I imagined her shaking her head at me while sipping Diet Pepsi from the back patio. My parents still live in Bend, Oregon; in a newer subdivision lined with tall Juniper trees and a private golf course. One of my mom's favorite pastimes is sitting on the back deck watching the golfers tee off on the par four that sits directly behind their house. But that's only when she isn't working at the hospital. She still puts in ten hours a week as a neonatal nurse because she loves her job and more importantly gets to spend lots of

time with babies—because I haven't graced her
with grandchildren yet…shame on me! Both my
perfect brothers have kids. In fact, Dave's wife
just gave birth to their second. I'm so far behind,
it's not even funny.

"Mom, please. She won't be any trouble
and you really don't have to do anything. She's
old enough to take care of herself, you just have
to make sure she's home at night and that she
doesn't get anything pierced…Paaallease. You're
my only hope."

"And where is it that you'll be again?" she
asked, not doing a very good job at keeping the
skepticism from her tone.

"I'll be out of town with Jack. He's taking
me to his insurance seminar and showing me the
ropes in case I want to go to work for his
company." There, that wasn't a huge lie…just a
little white one, but so much better than telling
her the truth. I could just imagine how that
conversation would go. 'Actually, Mom, Jack is
taking me to some remote international location
with the government agency that he works for
because, guess what? I want to be a super spy like
him and kill people for a living. Aren't you
proud?'

"Insurance, huh. Not a bad job, I guess,"
she said. "You know, your father would rather
see you take all that money you have saved and
use it to go to college."

"Yeah, well, we can talk about that when I
come and get Bella, I have to go. Can I send her
out, or not?"

61

"Sure, honey. Tell Jack we send our love and have fun."

"I love you and tell Dad I said hi." I disconnected with a sigh.

One problem down, one to go.

I took what necessities I needed from my room and left the rest for the bon-fire. Bella was so happy to hear that she was spending an infinite amount of time with my straight-laced parents in the middle of Oregon...NOT! She whined, moaned, and protested until I reminded her that she really, really wanted to go.

"Yeah, but with you. Not alone. What am I gonna do there?"

"You can walk Ruger and play chess with my father." I chuckled and tossed our bags into the backseat of my Expedition. My head was throbbing from the hangover I had subjected myself to by sipping apple martinis in the afternoon.

Hangovers suck!

I turned in time to see Gregory stuffing his giant Gucci bag into the front seat of his SUV. He looked as if his ass were on fire as he whistled for the dogs and got them secured into the back seat. "Greg, relax," I said, doing a mock imitation of my Yoga instructor. "Breathe in, breathe out!"

"Bite me," he snickered and then handed me a piece of paper. "Call me if you need anything. I'll be at Mom's in New Hampshire."

"Thanks." I smiled and returned his warm hug before climbing into the front seat of my own SUV beside Bella. "Bella, please don't look so

glum. I'll meet you there as soon as I can.
Everything is fine. Really, it is," I said for the
umpteenth time to dissuade her anxiety. "You'll
have fun. I know you will. Just give it a chance."

"Do they have MTV?" she asked, sliding
down her window to get some fresh air once we
left the enclosure.

I watched the garage bay close tightly
before pulling away. "No."

She blew out a disgusted breath and didn't
speak to me until we got to JFK International
airport and I hugged her goodbye. "If you get
bored or homesick, just call your mom. I left her
a message telling her where you'd be, just in case,
okay." I kissed her forehead and handed her a bag
of gummy bears.

"I'd rather eat shit." I heard her mumble
as she huffed away.

I so wanted to chase her down and
retrieve the quarter she owed me, but I had a
plane to catch and a speech to prepare. Somehow,
without sounding like a pathetic ninny, I had to
figure out a way to ask Jack to help me with my
rat problem. Oh boy!

# Chapter Four

I'd gone over it in my head about a
hundred times on my short flight to Baltimore,
but once I saw the grim expression on Jack's
face, I decided the rat invasion was a
conversation best left for the minute after he
climaxes.

"Hey." He somewhat smiled and grabbed
my hand, yanking the luggage from my other
hand. "This is all you brought?" He lifted my
pathetic bag and frowned.

"Long story." I grumbled and hurried
behind him as he nearly dragged me through the
crowd.

"Forget to do laundry again?" he
snickered and once we were out the doors, he
hailed for his car and a black Lincoln Towncar
pulled to the curb with a screech. He tossed my
bag into the trunk, slammed it closed and climbed
into the backseat beside me. It was nicely air
conditioned and had a roomy interior, much like a
limousine. Once the door was closed behind him,
a tinted window began to rise behind the driver's
head and Jack already had his hand up my shirt.

"Goddamn, I missed you." His kiss was intense and filled with promise. His tongue caressed mine with sudden urgency as he slid his hand further up my sweatshirt, seeking out an already taut nipple.

I'd had a glass of wine during my short flight, so my earlier hangover was gone and I was okay with the notion that I was about to have car-sex, despite the fact that I was scared to death of supposedly-dead, rat men.

I groaned low in my throat and wiggled under Jack's hand. He kissed my neck, trailing little kisses up and down the curve of my jaw, his fingers lightly tantalizing my bare-naked breast. I felt his erection against my leg and although I'm usually enthralled with Jack's impressive penis, I just couldn't get my mind off the deceased vermin.

I gasped, sucked in some well-needed air, and squealed. "Rats, dead ones. All over my bed!"

If I had an entire thesaurus to describe the look on his face, I still couldn't do it justice. I think mortified and highly disappointed would be an understatement.

He leaned back, adjusted the engorged bulge under his button fly, and eased back into the leather seat, keeping his eyes locked with mine. "Come again."

I squealed, wishing that I were coming again, instead of having this damn discussion. I have no idea why I had to blurt that out at that increasingly erotic moment. Why God, why?

"I got home and there were dead rats on my bed." Still unable to read his facial expressions, I bit down on my lip and sucked back a tear. "Are you sure he's dead?"

Something softened in his eyes when my first tear trickled down my flushed cheek. A muscle clenched in his tight jaw and he pulled me into his arms, rocking me gently, humming sweet nothings into my hair. I felt peaceful, and loved and Jack really does know a thing or two about what I need to hear when I'm upset. He's probably the best friend I've ever had and even without the hot monkey sex, I know that he'll be a huge part of my life, forever. I cuddled closer to his chest and tried to keep my tears from spilling on his nice white shirt.

That moment of complete and utter bliss lasted about twenty-three seconds and then the interrogation began. He withdrew his comforting embrace and narrowed his eyes on me. "I thought we agreed that you'd call if anything else happened."

"I would have, but I know you, Jack. You would have sent a team to kidnap me in my sleep," I said, brushing the tears from my cheeks. "My driver's license arrived too. In the mail, just folded in a piece of paper."

I could tell at that moment he was certainly attempting to keep his cool. His hands were clenched tightly and something short of rage was apparent on his face. He scratched his goatee and leaned toward me in a menacing fashion. "Who else knows that you call him The Rat?"

I had to think long and hard about that one. The air around us had somehow electrified and all I could smell was his musky scent. Jack reeked of testosterone. He was a pent up ball of luscious manliness all rolled into an impressive package and sometimes I couldn't think straight when he was touching me. Mostly when he had his hand clamped around the back of my neck and he was caressing the side of my throat with his thumb. Much like he was doing right then. Ahhh, I should have kept my mouth shut and let him take me in a very un-ladylike manner right where I sat. Double damn.

I fanned my flushed face and moaned, leaning closer to him. When I finally stopped my forward movement, he chuckled lightly and kissed me with extreme passion and unadulterated need.

I don't remember a time in my life when I've wanted something so damn bad as I wanted Jack at that particular moment. Call me crazy, call me emotionally unstable, but I couldn't crawl into his lap fast enough. I straddled him in two seconds flat and already had my hand down the fly of his jeans. I kissed him hard, mashing my entire mouth against his, moaning and begging him to do something really nasty to me. I think he liked my pleas because he was growing bigger under my hand and his breath was coming faster in his chest. He garbled a couple of hot obscenities, then sighed against my swollen lips.

"Charlie," he mumbled against my chest, burying his face against the fleece of my sweatshirt. "We're here."

As he said it I noticed the car come to a complete stop. The driver gave the window a little rap and Jack bucked his hips, teasing me before dumping me into the seat.

"We're not done with this discussion," he said, cocking a dark brow.

"I certainly hope not." I responded with flushed cheeks, hoping we'd be able to sneak off to the bathroom on the plane and join the mile high club on our way to wherever we were going. I still had no clue. Jack had just said, 'pack for hot weather.'

He winked, hauled me closer for a brief moment and then kissed me with a promise to finish what we started. "Get yourself together, then I'll bring you in to see the boss."

"What?" My voice cracked. "I'm not dressed right. Jesus, Jack. Thanks for the warning."

" It's not a job interview. He just wants to meet you." He tucked his long-sleeve, white oxford shirt back into his faded jeans and ran a hand through his short black hair. "And don't look at me like you want to fuck me. This is strictly professional."

My jaw dropped a couple of inches.
"Nice."

"And don't mention your upcoming interview with the Feds. Blackman doesn't like them too much."

My jaw dropped even further. I hadn't told Jack about the Feds or their interest in hiring me. Shit! The look on my face must have prodded Jack to explain further while stepping from the car.

"Babe, you can't hide shit from me. I don't know why the hell you even try."

The parking garage was small, dark and had only a few vans parked in it. I straightened my red UCONN sweatshirt and fumbled with my words. "I wasn't trying to hide it from you. Hell, this all came about before I even met you. I didn't tell you yet, because there's nothing to tell. I haven't met with this guy yet and who knows, maybe I never will. I haven't thought that far ahead."

"And that's fine. Just don't mention Special Agent Dean Williams to Dick Blackman." He grabbed my bag and handed it to the driver who had emerged by his side during our discussion. "Check this for me and see what else she may need. Be back in one hour."

The tall, lanky blonde man left without a word. He just nodded and did what Agent Sullivan had requested.

I was still trying to look presentable when Jack turned around to engage me with his killer smile. "You don't want to be a Fed, honey. The FBI is nothing but a bunch of pansy-ass college boys. You're military, Charlie. Remember that." He winked and took off in front of me, giving me special inside information about who I was about to meet and how I should stop looking at him the way I was.

70

"Every wall has a camera, so don't look at my ass when I walk by and stop doing that with your teeth."

"What?" I grumbled as we entered the elevator. Much to my surprise, Jack hit a button, entered a secret pass code and we went down…way down. Below parking structure level and into what felt like a deep abyss.

"You're grinding your teeth again."

"Sorry." I bit down hard to stop the grinding.

When we exited the elevator, we walked out the rear through a hidden door that slid open. The hall was long and white. Fluorescent lights flickered overhead and then Jack opened the door at the end of the hall. The only door, in fact.

"Blackman, this is Charlie."

"Charlie Ford. I've heard a lot about you." Mr. Blackman said from his wheelchair. He was probably around sixty-five years old. White hair cut military short. He was missing one leg; the other frail leg sagged lifelessly against the leg rest of the wheelchair.

"Nice to meet you, sir."

"Sir?" He chuckled, giving me a warm smile. "It's been a long time since anyone called me Sir. Around here, most people call me Dick."

I chuckled at his lame attempt at levity. I was quaking in my boots, to be perfectly honest. In the room, there were three chairs, one desk with nothing on top of it and it smelled like stale cigars. The carpet was frayed and old and the cement blocks in the walls looked chipped away by time and probably a couple of earthquakes. What I was standing in seemed to be a shelter of some kind. Probably built during the cold war or perhaps even WWII.

"Everything set then," Dick said to Jack, handing him a cigar. Jack lit the end and then did the same for Dick's cigar. The old man had a hard time keeping his hands from shaking as he lifted the cigar to his lips.

"Charlie, you smoke?"

I shook my head. I'm a purist at heart – with the exception of an occasional drink to calm my nerves, of course. I sat down in the chair and watched Jack inhale then exhale a cloud of gray smoke.

"We're good to go." Jack said to the old man, cocking a brow and clearly giving him a nod of good intentions.

"Don't let him get away this time," Dick said under his breath. "The leaky faucet has been plugged." The man's belly shook when he began laughing whole-heartedly.

I gulped loudly and twiddled my thumbs. I knew exactly what they were laughing about and I don't think being plugged was a good thing. It's most certainly not a laughing matter in my book. Then again, if the leaky faucet had succeeded in his evil plot and Jack had been in his car when it had been blown to smithereens a few days ago, then I would probably be laughing about the death of the son-of-a-bitch who had killed my lover.

I shook my head and took my eyes off Jack's ass.
Damn, I really do stare at his butt a lot.

He exhaled again and cocked a brow in
my direction. "You ready for this?"

"Yep." I quickly stood up and extended
my hand to Mr. Blackman. "It was nice meeting
you."

"The pleasure is all mine. I look forward
to having you aboard and no matter what you
hear about this guy..." He poked Jack in the
stomach with an outstretched hand. "Don't
believe a word of it. He's the best there is and
he's not as big of an asshole as you may think.
Big heart, this one has." He smiled in a loving
way toward Jack. "Take good care of him for me
and watch each other's backs."

"I will." I smiled and followed Jack to the
elevator. Once we were inside, I bent over at the
waist and steadied my breath. "SHIT!"

"Problem," he said, staring straight ahead.

"This shit is real. I mean, like really,
really real." I stammered, trying to catch my
breath. "I feel like I'm in a movie."

"Can you breathe?" He asked, still staring
straight ahead. "Or do you need mouth to
mouth?"

"Not funny," I grumbled with a small
smile. "Where are we going now?" I asked as we
stepped off the elevator. I'd just been to an
alternate universe and was wondering if maybe
Mars was our next stop.

"You're going straight to the airport.
Gilbert will get you onto the plane and then when

you reach your destination, I'll give you further instructions because I don't have time to brief you now," he said all this while walking swiftly toward another big black car. A different driver emerged. A tall black man with perfect white teeth and an unholy grin.

"You must be Charlie. Heard all about you."

"Oh yeah. All good I hope." I quipped playfully and was handed an airplane ticket, boarding pass and a couple of crossword books. "Thanks." I smiled at Jack. The man knows me so well.

"Get some sleep and don't worry about rodents. I swear, there aren't any rats where we're headed." That's all he said as he walked away and disappeared into a white van.

~~~

Gilbert remained quiet the entire way to the airport. We boarded a commercial airliner with a destination of the Bahamas, which I thought was odd, because I was sure that super-secret spies took their own airplanes everywhere, much like Air Force One. Boy, I was wrong. I was stuck in coach, sitting next to a large man who snores and passes gas in his sleep. Gilbert was across the way in first class, probably sipping mimosas and flirting with a pretty flight attendant.

I never used to fear flying. I did it all the time in the army and then of course all the times that I had flown home to visit the folks after being fired from my former nanny positions. Before I met Roald and Bella, I had pretty bad luck finding nice families. Most of the time, I got stuck with the spawn of Satan who had parents oblivious to their true evil selves. Lucky me. Anyway, my fear of flying came from last summer after being hi-jacked in the middle of Kenya. Now, I loathe flying.

"Can I get a drink?" I asked the flight attendant, handing her a five-dollar bill.

"What would you like?"

"Something strong."

She handed me a tiny bottle of Jack Daniels. "Drink that. It'll take the edge off." She winked and I twisted the lid. It smelled like cough syrup and hospital antiseptic. I couldn't believe that people actually drink that stuff for pleasure. I shivered and put it up to my lips. At first, I attempted to sip it and then I just chugged it down like it was Nyquil. It warmed me all the way down to my toes and I felt mellow enough to shut my eyes and take a couple deep cleansing breaths.

~~~

I must have fallen asleep, which is odd because normally I can't sleep on airplanes, but a deep voice boomed in my head instructing me to put my seat and table in an upright position for landing. I felt capricious and quickly did what the

Captain asked, while staring out the window at the lights below. It was my first time in the Bahamas.

Gilbert met me outside when we exited the plane. We had to walk outside and the humidity was already causing my clothes to stick to my skin. I was still in jeans and my sweatshirt, but Gil had apparently changed on the plane, because he now looked like a tourist, camera around his neck and all.

"So, what's our cover?" I mumbled with a smile, keeping my head down in case bad guys were around and could read lips.

I'm new at this--give me a break!

"Photo shoot for a fashion magazine."

"Oh," I perked up and straightened my spine. How flattering that Jack asked me to come along on this particular mission. He must think I'm beautiful. "Do I get to be a model?" I know I'm not a gorgeous Cindy Crawford look alike, but I'm pretty. My hair is about shoulder length and I'm five eight. With a little work, it could happen.

"No," Gilbert smirked at me, almost mocking me with his eyes. "Those are the models." He pointed to a gaggle of tall babes, smoking cigarettes and hanging out by a couple of Jeeps at the end of the parking lot. Six women, taller than me wearing nothing but string bikini tops and hot pants. Hell, I didn't think they even made hot pants anymore.

"Bon jour," one of the women said, kissing Gilbert's cheeks a couple of times. The others did the same and I suddenly felt really, really ugly.

"This is Charlie, she's the production assistant. Do you have everything?"

The tallest of the group smiled and extended her hand, she had an Australian accent. "I'm Liza."

"Nice to meet you," I said with a smile. The others just stared at me and then entered the Jeeps without as much as a hello.

We were driven to a lodge on the south end of a fancy resort that sat in between palm trees and the ocean. Four bungalows were set on the beach in front of the large main house. Exotic trees towered overhead and the air smelled of salt and barbecued shrimp. I could almost taste the ocean when I inhaled. I was very nervous, but that ended when Jack walked in the room and I couldn't help the smile when I saw a familiar face.

"Ladies," he said, giving each one of the babes a kiss on the cheek. The sight of it made my stomach churn. He glanced at me for a quick second, but that's all I got in the way of a greeting.

I watched them interact. Flirting would be an understatement. My stomach grew tighter and I could feel the acid churning each time one of them tossed their hair and gingerly slapped Jack's arm, or his back or shoulders. Ugh.

Jack is six feet tall, much like each of those models. One was even taller than Jack. That one was Liza and she was by far the most beautiful woman I had ever seen. Long, dark hair that cascaded down her perfect back and her smile was nothing short of amazing. I'm sure her teeth were fake, probably as were her perfect boobs.

Jack took her aside and I glanced at them from the corner of my eye as they walked down a long hall. Again, my stomach clenched and I felt the need to puke up my dinner.

"Charlie," Gilbert said. "You're in bungalow three. You'll find your bags already in there, along with an itinerary of tomorrow's shoot. Be on the beach at seven a.m. sharp. I don't like waiting."

I momentarily snapped out of my tizzy fit, wanting answers and some sort of direction. "Are you…" I bobbed my eyebrows as if we had a secret code of sorts "… the producer?"

"No," he chuckled. "Eddie is. I'm just the photographer."

"Oh."

I so felt like a fool because I have no idea who the hell Eddie was and I wish to God someone had given me the scoop before I left American soil. To me, this little operation was completely ass-backwards and I had an urge to hunt down Jack and get some answers. That and I really wanted to see where he had run off to with my worst nightmare. Instead, I grabbed my key off the table and headed to bungalow number three. When I got to it, I held my breath and prayed no cockroaches were skittering across the floor. Much to my surprise, the room was big and there were no bugs the size of my fist. On the nightstand, there was a small clock radio, three bottles of Evian and a single red rose. I smiled, wondering if Jack had been there. To my right there was a small kitchenette, a coffee maker and a large king size bed. My duffle bag was on the bed, along with another new bag that I'd never seen before. I opened that bag and found three pairs of denim shorts; tags still on. A couple colorful tank tops, a new pair of white Keds, a package of jockey underwear. I yanked out the underwear and noticed he got my size right, good for him. Underneath it all was a sleek nine-millimeter gun, much like the one I own, the one I left with Vinny for safekeeping. A pair of handcuffs was tucked into the side pocket, along with a funny looking walkie-talkie, an earpiece of some sort and another gun.

"Sheesh," I held up the gun and checked the magazine. "Fully loaded and ready to rock!" I placed it back in the bag and pulled out a map of the island and the itinerary that Gilbert had told me about.

The television worked. I got plenty of movie channels and could even watch the local Miami news. I didn't want to, so I turned it off, tucked my pillow under my head, and closed my eyes. I was overwhelmed, exhausted, and ready for my newest adventure.

~~~

It was the creak in the floorboard that first caught my attention. I flipped over and stared at the LED readout of the digital clock before sitting straight up and blasting Jack with a couple of really bad words while clutching my chest. It was only three a.m. for God's sake. I can't be loving and amiable at three a.m.

"Fuck, Jack. Don't do that to me, I could have shot you!"

"Funny." His grin was sexy; I'll give him that. "Having any fun yet?" He slid in beside me and curled his hand around the small of my back, dragging me toward him.

I succumbed to his insistence of being naked, but I still wanted answers. He lifted my sweatshirt over my head and licked his bottom lip. "I can't stay long," he said while unsnapping my unflattering white bra. I should have thought ahead and removed my clothes before climbing into bed. Who knew I'd be getting lucky tonight. From the looks of his earlier departure with the model, I thought I'd never get lucky again. I was so jealous and hadn't a clue as to why. Well, okay, I was jealous because I was the ugly duckling in the room and Jack kissed all the models...and not me. I know I'm supposed to be professional and mature, but come on. That was excruciatingly painful to witness.

My skin crawled with a feeling of bittersweet arousal. I wanted answers. I always wanted answers. I was strange that way, I know, but I like to know what's in store for me and I certainly wanted to know what we were doing in the Bahamas with a bunch of hot women. "Are you going to tell me anything about this, or is this a sink or swim test, because, frankly, I'm lost."

He nuzzled his chin against my then naked breast and groaned. "Babe, give me ten minutes, then I'll tell you whatever you want to know."

My breath caught in my throat when he slid my underwear down my thighs and slowly licked his way down my stomach and lower. "Only ten minutes?" I whimpered and grasped the back of his head with one hand and grabbed a handful of bedding with the other. "You're no fun."

And then I couldn't think, talk, or remember my name for the next half hour or so.

When my pulse resumed to a normal pace, I lifted my tired body off the damp sheets and gave Jack a long kiss on the lips. "Now, I want answers."

"Shoot." He grabbed a bottle of water and drank half of it before handing it to me.

"Why are we here? What's the objective?"

"Columbian drug cartel member, Sergio Benitez is on the lam. Cartel wants him dead, we need him alive."

"So, you aren't here to…you know, have him eliminated." I sipped some water and slid my toes out of the covers to let them cool down. The air conditioning worked rather well but let me

just say that Jack and I can burn up the sheets
when we're in bed together.

"I'm not an assassin, Charlie. Our unit
mostly works on saving lives, not taking them."

"Okay, so what do we do once we save
him?"

"We torture him until he tells us where the
missing drugs and money are and then we kill
him." Jack turned his head and laughed into his
pillow. I love hearing him laugh aloud. It rarely
happens, but when it does, my heart swoons even
more. He pulled me closer when my jaw
unhinged. "Don't worry, I won't make you pull
the trigger."

"You are so not funny."

"Don't worry about what happens next,
our objective is to keep him safe...for the time
being." He winked.

"How do you know he's here?"

"Got word from our informant that he will
be here. Likes to stay at the resort next door.
Usually has an eye for beautiful models, thus our
idea for a photo shoot."

"So, when will he be here?"

"A day or two, according to our source
with the DEA. We don't know how far behind
him the cartel hit-man is, so we thought it would
be best to case the area first. A secondary team is
handling the outer perimeter surveillance. All we
have to do is supply the eye candy and hopefully
get close to him."

I digested that information for a minute or
two and sat up in bed, curling my arms around

my knees. It sounded to me like one of these
models was going to have to get close to our
mark. That means one of them, if not more, might
just be part of the organization and not just
pawns. Ugh, I hated the idea of Jack working so
closely with such beauties so I dismissed the idea
and ran my fingers through Jack's short hair.

He moaned and incited me to continue
massaging his scalp.

"And who's Eddie?"

Jack's eyes flickered in the dim light.
Some-times when he looked at me, I could see
the love in his eyes and sometimes I just felt that
he was staring right through me. A second ago, I
felt the apparent love, right then, when I
mentioned the name Eddie, something changed
and his jaw tightened.

"I'm Eddie. Shit. Guess I should have
mentioned that sooner. Everyone calls me Eddie
on the unit, so don't go blowing it by calling me
Jack, okay."

"Does anyone know…about us, I mean."

"Hell no!" He sat straight up and kicked
his legs over the side of the bed. "In fact, I
shouldn't even be here. Fuck, Charlie, I'm sorry.
I have to go."

I didn't know what to say. I couldn't tell if
he was angry at me or simply angry at himself for
being weak when it comes to my flesh. He bent
over at the waist after his clothes were once again
on and he kissed me tenderly, sighing heavily
against my lips. "When this is over, how about a
nice long week in Hawaii? Just the two of us."

"And Bella?" I retorted, letting him know I already had plans when this was over. Hell, I still need to find a job and a place to live. He looked crestfallen at best. "You could come to Orlando with us."

"It's a nice offer, but I want you alone; naked and at my beck and call," he said on his way out the back door.

"Sex, sex, sex." I said to the closed door and fell fast asleep.

~~~

The alarm woke me at six-thirty. I showered, dressed in my new denim shorts, a purple tank top, and my sandals. I pulled my hair into a ponytail and headed out for a quick glass of juice and a muffin -- if I could find one. My fridge had been stocked with nothing but fruit and champagne, so I desperately needed to go grocery shopping before I starved to death.

The lodge was brimming with people having breakfast. Children were running by me with plates full of waffles, eggs, and smiley-face pancakes. My uterus seemed to clench when I looked at the families sharing a wonderful meal together. I wanted kids...by God, not now, but someday. Kids are wonderful and babies are the most precious things on earth. My brother Dave's little girl is just six weeks old. I was there in

Seattle when she was born, waiting to be the first of the family to meet her. Dave had asked me to be her Godmother, so I was insistent on being there when she was born. They named her Katie, after my grandmother and she was just a tiny precious bundle of joy.

A tall black man nudged my shoulder, ripping me out of my daydream and it didn't dawn on me that it was Gilbert until he smiled, and once again, I was blinded by his teeth.

"Do you have those whitened?"

He laughed and crooked his massive bicep around my neck, hauling me toward the beach. "No, I just don't drink coffee or smoke. Plus, I have a great complexion." He eyeballed me for a quiet minute.

"You're late. I said seven."

"Sorry, I was daydreaming about babies." I don't know why I felt compelled to tell the truth, but I did.

We took the short route to the beach and had to climb over a couple of nude sunbathers to get to the group near the water. The cameras were set up, the models were in their bikinis, and Jack was sipping coffee from his director's chair, in the shade of a large palm tree. "Take this to Liza, she's getting pink." He handed me a bottle of sunblock without as much as a hello.

I guess I should get used to it. Jack seemed to have multiple personalities at times. "Yes, sir," I grunted and plowed through the hot sand to hand it to Liza. Her long dark hair looked perfectly conditioned and not a strand was out of place, despite the hot breeze.

"Can you do my back?" she asked with false sweetness.

"Are you serious?"

"Never mind," she snapped and waved toward Jack. "Eddie, can you do my back, please?"

I grabbed the damn sunblock from her hand so fast, she didn't have time to blink. I grumbled, but by God, I did a good job lathering her up and keeping the white lotion from ruining her sequined bikini. "All set, is there anything else?"

"I'd love some more water," she said, clearly tormenting me.

When I was finished playing servant to the Prima Donnas, I sat down next to Jack and let my cheek fall into my open palm. "Models are a bunch of spoiled rotten bitches."

Jack chuckled, but kept his attention on his paperwork. "Can you get me a sandwich?"

"Are you serious?" I'd been reduced to a gopher-boy. "It's only nine."

"I've been up since three," he bobbed his brow playfully and then let his sunglasses slide back down to his nose. "Please. You know what I like."

I stood up and brushed the sand from my butt.

"And please get Liza a bowl of fruit, she's looking dehydrated."

I stormed off, indignant to the fact that there were six beautiful models and not just Liza, and yet every other second, he was looking at her and demanding that she be taken care of with kid-gloves. What the hell is up with that? My only guess was that Liza was his insider. His one shot at getting close to Sergio and probably a member of his permanent team. The thought made my blood run cold.

I continued up the sand, around the naked women and ran smack into a tall Latin man wearing a Stetson and a sinister smile. His black hair was tucked behind his ears, yet long enough to brush the backs of his shoulders.

"Pardon," he said, pulling me up by my arm. "I'm so sorry."

"No, it's my fault. I wasn't watching where I was going." I casually yanked my arm from his clutch. "Sorry."

"Don't be, it was sort of fun." He winked and continued down the beach. I watched him, only because something about his dark eyes set my heart a fluttering and not in a good way. Any one of these men on the beach could be a cartel assassin, or Sergio Benitez for all I knew. Except, I presume that Sergio would be surrounded by an entourage, just like in the movies. Have you ever noticed that in the movies, the bad guys are rarely alone? Huh, I watch a lot of movies. Mostly James Bond and anything with Bruce Willis or Roald Munson. I can't help it. I'm a nanny and there's not much else to do in my line of work.

I shivered and got my composure back. Had I just bumped into a killer or a major drug lord? I dismissed those thoughts also and begged the girl behind the buffet table to make me a roast turkey sandwich on wheat bread.

One of the things that the Army had taught me was to be aware of my surroundings. I could describe to a tee each person sitting at the tables by the Café. Not one second went by that I wasn't glancing over my shoulder keeping an eye out for suspicious people or assassins lurking behind palm trees. I had an astute sense of who was around me at all times. Never again was I going to be as careless as I was a minute ago. Tripping and being helped up by a strange man. That's unacceptable. What would Jack think? Besides the fact that we occasionally share a bed, there was no real promise that Jack would take me onto his team. I still didn't know if I wanted to be on the team, but it would be really shitty if I did and he suddenly told me I was too careless and clumsy.

I carefully tucked a bag of chips under my arm and walked back to the beach, carrying Jack's sandwich, and a Diet Pepsi for myself. I don't usually drink coffee so I rely on soda for my caffeine fix. I noticed the Stetson man sitting on the dune, watching the show. His hat was tilted low, shadowing his scruffy face, but he was definitely interested in the goings-on at our beach. Then I noticed Jack wasn't in his chair, he was in the surf, adjusting Liza's red bikini strap and whispering something in her ear. Her head tossed back when she laughed, exposing her very perfect, long neck, which Jack then kissed.

His sandwich didn't stand a chance. When I jumped in horror, it slid off the paper plate and into the sand. I quickly shielded my eyes from the horrific scene in the surf and scooped the sandwich up, shook off what sand I could and placed it back on the plate, sandy side down.

Jack came back, put his sunglasses back on and grabbed his plate. "Thanks."

I felt a twinge of remorse and couldn't watch him take the first bite so I turned my head and immediately heard him spit and wheeze.

"Jesus, Charlie, did you drop it?" He spit out a couple more chunks of bread and turkey.

I shrugged and felt a rush of immaturity flush my cheeks. "It may have fallen off the plate, but I didn't see it. I was too busy watching you kiss Liza."

I didn't get a groan, a moan of disapproval, or even a dirty look. He just turned his head to the side and looked back out at waves. The man was as cool as they came.

"Maybe you should go cool your jets and make yourself scarce before I throw you in the ocean."

"Maybe you should go to hell," I said with a huff and then stormed off toward Gilbert, grabbing my folding chair and dragging it behind me in the sand. I stayed glued to his side for the rest of the day. I was pissed off beyond belief and Jack knew it. Jack knows me well and when my sense of humor dries up, he pretty much knows he's pushed me too far. I'm usually a very fun and lighthearted person, so anger and spite doesn't look good on me.

An hour or two later, Gil looked over his shoulder at me. "What's up your butt?" he asked, still clicking away on his fancy Nikon camera. He didn't wait for my reply. It was probably a rhetorical question anyway. "Go tell Mia to take off her top and lay in the surf. Pull her hair off her shoulders and tell her to wipe that stupid grin off her face, she's supposed to be sexy."

"Fine." I slid my sunglasses onto the bridge of my nose and did what Gil wanted. I remembered taking orders in the Army. I hated it, sometimes despised it, but I did it just the same. Mia's long blonde hair was already losing its curl thanks to the misty breeze from the waves crashing behind her. I helped her remove her top and to my amazement, her breasts didn't move from their high position on her chest – obviously, they were fake.

"Gil said, 'stop smiling and look sexy'." I slid my hand around the back of her neck and adjusted her hair as she lay in the wet sand.

"Tell Gil to go fuck himself," she retorted with a gruff voice. I was taken aback. She didn't look like the kind of woman to say such things. She was a few inches taller than me, had dark green eyes, and was skinny as hell, despite her melon size boobs.

"Will do." I actually felt my cheeks pucker when I smiled. I laughed the entire way back to Gil's side, ignoring the incessant waving of Jack. "She said for you to go fuck yourself," I said with a smirk. I felt as if I was back in the Army, throwing out the insults and listening to guy talk.

"Maybe later," he chuckled along with me and then got serious and snapped a few shots of Mia in the sand.

Gil's walkie-talkie blipped and Jack's stern voice crackled from the speaker.

"Tell Charlie to get her ass over here and stop ignoring me."

I turned and glared at Jack who was sipping coffee again and glaring in my direction. His position on the top of the dune wasn't that far, so I could see the tight set of his jaw. "Now," he said again for good measure.

With an exaggerated grunt, I slapped my hand around my chair and hauled it up to Jack. The sun was relentless and felt as if it had grown in diameter in the last few seconds alone. "What?"

"Are you mad?"

"You tell me."

"Fine, you're pissed, but can you please curb your jealousy for ten minutes. I need you to do me a favor."

"You're hungry again?"

He gave me an odd look and shook his head. "See that man over there, sitting on the ridge. The one you bumped into earlier."

Damn!

I told you. Jack knows EVERYTHING. Even when I don't think he's watching, he sees things. It's spooky!

I didn't look at Stetson man; I just nodded and then stared down at Jack's paperwork.

"What about him?"

"Walk by and see if you can get him talking. I need a clear shot and my men can't see his face well enough under that hat. Accidentally fall on him or something." He actually smiled at me. "Come on, klutz, show me what you've got."

If I wasn't pissed off already, I certainly was then. The tiny hairs on the back of my neck stood on end and in no way did I find his laughter amusing, sexy or endearing. I muttered several obscenities under my breath, threw my hands in the air in resignation, and began acting like a complete lunatic; All the while watching Stetson man from the corner of my eye. I kicked the sand, mumbled toward the sky and then crashed right into the side of him, knocking him backwards. His hat flew off and into the sand and it took me a moment to climb off his lap.

"Oh for God's sake." I shouted. "What else can go wrong today? I am so sorry, sir. Christ, I'm a menace to society." I did my job well. I'm sure Jack was proud.

"You're just a bit preoccupied that's all." He said, rather calmly about me knocking him senseless. "Those girls have been running you ragged all morning."

I sighed and gave him a genuine smile. "Thanks so much for noticing. I was beginning to think it was just me, but my God, they are relentless. Get me this -- get me that -- brush my hair -- tweeze my eyebrows. My God, I want to scream." I finished with a grin. "I'm Charlie. Again, I'm so sorry." I extended my hand, which he took and then kissed never taking his eyes off me.

"Grady." He responded, quickly picking up his hat and re-positioning it onto his head. "How long have you been doing this?"

"About four hours. Just started and already I want to quit, but it's my best chance at becoming a fashion editor so I'm willing to endure the bullshit."

"What doesn't kill you, makes you stronger."

"True," I grinned. "I'm taking up your time, I should go. Need to get the boss another Pepsi."

"Don't work too hard. You're too young and far too beautiful to be running yourself ragged."

I smiled and ran up and over the dune. When I reached the top, someone grabbed my upper arm and hauled me behind the side of the Café. I was too startled to scream and too restrained to knee him in the balls.
He was taller than I was, stronger than I was and had the meanest damn look on his face that I've ever seen. His hair was long, blonde and pulled into a ponytail behind his beefy neck.

"Get your paws off me, pal." I shouted and waited until he spoke before attempting to nail him in the balls. He wasn't holding a gun, knife, or any other weapon, so I gave him the benefit of the doubt.

"Who the fuck are you?"

"Who the fuck are you?" I squealed with a great deal of bravado. I had moves too. I was just biding my time before maiming the poor lad. "And I'll kindly tell you again. Get your paws off me." I shrugged out of his grasp and to my surprise, he let me go.

"That was no accident. Who are you and what do you want with Grady Sanchez?"

"Ummm, I tripped." Best to play the village idiot. I straightened my shirt and took a well-needed breath. "I was mad at my boss and I tripped."

He glared into my eyes and scowled. "Just stay the fuck out of my way." He growled and left me alone.

Great, now to add to the mystery, there's a tall blonde man in the mix.

"Who was that?" Liza said from beside me once I was alone again and reining in my emotions against the bricks of the Café wall.

"Nothing I can't handle, thank you very much." I snapped. I didn't intend on taking my rage and jealousy out on Liza, but she was there-- in my face—just asking for it. Besides, I had just been mauled by a mean man and I was a bit distressed.

"I'll go tell Eddie," she said, taking her time, watching my reaction. "What's your story anyway?"

"Don't have one." I said. "And I'll tell Eddie. You just smile and look pretty for the camera."

"Is that what you think of me?"

"If the shoe fits." I tilted my chin in the air pushing my way past her, retrieved a soda from the concession stand, and headed back to my post.

Several minutes later, after taking the time to take a few deep breaths and reflect on how I had treated Liza, a tiny pang of remorse washed over me and I felt immature to say the least. I think I may have been hanging my head when I finally got back to Jack, because he stood up and began rubbing my shoulders, staring out at the girls still in the surf. Half of them were whining because they were hot and hungry and the other half were signing autographs on men's torsos.

"Nice move up there. They got a perfect shot. I'll have to thank you later…that is unless you're still mad at me." His touch reminded me just how much I enjoy him. All of him and I didn't want that to ever end.

"I'm not mad," I said solemnly. "I guess I just wasn't expecting any of this. Each and every time you leave me to go on assignment, I envision you with a group of ugly, hairy thugs…not women like Liza." My shoulders somewhat relaxed under his capable hands. "She's one of yours, isn't she?"

"How'd you know?"

"Women's intuition." I chuckled.

"You're a smart woman, Charlie. Now let's wrap up this charade and get some dinner. I'm starved."

# Chapter Five

I helped Gilbert with the equipment and then carried the folding chairs back up to the Café, thanking the owner for letting us use them. Jack had ditched us all, probably to do something secretive with the secondary team and I was a bit disappointed, because when he suggested dinner, I expected room service for two in my bed. What I got instead was six anorexics and one excited Gilbert, sitting at my table—in my bungalow.

"Where'd Eddie run off to?" Mia asked, forking a baked potato and slamming down imported beer like a frat-boy. Her behavior bordered on suspicious because I didn't think models ate carbohydrates and drank high calorie regular beer.

I was about to speak up when Liza cut me off.

"He had to check on some things. Said he'd be back in the morning."

Highly, highly disappointed to hear that. Dang, I feel so alone.

The women engaged in small talk over the barbecued oysters and I made good timing finishing off my plate of Caesar salad while

sitting cross legged on the middle of my bed.
There weren't enough chairs to go around and it's
not like I'm actually interested in their small talk
anyway.

"So," Mia bobbed her brow at Liza and
wiped the drawn butter from her chin. "Anyone
heard the latest?"

"About what?" I was the first to speak.
Okay, so I wanted to be involved in their small
talk. When I was a girl, I opted to stay away from
slumber parties and girl talk because I was too
busy rebelling and pretending I was just as tough
as my brothers. I'd missed out on a lot and was
trying to mend my ways. Bella works well for me
in that department. I know all the juicy gossip at
her junior high school. Lucky me!

Thinking about Bella made me realize that
I missed her terribly.

"Eddie's girlfriend," Mia replied.

Jesus Christ! I almost choked on my
jumbo prawn. The entire table of people turned
and stared at me as I wheezed and gasped for
breath.

"Geez, don't die on us…yet!" Mia joked
while jabbing Gilbert with her elbow. He quickly
handed me a bottle of water. Everyone stared at
me with wide-eyes, wondering if I was going to
live or die. "Anyway, what was I saying?" Mia
asked with a flick of her wrist.

"Girlfriend. What about her?" one of the
leggy brunettes said. I think her name was Kaia,
but I wasn't sure because she looked just like the

other dark skinned woman named Serena. I got them confused all day.

"My brother thinks he's about to…"

I had to cut her off at that point because I didn't want to know. My life is private and hearing about my relationship with Jack was just too much for my ears and my heart to take. It could be bad, it could be good, but it's sort of like getting your palms read. Do you really want to know the exact moment that your boyfriend is going to break your heart? I personally would rather have it be a horrific surprise.

"Wait…how does your brother know Eddie?" I asked with wide eyes. I was attempting to change the subject and I thought it was quite odd.

Mia narrowed her eyes at me, probably pissed off that I interrupted her gossip session. Her eye twitched for a second and then her nose began twitching too. With one fluid movement, she reached up and yanked the blonde wig off her head, exposing an almost-bald head. Her hair was almost as short as Jack's and it was dark brown, not blonde. I was floored.

"Damn that thing is itchy." She tucked it into her bag and ran her hand over her hair. "Now, what are you babbling about?"

"Umm," I said.

"I thought Eddie said she was smart." Kaia pulled her hair up into a ponytail and shook her head at me.

"And nice." Liza shot at me with a scowl.

"Wait!" I put my hands up and furrowed my brows. "You're all on the…I mean…" At that point, I wondered if they were all part of Jack's unit. It seemed fitting, somewhat. Fitting -- yet completely disturbing and nauseating at the same time.

"He told me she was quick too," Gilbert added with a smirk. "and articulate and well educated."

"Yeah, Charlie. We're all on a team and as a team, we are supposed to work together." Liza's brown eyes softened as she turned her chair around and slid it closer to me. "Now what really happened with the guy outside the Café?"

"Uh," I felt sick to say the least. "You're all…Wow!"

"Wow! That almost sounded like a disappointed Wow. What were you expecting?"

"Honestly," I chuckled nervously. "A bunch of thugs."

"Hey, we can be thugs." Mia said, scratching her chin and downing more beer. "Eddie personally chose each and every one of us for a damn good reason."

I'll bet, I thought. I could just imagine him in bed with each of them, telling them that they'd be good together, just as he had said it to me. Ugh. My life as I know it is over.

"I need air," I got up and headed toward the door.

Liza met me outside, just as I slipped on my sandals and started for the crashing waves. I was thinking about jumping into them without a life preserver. My head swam with horrific images and I just wanted it all to stop. Mostly, I just wanted to kick Jack in the balls, but that would only make me feel better for about a second. This kind of pain ran too deep.

I was still trying to take a deep breath when Liza appeared at my side.

"Did you tell Jack about that guy yet?"

"You know what, I can't do this right now. I need some air..." I paused to narrow my eyes in suspicion. She just called him Jack!! Ah ha, the plot thickens!

She grabbed me by the arm and yanked hard. "This isn't a game, Charlie. People's lives depend on us and we all have to bury our shit when we're out in the field. If you can't deal with that and keep it together, then you have no business risking your life and the rest of our lives too. Now, what did he say to you?"

"He just asked me what I wanted with Grady Sanchez and then he told me to stay out of his way. That's all, I swear and as soon as I see Eddie, I'll tell him."

Her dark eyes flickered with irritability. "Tell him now. He's in my bungalow." She handed me the key to her bungalow and then stepped back inside.

My spine lengthened and I grew a couple of inches as I walked straight to her bungalow with a fire in my belly. If he thinks I'm about to become another one of his harem, then he's sorely mistaken.

I inserted the key, opened the door slowly, and was immediately tossed against the wall by a short bald man with biceps as big as my neck. He had me pinned against the door, spread eagle. My heart thumped harder in my chest and it was a good thing that I was already good and pissed off because my adrenaline was already surging and I had some kind of super strength that allowed me to turn my head and viciously rip one arm from his grasp. I twisted at the waist and caught him in the groin with my knee. I then sucker punched him in the temple, rendering him totally unconscious.

I leaned over his body and gasped for a well-needed breath. I could feel my heart ka-thunking against my rib cage at a rapid and probably unhealthy rate. Quickly, I gathered up his sidearm and checked for ammo. It was fully loaded, so I clicked off the safety and held it to his back, waiting to regain some sort of composure before screaming for help.

Before I had time to do anything else, Jack emerged from the back door, holding a couple of Styrofoam to-go containers and a six-pack of beer. The door slammed shut behind him and his jaw dropped when he saw me standing over a body.

"Fuck, Charlie. What the hell are you doing?"

I brushed the hair from my eye with one hand and kept the gun on the assailant's back. "I was trying to find you and this jackass attacked me. Should I shoot him, or do we want to ask him questions first?" I asked sarcastically, still angered by my harem theory.

"Very funny," Jack said. "Put down the gun."

"Why?"

"Because that's a good guy and I don't want you to accidentally kill him. He's sort of a friend." He crossed the room quickly so he could be by my side.

"Oh," I put the safety on and stepped back. "Sorry, but he grabbed me and I was pissed."

"How'd you do that?" He looked down at his friend and then back up at me. "Randy's one of my best men."

"Adrenaline I guess." I shook my head and made my way toward the sink. Filling a glass of water, I drank most of it and then poured the rest on Sleeping Beauty's face.

He sat up, gasping and sloshing water from his face. "What the fuck?" He tried to grab me, but Jack grabbed his hand before it made contact with my ankle.

"Meet Charlie," he said and then handed Randy a cold beer. "Charlie, this is Randy Sutter, my right hand man."

"Sorry," I said sheepishly.

He wasn't as macho and hotheaded as I expected. "Nice moves…for a girl."

Then again.

"Did you eat?" Jack asked, holding out half a sandwich to me.

I nodded and fidgeted with a hangnail that had been bothering me all day. "Can I talk to you?"

"Yeah," he said warily.

"Alone?"

He glanced at Randy and then back at me. "We're sort of in the middle of something here. Can it wait?"

"Liza doesn't think so."

"You can talk in front of Randy. He's on our side you know."

I rolled my eyes and leaned back against the countertop. My tank top was sweaty and clinging to my breasts due to my wrestling match--which I won. I was still smiling on the inside.

"A guy sort of jumped me behind the Café today. He asked me what I wanted with Grady Sanchez and then not-so-nicely told me to stay out of his way. Liza saw it all and thought you should know."

The men exchanged glances. "Describe him."

"Six two, two twenty. Long blonde hair, pulled into a low ponytail. Blue eyes, scruffy face and a scar above his left eyebrow." I inhaled sharply and started again. "Blue jeans, white tank top and black boots. Sounded American, but I've been fooled before. What do you think?"

"I think you should have told me this afternoon."

"I was preoccupied," I said, still trying to rein in my desire to kick him in the balls. "I really need to talk to you."

"Give us a minute," he said to Randy and finished off his sandwich. "What's up? You look pissed off again."

"Damn straight." I growled. "Your entire unit consists of probably six of the most beautiful women I've ever seen and you never happened to mention that to me," I quietly shouted. "Oh, and you just happened to personally pick them all. You were the one who recruited them...just like you're trying to recruit me. Jesus Jack, this is sick!"

He started to respond but I interrupted him.

"Sick, I tell you, it's just sick and wrong and, oh God, I feel like such a fool." I sat down and began grinding my teeth to halt the tears. "I want to go home. I'm not cut out for this, Jack. I'm not a spy. I prefer to be on the outside looking in. I'm a sniper for God's sake. I can't do this up close and personal shit. I need air...I need space...I need air." I gasped and ended up on the bed, clutching my chest in a dramatic fashion. "This just isn't what I had in mind."

"Honestly, Charlie, neither did I." He knelt down beside me. The mattress sank down from his weight. "I had no intention of throwing you in like this, but what choice did I have. I couldn't let you go gallivanting around at Disney World with a psycho on your heels."

"What?" I snapped at attention. "What the hell is that supposed to mean?"

He raked a hand through his hair a couple of times, clearly not happy about what he was about to say. "They couldn't identify his body."

That's what I was afraid of.

My tears steadily streamed down my face. "And you knew it was a possibility that he'd come for me, didn't you?"

He stood up and moved away from me, which was a good thing because I was still itching to kick him where it counts.

"So, he is after me?" My God, the Rat is coming for me. I violently shivered at the thought.

"I didn't say that." His tone turned guarded. "All I said was that they never identified his body."

"But you thought it was a possibility. That's why I'm here, you just said it yourself."

"Yeah, but it doesn't necessarily mean it's Malcolm Rchevicha. Anyone could have done it. That's why I need to know who else knew you called him The Rat?"

I didn't know what to say. Sure, only a handful of people knew about my pet name for the fascist pig, but what hurt was that Jack had gone back into cop-mode and was staring at me with narrowed eyes. "I guess just Du Lucere, Russo and the men from the hospital where I was kept."

"That's it?" His arms folded across his chest and he seemed to relax a bit, but was clearly trying to work something out in his head.

I climbed off the bed, grabbed a bottle of water from the fridge and then caught a glimpse of Liza's silky gown hanging from the bathroom doorknob. Who knew that my jealousy would outweigh my fear of death? "So, are you sleeping with Liza…and how about Mia? Hell, no wonder you're so damn good in bed. Lots of practice, huh?"

I saw his jaw clench out of the corner of my eye, but I was too afraid to look at him.

"I know you just didn't say that," he said with a slow, disapproving headshake.

I shot him a serious glare. "Well, it seems fitting. They told me that you picked each of them…personally. What else am I supposed to think?"

Just then, before he could utter his -- what I assumed would be – pathetic rebuttal, there was a loud knock on the door and Randy was mumbling about eating.

I walked over to the door, wrenched it open and looked back at Jack over my shoulder. "We're finished here." I muttered and headed down the dune, past the towering palm trees and into the cool sand.

The sun had set and the stars were just starting to emerge against the indigo sky and I was heartbroken, scared, and for the first time since I had met Jack, I felt alone.

Jack was so much more to me than just a boyfriend, lover, or friend. He was the one person that I counted on to keep me at peace. The one constant in my life that I looked to for comfort and camaraderie. That moment that I walked out that door, I felt as if my world had crumbled and nothing would ever be the same between us again. I'm just not that kind of girl. I don't accuse him of staring too long at women on the street. I never ask him where he's been or who he's been with because I know him and I trust him. I used to feel secure in my relationship because I knew that Jack had me... and his job.

I guess that's where I took a pounding, because his job entails spending more time with Liza, Mia and the sexy Kaia and Serena, and less time with me.

I was determined not to cry and turn into a wimpy girl and that's why I wasn't paying any attention to where I was walking and who was walking beside me.

"Are you okay?" The Stetson Man asked me with a warm smile, once he finally paced his stride to match mine. "You look sad."

My heart jumped into my throat, but I managed to smile. "I'm fine, thanks." I looked around, panicking that I was alone with a potential hit-man. "I should get back."

His fingers curled around my bicep, which incited me to suck in a breath and then gasp loudly.

His hand dropped from my arm. "I'm sorry, I didn't mean anything by that...I was just...well, I thought we could walk...together. It's a beautiful night."

Oh, I so wanted to scream for my Daddy, but I'm a big girl and I pride myself in the fact that I can remain panic free in times of discomfort.

Yeah right.

I looked around and saw no one that could possibly help me.

His dark skin contrasted the flash of his white teeth as he smiled widely. "I won't bite you."

"It's not that," I laughed nervously. "It's just that..." I rolled my eyes. "I quit my job tonight and I should be trying to get my plane ticket changed, or packing or at least calling my boyfriend to tell him I'm coming home early."

Little white lies never hurt anyone.

"Oh."

I nodded and bobbed my eyebrows while rocking back on my bare heels. "Thanks for the offer, but I really should be going."

He took my hand, gave my wrist a small kiss and smiled a tight-lipped grin. "Maybe some other time."

I ran back to my cabana. It was dark, everyone was gone, but it still smelled like crab, shrimp, and French fries. I know I left my sandals in the surf, but all I could think about was opening my door, crawling into bed and ramming my fists into my pillow a couple of times. My heart was beating out of control and when a man wrapped his hand across my mouth, I bit hard.

"Jesus," Jack half shouted, half whispered, letting me go and stepping back to evade my flailing appendages.

"Don't do that to me!" I clutched my heaving chest and glared. "I quit! Get out and leave me alone!"

"What did he want?"

His legs were nicely tanned, he had a sexy five-o'clock shadow going on and he smelled amazing, but I was having no part of his sick little world.

"Why do you care?" I stumbled into the bathroom, brushed my teeth in record time, and undressed, covering myself with a very unattractive oversized t-shirt.

When I came back out, Jack was lounging on my bed, sucking on a half-eaten apple, and pounding away on his laptop.

I stopped, stared at his nice ass and tanned torso, and then sucked back the trickle of drool, reminding myself that I was mad and he was a pig!

"So, what did he say?" he asked without looking up.

"Am I not making myself clear here. I said I quit. What part of I quit don't you understand?"

It was then that he turned his head and narrowed his eyes at me. "Is this still about sleeping arrangements?"

"Yes...no...fuck, Jack!" I mumbled before yanking back the sheets and attempting to climb under them.

"You're serious?"

"What do you think?" I snarled.

"I think Grady Sanchez has a crush on you and that you could help me out. We're running out of time."

"Now you want me to sleep with the man. What's next?"

He rose slowly, checked the locks, peered out the window, rechecked the locks, and then grabbed an imported beer from the fridge.

I pounded on my pillow, got my head snuggled in nicely and then shut my eyes tightly, hoping he'd get the picture. I was fairly sure he thought I was full of crap because I never go to bed before ten and it was only eight-fifteen.

I felt his breath hot on my lips before he spoke softly. "Charlie."

I moaned.

"Pretty please."

"No," I groused.

His lips moved closer, he was the master of seduction after all. "Baby, if you won't do it for me, do it for your country." I could almost sense the smirk on his face.

He caught my lower lips between his, suckling it slowly. My body was betraying me once again, as I whimpered and struggled to catch my breath. Then I popped my eyes open wide and pulled back.

"Seriously, Jack. You're not helping yourself here. If anything you're digging yourself in deeper," I said seriously. "You're a sick pig!"

He laughed hard and plopped his body down next to me, chuckling and brushing my long bangs from my eyes. "Babe, I was kidding…Kaia does all the sleeping around."

I wanted to hit him, but instead I pursed my lips tightly and ran for the bathroom. It was not funny and I wanted no part of his twisted spy games. I wanted structure and ops that made sense. I want all the information in front of me and I don't like playing games.

FBI here I come!

~~~

I slept in the bathtub, because I have the most stubborn boyfriend in the world and he refused to leave after my latest temper tantrum. I woke with a serious crick in my neck and waterlogged toes. The faucet had leaked all night and let me just say, I was a bitch when I finally emerged from the bathroom.

Jack was smart and was already gone.

I showered, shaved my legs, and then called the airline to see if I could up my flight. I was eager to return to the states, set an appointment with Special Agent Dean Williams of the FBI and take my rightful place beside the pansy-ass college boys.

"What do you mean, no?" I shouted again at the customer service rep for my airline of choice. "I'll gladly pay the extra amount to change it...I need to leave – now!"

There was a loud knock on the door. My pulse raced. I hurriedly grabbed my gun, rammed it into the back of my Capri pants and peeked through the window near the front door.

It was Grady Sanchez, adorned in his Stetson, holding my sandals and two cups of coffee.

I had trouble swallowing, but managed to get out a short nod of acknowledgement before returning to my conversation with Stacy at American Airlines. "Tonight...that's fine. Tonight is good." I rolled my eyes, thinking I could make it through one more day in this God-forsaken paradise. I jotted down my new flight number, gave her my credit card information, and then hung up. Swiping the sweat from my palms, I opened the door and smiled.

"Good morning," he said sweetly. "Thought you might need these. You left them on the beach last night, but I saw that you had company...didn't you say you had a boyfriend back home."

Jesus! Did I say that?

I felt my cheeks flush. "Oh...last night. That was just my boss. He's gay." I couldn't help myself. It just came out.

"Oh." He smiled brightly and I think he bought it. "Breakfast?"

Oh what the hell? Maybe I could be a seductress after all. Not. I was just starving, that's all. "Sure," I said. "I'd love it."

~~~

I made sure we ate at the main restaurant that I had frequented the day before. Lots of people milling around and Jack just a few hundred feet away, looking out at the waves and the babes in bikinis.

My stomach growled, so I excused myself from the table and headed to the buffet before the waitress could even offer juice.

"You don't eat like any woman I know." Grady said from beside me. The buffet was magnificent. Every kind of breakfast meat, three kinds of scrambled eggs; fruit of every color and even omelets to order. I couldn't even wait to get the food onto my plate.

I finished off the chunk of bacon I was chewing and gave him a wide-eyed look of horror.

"I meant that in the nicest way possible. It's rather refreshing to meet a women with an appetite," he said, after clearing his throat loudly.

"Oh," I really could have cared less, but it was an odd thing to say to a woman. "Are you married?" I asked, shoveling pancake after pancake onto my platter. "Got kids?"

He shook his head solemnly. "No."

I think I hit a nerve and a tingle of trepidation raced up my spine.

To my left, I saw the tall ponytail guy who had attacked me the day before. He was watching us like a hawk, and not being very covert about it. Clearly, he wasn't a super spy like Jack because at least when Jack glanced our way, he did it surreptitiously, pretending to be stretching, or adjusting his sunglasses.

I knew he'd be watching, probably happily gloating about it too.

Grady and I ate, talked, and then filled our plates again. Besides the fact that he's probably a cartel hitman, he seemed genuinely nice.

When I was full beyond the confines of my khaki colored Capri pants, I thanked Grady and sauntered onto the beach with a Diet Pepsi. The cabana boy, Ricardo was carrying my lounge chair and beach towel. I walked past Jack, winked at him with attitude, and then let Ricardo lather my naked back with suntan oil.

It took Jack three and a half seconds to jump out of his chair, scurry through the sand, and tell Ricardo to take a hike. Jealous perhaps? He didn't look happy with me one bit, but he did finish where Ricardo had left off. "Well, what made you change your mind?" His hands were massaging with great urgency. I could feel his angst in the tips of his fingers.

"I didn't. I was hungry; he offered pancakes. End of story." I turned my head so he could lather the left shoulder without getting his hands caught in my hair. "You're gay by the way, so don't look like you're having too much fun."

He laughed hard. "Want to tell me about it?" He asked, before whistling at the tall hunk who had just bent over in front of us.

I just about lost bladder control and then quickly stifled my laughter. "Nothing to tell. We talked about my fake job, my fake boyfriend back home, and his ranch near Miami. That's all. I don't think he's your man, but the ponytail guy sure was interested in us."

"D.E.A," he said through clenched teeth and then leaned over and kissed my shoulder, sending tiny aftershocks of joy across my oily skin. "Does this mean you're staying?"

"No," I said. "I could have an appointment with Dean Williams by tomorrow afternoon."

"Has anyone ever told you how damn stubborn you are?" I heard a gush of breath leave his flaring nostrils. It was silent for a minute or two, which in and of itself was completely unnerving. "What about The Rat?"

My heart leapt in my chest, then it tightened slightly. Rolling onto my back, I glared hard. "That was low." I had completely...well, almost completely, forgotten that I was still being stalked by Vermin Man.

"Don't go," he pleaded. "Both my teams are here and I can't watch you back home. Three more days, tops."

"I can't."

He blew out a breath of defeat and left me alone with my Harlequin romance and Diet Pepsi.

Jack stopped talking to me after that, or I stopped talking to him. I couldn't tell the difference. I spent my last day in paradise alone on that beach, sulking in my soda, rethinking my life. Did I really want to return to the states where The Rat was waiting to torture and kill me? Not particularly, but the only other option was to stay in the Bahamas and watch Jack interact with Liza and that was making me ponder suicide, so it mattered not what I did. I was dead either way.

# Chapter Six

Vinny was kind enough to meet me at Newark Airport. I figured I had a few more days until Bella completely lost it at my folks' house and called me, begging for me to come and save her from small town America. I was going to take advantage of that time and I was not going to be scared of The Rat. The Rat was the least of my problems. Jack was furious and I mean, furious at me. When he dropped me at the airport, he didn't even demand that I call him when I got back. Not at all like the controlling, skittish Jack that I know and love.

It was very early morning by the time Vinny pulled the limo into the garage bay at the Munson house; six fifteen to be exact. I was tired, irritated, and honestly terrified to step from the vehicle.

He opened the door and extended his big burly hand to me. Vinny looked like Jesse Ventura…but on super steroids. The man was huge, but he rarely spoke, so it surprised me when he grinned and said, "Nothing weird's been going on here. You're cool."

"Thanks," I muttered with a yawn. "Can I sleep with you just in case?"

His big white cheeks burned with a light rosy glow and he stuttered.

"Kidding," I said before he got any wild ideas. He opened the door that lead into the kitchen and I hesitantly followed. Without the benefit of having Greg around, the kitchen smelled like barbecued beef. The counters were cluttered with body building magazines, a couple of Playboys and some empty protein shake containers. Before I made it past the mess, my cell phone blipped from the bottom of my purse. To my dismay, it wasn't Jack.

"Yes, Randy. I made it. I'm fine. We just pulled in."

Randy was the second best thing, I guess. I know he's the only one of the members of Jack's team who knows anything about our little romance, so my guess is, Jack put him up to it. I climbed the stairs two at a time and opened the second door on the left. "Tell Jack, I'm fine."

"You need anything, you just call. We'll be back in two days."

"Over and out!" I flipped it shut and fell fast asleep in Bella's bed.

The following morning, I did what any other normal paranoid woman would do; I showered, (without closing my eyes while washing my hair.) I wore jeans and tennis shoes in case I had to make a quick getaway and then I tucked my gun under the waste band of my Levis and ate three peanut butter and jelly sandwiches. I checked my cell-phone again, just to make sure it was working and I hadn't missed Jack's apology call. Much to my dismay, it was working. Damn! There was one message and one message alone from Agent Dean Williams and of F.B.I instructing me to please meet him this afternoon to get the ball rolling.

~~~

My interviewer was waiting for me in the lobby of the Hilton Hotel promptly at three P.M. He wore a dark gray suit, white oxford and a burgundy tie. Pansy-ass college boy incarnate.

"Miss Ford," he said, extending his hand to me and introduced himself as Agent Dean Williams. "Good to see you. Can I get you some coffee?"

"No, thanks." I shook his hand firmly and looked right into his hazel eyes. His hair was blonde, as were his fluffy eyebrows. I wondered if pansy-ass college boy had muscles like Jack did. My mind began wandering to places it had no right to go. Just because Jack's final words before I left weren't so nice and he had given me that stupid ultimatum doesn't necessarily mean that we are over…it just means he's a big horse's ass!

He smiled warmly and dropped his hand from mine to grab a large briefcase from his side. He motioned to the conference room and I led the way, entering the room filled with two other serious looking men and a very familiar scowl. My heart leapt into my chest. I felt weak-kneed and then I was not so nicely asked to sit. The doors closed tightly, the lights seemed to dim slightly and the big man in the corner rounded the table and put his hands down on the table in front of me. I felt his breath hot on my face, drying my eyes -- that for some reason were frozen in terror.

I tried to speak, but no words would come. Was this some sort of sick joke? One of Jack's not-so-funny spy games? No one in the room seemed to understand my state of angst.

He got words out before I could. "Eddie Malone isn't who you think he is." The tall blonde man with a ponytail said through clenched teeth.

I looked around for help from the nice FBI guys, and then I realized that they probably weren't FBI guys. This supposed D.E.A agent who was breathing down my neck – the same man who had attacked me at the Paradiso Café in the Bahamas – had probably somehow intercepted my phone call and this was a set-up. But why? And as long as I was rationalizing in my head…who the hell is Eddie Malone?

I remained quiet and he went on. "This is important, so make sure you don't leave anything out." A tape recorder the size of a deck of cards was set in front of me. He pushed the record button and slid it even closer to my chest. "Start at the beginning. Why were you in the Bahamas and what did you want with Grady Sanchez?"

Jack had told me that this big jerk was D.E.A. Was he lying to me, or was something else going on? I hadn't a clue, but I still remained silent.

The big man was dressed much different from the last time I saw him. On the beach he looked like a sloppy biker. In this small room, he looked like a trained professional. Faded jeans, dark blue oxford shirt, rolled up his beefy forearms. Oh my. He definitely didn't look like a pansy-ass college boy.

I remained tight lipped and tried not to squirm in my seat.

His eyes bulged out then narrowed slightly. "Grady Sanchez was found murdered late last night."

I gasped then swallowed hard, pressing my lips even tighter together. I guess Jack got his man...but why would the DEA be breathing down my neck? Eddie...Oh shit. Eddie is Eddie Malone. Jack is Eddie. Ah Crud! What the hell is going on?

He made a gesture to the other agent-type-men and they swiftly left the room.

Terrified? Sure, I almost peed my pants.

He sat down and leaned his chiseled jaw into the palm of his hand. "Let's start at the beginning. How did Eddie contact you and what were you supposed to find out by getting close to Grady Sanchez?"

"I don't know what you are talking about." I said with a completely trembling jaw.

"And I don't know anyone named Eddie, or Grady for that matter."

"We know who you are, Charlie. We know that you spend time with Eddie Malone," he said with a cocked brow. "...alone."

Gulp!

"I don't know this Eddie person," I repeated.

That's when at least thirty 8x10 glossy photos were pulled from a manila file and tossed in front of me. Jack and I outside a hotel in Westport. Jack and I in the Bahamas. Jack and I at the Nassau airport. Even in the photograph I could see how mad Jack was at me for leaving early. Maybe he does love me. He looked pissed!

I said nothing shoving them away with a perfect poker face. "What do you want?"

"Grady Sanchez," he replied with quite a bit of spit flying from his lips. "Why were you following him and what did Eddie want with him?"

I hated how he kept calling Jack, Eddie. Mostly because when I first met Jack, he had told me his name was Duane, Vince and Ryan and now, after many months of intimacy and grand orgasms, I would be very angry and hurt if his name really wasn't Jack. I'd hope that I have better sense than to be involved with a man whose real name I didn't know.

"Look," I glared; panic fluttering in my tummy as if I'd swallowed a handful of jumping beans. I could smell bacon and eggs and syrup when I took a deep breath. "I don't know anyone named Eddie. I think you have me confused with someone else. Can I go now?"

He looked at me with a heinous glare, as if he wanted to pick me up and toss me against the far wall. A pale blue vein bulged in his neck. "Be very careful, Charlie. This isn't a game and Eddie Malone is a very dangerous man." He left me alone after that life altering statement and I could taste my own vomit in the back of my throat. My three peanut butter sandwiches were still sitting in my churning stomach. I had no idea why I was so nervous. With seven little words, that big man that I didn't even know, had single-handedly made me doubt Jack Edward Sullivan, the man I sleep with – the man who is my best friend in the entire world – the man I probably love. I left that room with a heavy heart and then quickly decided that this had to be some sort of mistake.

I flipped open my cell phone, called Jack's number and was mortified when it was disconnected. It hadn't been disconnected last night when I called him and hung up on him twelve times. It hadn't even been disconnected very early this morning when I called just to hear his voice…and then hung up on him again. Crap, what does this mean?

I knew that nothing made sense. I quickly decided that because of my fear of Vermin Man and the fact that my mom and Bella weren't expecting me for another couple of days, that it was time to find out what the hell was going on. My first order of business was to call Randy.

Surprisingly, his phone was also disconnected.
Next, I entered my SUV, grabbed my gun from
under the seat, placed it beside me in the
passenger seat and then stared at it for a good ten
minutes while I calmed my nerves and tried to
talk myself out of driving straight to Baltimore.

~~~

The drive to Baltimore was nice and
quick. I had been daydreaming about what I was
going to do to Jack once I found him, but when I
merged onto Interstate 95, I quickly decided to
give him the benefit of the doubt. That, of course,
changed again once I drove through Philadelphia.
My nerves were shot after stopping for a Grande
mocha, which I normally don't drink. By the time
I entered downtown Baltimore, I was jittery and
cursing like a sailor.

I'd only been to Jack's apartment a
handful of times. It wasn't very homey. It was a
studio in the industrial part of town, just off
Harborview Drive. The building overlooked the
Patapsco River and the air around it smelled like
rotten broccoli. There was a bed, a small
bathroom and a poor excuse of a kitchen; it was
more like a place to keep his hotplate and can
opener. Needless to say, I don't think Jack spent
too much time at home. Hell, he's never home.
He's always off saving the world from
international terrorists...or was he?

When I pulled up to the building that housed Jack's apartment, I couldn't hold back the tears or the obscenities. It looked like something out of a movie. The smoke was black and red with little puffs of blue around the edges. Flames were licking the side of the adjacent building. The entire building was blown to smithereens. In fact, all the damn firefighters could do was stand back and watch. It was an inferno. I felt my world implode. More so then, than when I had quit the Army four years ago. I hadn't felt that big of a loss since that day and it just reminded me more and more about how my life was still anywhere but on track. And now this? Finding out that my relationship with Jack was a lie...or worse, that he was dead. I curled up in a ball and cried for what seemed like an eternity.

Moments later, a fireman tapped on my window and asked me to leave. Nice, I was in tears.

What if Jack had been home? What if he were dead?

I pulled out onto Grindall Street and headed toward Jack's favorite joint.

"Serves him right!" I shouted to myself, looking like a deranged psycho at the diner up the street. Jack, or whatever his name was, probably didn't want to be found. If he were dead, then good riddance! I cried some more, loudly blew my nose into my soiled napkin again and finished off my second piece of apple pie. I paid for my pie and hot cocoa and then drove two blocks up the street to Federal Hill Park and reminisced about my time with Secret Agent Man. I should have known that someday this would happen. Just like the attempt on his life in California, shit happens, and I should have better prepared myself for an unhappy ending. It sucked though, because our last words to each other weren't nice ones. He never did tell me that he loved me and I never had the chance to tell him how I felt either.

I stayed the night in a tiny hotel room all alone with my gun, my tears and my broken heart.

Early the next morning, I got on a plane for Portland, Oregon, still scared of Vermin Man and still unsure of my future. What I did know was that I was lost without Jack. Jack made the world seem less horrible. He made me smile. He made me laugh and for the past eighteen hours, he had made me cry, harder than I had ever cried in my life.

# Chapter Seven

I opened the door to my parents' house in Bend, Oregon after a three-hour drive from Portland, and dropped my luggage on the hard-wood floor with a loud thud. I hadn't bothered unpacking from my Bahamas trip, so I was in need of a washing machine and a place to hide my guns.

"Charlene," my mom cooed as she hugged me tightly. "What's wrong, sweetie?"

Okay, so I was still in tears. Bad move on my part, as I usually try to keep my mother out of my love life. I was so damn mad. I was hurt and I was scared to death that Jack was sitting in a hot tub in some remote, romantic location with his team of highly trained sluts! I couldn't help the tears.

"Nothing," I lied. "I'm just glad to be home." I looked around and saw no sign of Bella. That scared me beyond words and had me moving past my mother with quick, impatient steps. "Where's Bella?" I asked calmly.

My mother wiped her hands on her apron and grinned. "She had a date."

"A date?" I almost screamed. "Mom, she's 13. You didn't let me date until I was 16 -- and, even then, Dad met my dates at the door with his shotgun! What were you thinking?"

"Don't exaggerate, darling," She chuckled slightly. "and let's not kid ourselves, you only had one date."

Completely beside the point...but true. I wasn't a typical girl.

"I dropped them off at the movies." She continued. "They will be home any minute. Sheesh." She hurried past me and grabbed a Diet Pepsi from the fridge. "How's Jack...and why are you two days early?" She glanced at me again, and then shook her head. "Did you two have a fight?"

Well, how could I answer that one? "Yeah, Mom. I told him to take a hike when he all but begged me to solicit information from a Columbian hitman with my body..."

"No, we didn't have a fight. I just – well – hell, Mom!" I shifted in my tennis shoes and glanced up at the clock. "Oh, General Hospital is on." I sidestepped my way into the living room and clicked on the TV to change the subject. It worked and she left me alone.

Twenty minutes later, the door opened and Bella walked in with a beaming smile.

"A date, huh?" I grinned over the arm of the couch and she shrieked with excitement.

"You're here! Oh God, Charlie. He's sooooo cute and he's 16!" She shouted and clearly wanted to give me all the horrific details.

I cocked my brow at her and she shut up, knowing full well that I was about to lecture her on older boys and those things in their pants that make them so dangerous! Sometimes our nanny-child relationship got a bit foggy, but one cocked brow usually put her back in her place.

The excitement receded and she sat down beside me. "What's wrong? Why are you early? I have a date tomorrow. We are going to go to the lake."

Wow, I felt so welcome. I leaned back and got comfortable. "I thought you wanted to go to Orlando?" I felt another sting of remorse and regret. I had finally gotten Jack to agree to come with us and now he was gone. Out of my life... forever.

She looked down at her hands, back up to me and I could tell she was trying not to cry. "I think I love him."

My lips tipped into a feeble smile. Her first love. Oh, how I wanted to smack the crap out of her and tell her that love sucks. That love will only break her heart. "I guess we can stay another day or two." I held her hand and attempted a smile.

"Is everything okay, Charlie?"

"Sure." I said and turned back to the television to escape her gaze. "It sounds like you've been having fun here. See, my parents aren't so bad, are they?"

She shrugged a couple of times and played with the pillow by her side. "You're dad is so cool, Charlie."

I whipped my head around to see her smile. "Really, you think so."

"Yeah, he took me to the hospital a couple times. I got to take someone's blood pressure and help the nurses with lunch. It was so fun. I think I want to be a doctor," she said dreamily. I remember having those same aspirations when I was her age. Thinking of my father made me realize I was home and had something important to tell him. But now that my FBI interview had been faked and Jack was MIA and apparently out of my life, I wasn't all that thrilled about telling him just yet. I decided it was a much better discussion to have once I got my life back on track.

I spent the rest of the day with Bella out on the back deck looking at golfers, as my parents live on the edge of a very busy golf course in a newer subdivision. My father came home around seven pm and greeted me with a big smile and a hug.

"You look good. How's everything?" he asked, then gave Bella a hug too. It warmed my heart to see him embracing her. It also made me sad because she may be the closest thing I ever come to having any kids of my own. The way my luck was going, I'll be old and gray before I find a good honest man to marry.

"Good, Dad." I said. "How are things at the hospital? Are you getting any closer to having your own practice?"

"Nah," he groaned. "Too much work. I'm better off just cutting back my schedule at St. Charles. You're mother wants me to take her to Ireland and Scotland this fall." He sipped from the martini that my mom had put down in front of him. "Your mom told me about Jack. You okay?"

I rolled my eyes. "I'm good. Things are just fine."

NOT!

We remained quiet for a heartbeat, staring out at the golfers.

"Dad," I cleared my throat and got serious. "Do you think I'm stubborn?"

He nearly laughed, but kept his composure well. "Honey," he said. "You joined the Army just to make your old man mad. You refused to eat spinach your entire life. When you were seven you refused to let me help you ride your brother's ten-speed -- You fell and skinned both your knees badly, don't you remember? I think when you were born, you even refused to cry when the doctor tried to get you to take your first breath. Do you see my point?" He sipped some more martini and smiled. "What happened with Jack?"

I shrugged and kept my eyes diverted, but he continued on.

"I can't believe I'm actually about to say this aloud, but I like Jack. Jack is good for you."

I smiled. I knew Jack was good for me too. He was macho as hell and even more stubborn than I, but he made me laugh. He inspired me to do my best at everything and he made me realize that I don't have to try to impress him with every breath I take. I'd been trying to impress men my entire life. I used to blame that on my perfect brothers, but after last summer, I realized my brothers weren't the problem. I was.

Boy, I really wanted to break down and tell my father everything. I couldn't remember a time in my life when I was more comfortable talking to him than I was right then. "It's nothing. We just had an argument."

"You're mother said you're thinking of going into the insurance business with Jack. How did this come about? What about college?"

"About that," I said, and then an errant golf ball flew by our heads and bounced off a tree. It landed on the table and shattered Dad's martini glass. I guess that was my sign from above that the timing really wasn't right after all.

~~~

Two days later, Bella was heartbroken when her first love found out she was only thirteen and decided to stand her up at the movie theater. Frankly, I was thrilled because it meant we were on a plane headed toward a happy place with sunshine, portable margaritas and a myriad of men to flirt with. I guess we were both brokenhearted and for the first four hours of our flight to Florida, neither of us said a word.

"You okay?" I finally asked, while pulling her headphones off her ears. "Bella?"

"He's a jerk," she said, tears streaming down her cheeks. I'd endured her sad taste in music since we left the Portland airport. I'd had enough.

"They all are, sweetie." The minute I said it, I wanted to take it back. I had no right to taint her image of men. Especially at her young age. That was a horrible, horrible thing for me to say. I should have said something nice, like… "Well, he's just immature and when he's sixty and you're only fifty-seven, he'll be thinking differently about his choice to dump you." I really need to work on my spiritual side.

She sighed heavily and put her hand on mine. "What happened with Jack? Did you break up?"

I nodded slowly, tightening my lips. "It's okay though. I have you and a master's degree. Who needs men?"

~~~

A limousine picked us up and took us straight to our grand hotel. Greg had done a great job with our reservations. We had prime real estate staring right into the heart of Universal Studios. The enormous suite with a view had two bedrooms, a kitchen and a big-screen TV. Good times indeed.

I dropped my luggage onto the paisley comforter and Bella headed for her room. My first order of business was to clear the air with a certain FBI dude, but before I could do that, there was a knock at the door. I opened it and was handed a basket of oranges, a pineapple, apples, nuts and chocolate. "Thanks," I said to the young bellhop and then burrowed in my pocket for a couple of dollars. He grinned, said thanks and left me alone.

"Bella!" I shouted. "Did you order room service?" There was no card attached, just a big red bow. I looked harder through the transparent wrapping, it seemed okay. "Never mind." I quickly opened it, dug around for all the chocolate I could find and when I lifted the large Tobelerone bar, I saw the distinct fur of a rat. The basket dropped heavily to the floor as I screamed like a girl and slammed the upper lock on the door. Bella ran in with her hand over her heart.

"Geez, Charlie."

"Sorry, I dropped it on my toe." I lied.
She narrowed her eyes. Her hands shot to her hips. "What's going on with you?"

"Nothing. Go watch TV."

She was already primping for our big day out. Brushing her long blonde hair, she paused to give me a contemptuous glare. "We're in Orlando…and you want me to go watch TV?" Her head shook from side to side. "Let's go!"

"NO!" I shouted more vocally than I realized. "I'm…I'm tired. Let me take a nap and then we'll go, okay?"

"What-ever." She turned and left me alone with the basket of dead rats.

I walked toward the bed, called the hotel janitor and had the basket removed. Then I bit my lip until it bled, cried into my pillow, hit my pillow and then rummaged through my purse, found the number to Inspector Russo with Interpol and I got him on the sixth ring.

"Carmelo, It's me, Charlie Ford."

"Charlie?" I think it was probably the middle of the night in France, so he sounded quite out of it, and rightfully so. "Vat's wrong?" Carmelo Russo had been there in Eastern Europe when The Rat had stolen my underwear, my purse and my faith in mankind. I hated that I was as scared as I was, but I had to suck it up and find answers. I tried to remember The Rat's real name, but it was hard to pronounce and, really, I'd only heard Jack call him that one time. Crap.I knew I was going to sound like a fool, but it was my only hope.

"Look, I know this is silly, but what happened to the man I called The Rat? I heard he

died, but strange things are happening here and
I'm really scared that he might be after me."
I heard rustling and some creative foreign
cursing.      "Vat happened there, Charlie?"

"Just some things, dead rats showing up
out of nowhere, my belongings came back to me
and it's the strangest thing -- I was told that he
was killed in prison, but they never identified the
body."

"I believe him to be dead, Charlie," he
said, not making me feel any better. "Could there
be someone else?"

"That's what I need to know. I don't know
who to call, I don't know what to do!" I sighed
heavily and laid back onto the bed, staring at the
ceiling and cursing Jack, or Eddie, or whoever the
hell he was.

"Vere are you now? Home?"

"No," I said. "We're in Orlando. Bella
and I."

"Tell me exactly vere you are and I'll
have someone meet you. Give me an hour, okay,
Charlie."

I rattled off our hotel information and then
asked him to do me a big favor in case anyone
was listening. I was having serious trust issues.
"Have him tell me what I used to call you. That
will be the password."

He laughed hard and agreed with me.
"You'll be fine. I'll send you the best man I can
find."

~~~

I nibbled my fingernails until there was nothing left. I watched part of a Drew Barrymore movie, ordered shrimp cocktail and then opened the door when a man knocked and said, "Bifocal Man sent me."

I opened the door and almost wept against his broad chest. He was tall. Tall and muscular and had a warm smile. It was easy to let him into my hotel room.

"Charlie, I presume." He nodded. He wore dark Dockers, a light colored shirt and tie and, despite the sweltering heat, he was wearing a long dark trench coat. It made me think of Kevin Costner as Elliot Ness. He was American, chocolate brown hair, hazel eyes. Cute as heck. Probably married, with my luck. Then again, the last thing I needed was another Secret Agent Man in my life. I'd rather stick a hot poker in my eye than get involved with one of those ever again. I nodded in lieu of words.

He smiled and looked around. "I understand you need an exterminator."
I tried to smile at his obvious attempt at levity. I failed miserably.

"Okay, Russo filled me in on what happened in Armenia. You just need to tell me what's been going on here." His voice was husky and deep.

"Do you have a name?" I asked.

"Joey Potter, CIA." He held up his identification.

I critiqued it carefully before stepping back and offering him bottled water.

"No thanks."

Bella came out of her room, dressed in shorts and a tight black tank top. Probably ready to find another boy to break her heart. "Who're you?" she asked.

"Joe," he said carefully. "I'm an old friend of Charlie's." He did a great job lying to the girl.

She must have bought it. She smiled at me, winked and went back into her room.

I motioned to Joey to step into my bedroom because I feared she'd be listening at the door.

He grinned, stepped into my bedroom and I closed the door. "The girl can't know anything. She's had enough trauma in her life to last a lifetime and she was just crushed by her first love."

"I see." He fidgeted with his hands and leaned back against the small Mahogany table across from the bed.

I went into great detail about the strange goings on and asked him if he knew anything about Malcolm 'whatever his name is'.

"No, I'm not familiar with Malcolm 'whatever his name is'." He actually laughed and then joined me on the bed. "So, what do you think is going on?"

"I don't have a clue. I just know that it's getting out of control and I'm scared to leave this

room. I think he's alive and after me…but I don't
know why."

"You're cute, I'll give you that, but I
don't see why he'd fake his own death, follow
you around, give you dead rats and not do
anything about it. If he wanted you dead, you'd
be dead, right?"

I blushed and then choked on my own
saliva when he finished his sentence. "Nice," I
grinned.

His hand slid over to mine and he
wrapped it around my trembling one. "I'm sure
it's nothing, but if Russo called me, then I'm here
for you as long as you need me."

"Really?"

"Really."

That made me feel so much better. My
own private bodyguard.

Joey left the room, made some phone calls
in private and then took us out to the theme park,
never leaving our side the entire time. He bought
a goofy hat and a disposable camera was
constantly hanging around his neck. The Perfect
Spy. In fact, when he stopped and bought a root
beer snow cone for Bella, I found myself cocking
my head to the side and watching his jaw clench a
couple of times. I just stood back and watched
them interact. It felt like an awful case of deja vu.

"You want one?" he yelled over to me. I
shook my head and went back to my thought. He
sauntered over and brushed the bangs from my
eyes. "What's up? Do I have mustard on my

chin?" With a swift brush of his hand, he whisked his chin a couple of times and grinned.

"No," I said. "You just really remind me of someone."

"Old boyfriend?" He chuckled, clearly amused with himself.

"Funny!" I snarled and kept my thoughts to myself for the rest of the day.

I woke early for some reason that next morning. I never really sleep all that great in hotels anyway, but this was different. An odd sense of panic came over me, causing me to sit upright in bed, clutching the sheet to my chest. My purple tank top and boxer shorts were damp from sweat. For a minute, I thought I was experiencing my first hot flash. Then I closed my eyes and remembered the last detail of the dream I was having. Or should I say nightmare.

"You okay," I heard a voice, husky and tattered.

I clutched the sheet tighter, holding it with trembling hands, wondering where the voice had come from. Then Joey's head popped up over the end of my bed. My heartbeat returned to normal.

"Geez." I groaned. "What the hell are you doing in here?"

He leaned onto the edge of the bed and grinned, while trying to latch onto my toes under the covers.

I retracted my foot and flailed, waiting for his response.

"I was trying to keep up the illusion that I'm your special 'friend'. Isn't that what you wanted?"

I had to think about that one. I guess having Joey in my bedroom was better than Joey on my couch with gun in hand, staring at the door, waiting for disaster to strike. I shrugged in lieu of words. He was certainly handsome and dangerously familiar. I had to shake the wild thoughts from my head. Although, thinking wild thoughts about Joey was a hell of a lot better than re-hashing my latest nightmare.

I sent him a small smile that I hoped wouldn't be construed as an invitation to join me in that giant, comfortable king-size bed. "Good plan." I glanced at the clock. It was nearly six A.M. I wondered if he'd been awake, watching me sleep.

He inched higher on the bed, getting to his knees. I could see now that he was completely buff from the waste-up. His upper body was shamefully delicious; completely hairless. Muscles taut like he was fresh from a good, sweaty workout at the gym. I could also see a partial tattoo on his left upper bicep. The sun was just starting to peer in, leaving a line of sunlight across his jaw. Sexy as hell.

Again, my mind was wandering. I cleared my throat in an attempt to speak. "You want coffee?"

The look in his eyes didn't read coffee, but I think he definitely wanted something. "You're very pretty when you sleep."

I swallowed hard.

"And you make the cutest damn noises," he replied with a wink.

Jack used to say the same thing. Damn, then I was thinking about Jack again. Why did this guy have to exude Jackness? Why the hell couldn't he look like Captain Kangaroo or something? Are all spies gorgeous and so nicely put- together? I'd like to think that the US government would be smarter than that. That they'd make ugly, chubby couch potatoes be their secret agents.

I continued staring at him with a stunned look of confusion. That is until he winked and stood up. Then I think my jaw dropped and I most certainly checked out his package.

"Want to tell me about it?" he asked, as he stepped into his Levis.

"Huh," I half-groaned, half-moaned. "What?"

"Your dream? You were screaming for someone named Duane."

I fixed my eyes on his. "It was nothing. I'm fine."

"Who's Duane? Your boyfriend?"

"Uhhh," I said. "No." Then I bit my lip and quickly retreated from bed. "Why, did it sound like he was my boyfriend?" I hoped I hadn't been ecstatically moaning in my sleep. I couldn't remember the whole dream. Just the part where The Rat was stringing me up by my ankles, about to feed me to a hungry school of piranhas.

He shrugged, then pulled on his t-shirt. I could still see the tattoo peering out from the bottom of his sleeve. It was an eagle, perched above the American Flag. I guess seeing that made me even more comfortable with the fact that he'd been sent to keep my nightmares from coming true.

~~~

Day two ended with a game of Scrabble and a late night movie that had me feigning a yawn.

"It's Pacino." Joey's eyes were wide open like a toddler at FAO Swartz for the first time. "How can you not like Pacino?"

"I love Pacino." I bit into my sub sandwich and finished swallowing before continuing. "I just don't happen to like this movie." Big fat lie. I love Pacino in every movie, but after spending two long days with super-spy here, I was afraid to sit next to him on our tiny hotel sofa whilst watching a very sexy movie. It wasn't gonna happen.

"Fine," he flipped through a couple more commercials and found Bull Durham.

"Uh-uh," I blushed to a crimson shade and grabbed the remote, quickly changing it to the Disney Channel. "Look, the Suite Life of Zack and Cody," I said with triumph.

"You've been a nanny for how long?" He did that damn eyebrow-cocking thing that reminded me so much of Jack it made my breasts simultaneously heave and sweat.

Swallowing became more difficult at that time because he was a little closer to me than he had been a minute before. How did that happen? Oh God, it was me. I was staring at him. Probably drooling. I felt myself stiffen when our thighs touched.

"Goodnight." Making a beeline for my bedroom, I turned and nervously smiled. "I'm locking this." Then I twisted the lock and jumped into bed with a squeal.

He slept on my sofa, answered the door for room service every morning and even rubbed my feet after day three of being dragged around the park by Bella, who was bordering on obnoxious with her Energizer Bunny routine.

"Ahhh, God that feels good." I groaned, trying to keep my toes from curling when he touched the ball of my foot. I'd stayed far away from him all day because the more I looked at him, the more I saw Jack. I blamed all this on my sorrow. In a moment of weakness I succumbed to his pleas and he had me lying on the couch with my feet in his lap. "Where'd you learn to do that?"

"High School." He grinned. "I found foot rubs were a great way to loosen up the girls."

"Ahhh." I said again and then got immediately rigid. He must have felt the change in my demeanor as I was in no way ready for any

part of that. I was still angrily in love with
another secret agent man.

"Oh, I didn't mean anything by that...I
mean, I'm not trying to..." He dropped my foot
and stood up from his relaxed position on the
couch. "I should go get some dinner."

"Okay," I said and then ran in to take a
quick cold shower. When I returned, cleaned and
refreshed, Joey was back with dinner. He dropped
the cartons of Chinese food on the counter and
turned to leave.

"I forgot chopsticks." His smile was
unnerving. He winked and was out the door
again. I scrounged around for my fried rice and
yelled for Bella. She didn't answer, so I peaked in
on her. The light was off, her bed was mussed,
yet she wasn't in her room.

God Bless America!

I shrieked wildly and then had to lie down
on the floor to encourage the blood to return to
my brain. What had I done? Bella was gone.
Probably abducted by That Dirty Rat while I
imagined what Joey looked like under that goofy
tie-die shirt. She could be anywhere by now.

I must have remained on the floor for at
least a half an hour and it dawned on me that Joey
hadn't returned. How long does it take to run
back down to the lobby? I really wished at that
point that I had brought my gun. It was still
hidden at my parents' house under my old
camping gear. Crap, crap, crap.

I called the front desk, put out a hotel
wide APB on both Joey and Bella and then left a

note and went looking for them myself. I spent an hour in that damn lobby, looking in every restaurant, every shop, every nook that might house a sneaky teenager or a Rat Man with an evil agenda. The place was huge. Like a three block radius, huge! I was spent by the time I made it back to the room.

When I returned, Bella was safely inside but we never saw or heard from Joey Potter again.

The following morning, I called Russo and I finally calmed down enough to look Bella in the eye.

"I said I was sorry," she said again for the umpteenth time since pancakes and eggs. "I didn't think you'd miss me. You and Joe looked pretty cozy."

I held up my hand to stop her incessant apology.

"Russo," I stammered and told him about Potter's disappearing act. He helped calm me down, told me to hold tight and said he was sending in a pro. What, like the CIA wasn't good enough. My God, what's next, Rambo?

"No thanks," I said adamantly. If the Rat found me in Florida, then I obviously wasn't safe anywhere and I needed home-field advantage, that, and my gun. "We're taking the next plane home and I'll think of something there. You just try to find your man, okay."

I disconnected, called American Airlines and Vinny, and we were on our way home.

# Chapter Eight

It took me two days to get out of bed once we were home. I had informed Vinny that Bella was not to leave his sight. Then I informed him that if anything weird should happen to me, he should call Russo and then my parents. I also informed him that I had a gun and I was prepared to use it, so he better not let any strangers into the house for at least another week. I called Greg at his mother's place and begged him to come home. Depression had sunk in big time and my life seemed meaningless.

"Rise and shine!" I heard him yell from the doorway of Roald's guest room. There was no way that I was spending even one night alone in my little cottage. Roald was still in Greece, Nicole was still in Paris with her latest fling and the house was at my disposal.

"What the hell is wrong with you? You love excitement and intrigue. Why aren't you out there kicking ass?" Greg bounded across the room and landed next to me in bed. "Bella told me about Jack. Sorry, Sweetie." He kissed me on

149

the lips, then frowned. "You need to brush your teeth. Come on, get your lily-livered ass out of this bed, right fucking now!"

I groaned and hid my head under my goose-down pillow. "I have no reason to get out of bed. I don't have a job. I have no friends. Jack is dead! The Rat wants me dead and I inadvertently killed a very nice CIA agent, who had a very nice ass, by the way. What the hell is wrong with me, huh?" I shouted and began kicking wildly, somewhat feeling my gumption and grit again. "I've been in this bed for two days. My muscles are degenerating. All I have eaten is crap. My hair is even falling out! Look at me!" Full meltdown, taking place right then. "I'm losing it!"

"You're not losing it. You've just been dumped and you're depressed. There's nothing wrong with a day or two of wallowing, but it's over now. You have phone calls to return. You have a kick-ass job to find and you need a shower. Get the fuck up and let's go jogging."

I slammed my hand down on the bed. "Hell yeah." Who knew all I needed was a pep-talk by the gay man in my life. I think we all need one of those every once in awhile. I pulled on a pair of Jack's old gray sweats, my Seattle Mariner's tee-shirt and my running shoes.

Our run lasted about thirty minutes and then Greg's attention span died. I guess he was sick and tired of running up and down the driveway, but there was no way in hell I was

about to venture out in the open and be shot at by
Vermin Man. I flat-out refused to die that way.

"Coffee," he groaned. "I need coffee."

"Fine, you pussy!" I laughed hard and
raced him inside. Bella was on the phone when
we made it to the kitchen counter. She handed the
receiver to me and went back to flittering about,
like she always does.

"Hello," I said cautiously. "Yes, I'm fine
thank you." I grinned into the phone. "I would be
very interested in talking to you." With wide
eyes, I looked at Bella and Greg who were
hanging on my every word. "Ten it is. See you
then." I hung up and jumped up and down.

"Well, who the hell was that?" Greg
asked.

"FBI," I bit down on my lip, "I think." I
shifted my stance, trying to stretch my legs and
think at the same time. "Oh hell, what if…" I bit
down hard on my lip again and thought more. I
had to use my instincts, my gut reaction, my
woman's intuition. This time it seemed legit, but
I'd been fooled before. I wasn't thrilled to be
leaving the confines of the Munson house, but I
was armed and I was on my way to meet Special
Agent Dean Williams of the FBI. This time, I was
prepared for the fact that I might just get abducted
and taken to a remote location where I would be
tortured and then killed. But really, I was meeting
Dean at the FBI headquarters in New Haven, so I
had faith that this was the real deal.

After a two-hour drive, I parked on State
Street, got out, stretched my legs, looked around

for fascist thugs who looked like albino rats, and then slid my gun under the seat of my Ford Expedition.

The building was taller than most others in downtown New Haven.

When I got inside, via the large swinging double doors in the lobby, a man approached me.

"Miss Ford," he said with a warm smile and an extended hand. "Agent Fairchild. Glad you could make it."

I shook his hand firmly and kept my eyes gazing into his. "You can call me Charlie." I finally smiled and let out the breath I'd been holding.

"How was the drive?" he asked, motioning the elevator in the corner of the lobby.

"Fine."

"I've heard a lot about you." With a quick push of a button, the doors closed and we moved upward. I nodded in lieu of small talk and then felt the jolt when we reached the seventh floor.

The room was abuzz with activity. Nothing like I'd ever seen in the movies. Agents were rushing around with cups of coffee, files in hand and some rather grim expressions. I felt the tension in the air as I followed Fairchild to the conference room at the end of a long hall. The lights flickered on when we stepped inside. On the oblong table sat a water pitcher, three glasses and three navy blue files.

"Army, huh?" Fairchild spoke again. I guess he was uncomfortable with the silence. I actually prefer silence in the company of strange

FBI agents. I felt like if I said something, it might be held against me in a court of law, and lately, I had plenty to keep quiet about. Things in my life had gone from eerie to downright terrifying. What actually did happen to Joey Potter? Did he find a hot babe and run off to Havana, or did The Rat dispose of him in the back of the Thai restaurant? I was afraid that I would never know and that bugged me beyond words.

I shook my head to return to my potential coworker. "Yeah," I smiled. "How about you?"

"University of Florida." Yep, pansy-ass college boy -- and he didn't stop there either. "Masters in Political science. Law degree from Columbia." He looked me up and down with wonderment, or a sense of satisfaction that he was smarter than me. "Where'd you study?"

Thank God another agent stepped into the room. He was taller than Fairchild, with salt and pepper hair and a dimple in his left cheek that puckered slightly when he winked and gave me a sideways glance. "Charlie Ford!" He rounded the table and looked at me as if he'd known me for years. For one panicked moment I thought he was going to hug me. He didn't, but he did extend his hand and give me a firm yet friendly handshake. "Dean Williams," he said, motioning to the chair I was supposed to take. "Professor Schneider didn't do you justice."

"Thanks." I felt my cheeks flush slightly. I wore a nice white blouse and khaki pants. A navy blue blazer completed my FBI interview ensemble and I felt like a man to say the least. Or at least I had felt like a man until Dean Williams surprised me with his compliment.

"So, how was your drive?" He got right to work, looking through his notebook and opening a file that probably included my bra measurements and what size tampons I buy. "Do you have any questions for us before we begin?"

Sure, I had questions, but none that this man could answer, so I shook my head and sipped some water.

Two more men entered the room. "Agent Ron Devlin and Kurt McKay," Dean said with a more somber expression. "Agent Devlin is our training tech advisor and McKay is here from Human Resources."

"Nice to meet you." I finished shaking hands and then sat back down and twiddled my thumbs. Maybe Jack was right. Maybe I'm ready for something more exciting and intriguing and well…less structured. As I sat and listened to the entire FBI spiel down to the last detail and nodded my head on cue and tried not to count the large dots on McKay's tie, I had a vision of myself dressed in a woman-suit every day. Coming to an office like this and drinking bland coffee from Styrofoam cups. Having discussions about the wicked secretaries at the water cooler, shining my loafers every night before climbing into my lonely bed. Did I want this?

"Any questions?" Dean asked a third time. Three times in two hours and yet, I still had no questions. I heard the deal. I knew it meant a six-week training course and after what I had been

through in the Army, I knew I could do anything
they threw at me. Yet, I was still envisioning
having to wear the woman-suit.

"Where would I go next?" I pleaded in my
head as the words came from my mouth…Not
South Dakota, or Kansas. I hate Kansas, there are
tornadoes in Kansas.

"That will be up to you."

"Really?"

"Well, you're usually given a choice of
three locations depending on your area of
expertise and our needs at the time. You have to
know that you will be starting from the bottom
here, Charlie. We recruit a hundred applicants
each year by referral, but that doesn't mean you
get special favors. Everyone starts from square
one." Dean explained, folding his hands in front
of him on the table. "The next training session
starts in three weeks. You have about a week to
come to a decision and then we will need your
answer." What started off as a given quickly
turned into hurry-up-we-have-others-in-line. Like
I was nothing special.

Devlin leaned back and adjusted his
burgundy tie. "We have applicants who speak
Japanese and Iraqi. Law school graduates with
twice as much education as you." He leaned
forward and rested his elbows on the table. "All
we are saying is that if it's not you, it will be
someone else more qualified. But what we are not
saying…" he looked at his counterparts. "Is that
we'd love to have someone with your
background. We have an abundance of brain

power, but sometimes we need something extra special." He grinned. His lips bowed up into a smile. That something special was most likely my ability to accurately kill people from very far away. I shivered at the thought. "Give it a week. Talk to your significant other, family, best friend and then let us know. We'd love to have you aboard, Miss Ford."

All three stood up at the same time.

"Thanks. I will let you know." I smiled and left the room, walking tall; yet still undecided.

I left the building and started for my SUV. Jack was right about one thing. I didn't see myself on their level. Sure, I had slowly finished college, gotten my master's degree in Criminal Justice, but that meant nothing. What I had to offer came from inside me. From a place deep within that the Army had taught me to discover. I knew I had a lot to learn about life, but I was ready to make that kind of decision. It was my time to think of myself. Jack was gone. It's just me again and that had me quickening my steps. I was walking swiftly; talking to myself in a soft voice, mumbling to my inner child that it was time to grow up. So what if I had to wear ugly clothes and go to an office every day. It's not like it wouldn't be exciting.

I stopped abruptly and clenched my jaw, turning to look up at the tall building that I had just left. I dug in my pocket for my keys and then remoted the alarm off on my SUV. Half a second later, I was on the asphalt losing consciousness, a warm trickle of blood seeping from my ear.

~~~

I blinked a couple of times, feeling the painful sting of the world's worst headache. The lights were off, so I couldn't see much, other than the flicker of the television in the corner. It smelled like antiseptic and orange Jell-O, so I was fairly certain I was in a hospital.

"Good morning," Gregory said from my side. It took me a moment to focus on his face. His scruffy five o'clock shadow scratched my cheek as he kissed me softly.

Instinctively, I brought my hand up to feel the large bandage on my head. It was wound around the back, covering one ear, so everything I heard was slightly muted. "What happened?" I tried to sit up and failed miserably, yet I caught a glimpse of hot pink legs that I reasoned were Bella. She was asleep in the couch in front of the TV.

"You don't remember!" Greg gasped and ran his fingers down my cheek. "Oh honey. Do you know who I am? What's your name? What day is it?"

I just stared without expression. Of course, I knew my name. I just wanted to know why I was lying in a hospital bed.

I closed my eyes and remembered the horrendous noise and bright flash of light before it all went black. "My car?"

"Totaled beyond recognition." He chewed his lip.

The door creaked open and Greg waved a couple of police officers in, along with Agent Dean Williams of the FBI. "It's okay. She's awake."

"Well, well, Miss Ford. Seems like someone doesn't like you all that much." Dean said, pulling up a rotating stool beside me. The two officers stood at attention near the door. "Any idea who might have put an explosive devise under your transmission?"

I knew I had to tell someone sometime. But really, who would believe me? I somewhat wanted to keep my personal life a mystery as to discourage the FBI from tossing me into a mental hospital. I mean, really. Who would believe my story about The Rat...besides Jack, Russo and the cute deceased CIA agent with a great ass? My life as of lately seemed to be something out of a Robert Ludlum novel.

I shook my head very carefully as to not upset the tiny cerebral nerve endings that were causing me extreme pain.

"No?" Dean said, narrowing his eyes on me.

Greg cleared his throat loudly, which he tends to do when he's nervous, and retreated to the sofa next to Sleeping Beauty.

I stared at the ceiling and blinked a couple of times.

"I have a feeling you are lying to me, Charlie."

"Oh yeah," I said, digging into my lower lip to stop the tears. "What makes you say that?"

"I'm a fairly good judge of character," he grinned and then put his hand on mine and gave it a warm squeeze. "Greg and Bella were fairly adamant about not calling your parents. Are you sure you don't want me to call anyone else for you?"

I did cry then, by God. What would my parents say?

I shook my head. He handed me a box of tissues and turned to leave.

"The local police would like to ask you some questions, but if you'd like I can have them wait until you're feeling up to it."

"Thanks," I sent him a weak smile and watched all three men leave the room, closing the door behind them. "Shit!" I cried out in pain and was comforted by Bella and Greg until there were no more tears to cry.

"This shit is serious, Charlie," Greg said, holding my hand once Bella was back to sleep again. Greg had run out after my breakdown and smuggled in a pint of Ben and Jerry's Cherry Garcia, which we shared. "Why not tell the Feds. They're here and he seemed nice."

"Nice," I said. "Yeah, he's very nice and just minutes before someone tried to incinerate me, he offered me a job. So, no, we are not telling

the Feds a damn thing. I don't want them
knowing anything about it."

He scooped up a giant spoon full and
lifted it to my quivering lips.

It was heavenly and reminded me so much
about how the little things make life worth living.
"Did Dean call you? How did you get here?"

"Actually it was a beat cop. Said I was
number one on your speed dial." His smiled
widened and he fed me another bite. "That's
pretty pathetic."

"Well, who else should it be?" I huffed.

"Where's a good secret agent when you
need him, huh?" He read my mind well. I'm sure
he fully understood that Jack used to be number
one on my speed dial, but since his rather bizarre
departure from my life, Greg had been bumped
into the top position in my cell phone. It's a good
thing too because there wasn't another person on
earth I wanted beside me. How would I ever
explain this to my parents?

"You should get some sleep." He kissed
the top of my head and winked. "Who should I
call? CIA? NSA? The Governor of California?"

I giggled slightly and closed my eyes. "Is
there still a cop outside my door?"

"Yep!" he said with a bounce of his brow.
"And he's hot."

~~~

I'm in no way exaggerating about what time the cavalry showed up the next morning. The entire state of Connecticut was up in arms about the fact that there was a car bombing right in front of the damn FBI headquarters in New Haven. I was just up in arms that my room had suddenly turned into a circus. Three FBI agents, a plainclothes detective, two uniformed cops, one of which was gorgeous just like Gregory had mentioned the night before, a clueless candy striper who was flirting with Gregory and a nurse who was trying to take my blood pressure.

"Let's try this again," she said for the third time, not liking the results. "Try to relax. Breathe easy and let it out slowly.

It took a minute for her to pump up the cuff again and then when she started to release the pressure, all I could hear was the racing of my heart.

She shook her head at the results. "You have to relax. It's off the charts!"

"Tell them that." I nodded toward the crowd.

She frowned and then gave my hand a little caress. "I'll be back in fifteen minutes to kick them all out." With a wink she was gone.

"You ready?" Dean Williams asked from my side.

I nodded and sat up a little straighter to see who I was talking too. The plainclothes

Detective started with his questions, that I
answered the best I could -- by lying.

"And you didn't stop anywhere on the
way," he asked while doodling in his little black
book.

"No," I said again. I too was going over
the events in my head, wondering when exactly
the bomb was placed in my car. It could have
happened anywhere, anytime.

Agent Williams was becoming antsy by
my side, probably waiting for the locals to leave
before grilling me one more time on his theory
that I was lying.

"I guess that's all we need." He handed
me a card and thanked me for my time. "Call us if
you think of anything else."

"I will." I watched four of the men leave
the room and then two more entered. They were
also in suits, but seemed to be a bit more
distinguished. Dean introduced them both as
National Security Agents. One walked straight
over to the window, pulled down the blinds and
then peered out. The other stood at my feet and
engaged me with a serious gaze.

"We can't help you unless you help us."

"I have nothing more to tell. That's all I
know," I stammered, hearing the angst in my own
voice. "Really. I don't know who wants me dead.
Perhaps it was a case of mistaken identity."

"The device we found was extremely
high-tech, Miss Ford, United States Government
issue. We have reason to suspect that you know
more than you are letting on." He looked at his

partner, then back to me. "Who are you working for?"

"I already told you. I work for Roald Munson. I'm a nanny."

"A nanny?" He stated with quite a bit of skepticism. "So, you have to travel a lot in your line of work? London? Africa? The Bahamas?"

I swallowed the large lump in my throat. "Yes, I was working on two of those occasions. The Bahamas was just a vacation."

Both men looked at one another before looking back down at me.

"Ever heard the name Grady Sanchez?" he asked, carefully watching my face for any signs of weakness.

I felt my throat tightening and swallowing was difficult, but I played it cool.

I knew that he didn't believe a word I was saying. I wasn't stupid. He was humoring me, I was sure of it. I know that National Security knows each and every move that each of us make. It's a known fact that they are the eyes and ears of America and my travels, I'm sure, were well noted.

I remained tight lipped until they left me alone.

The phone rang shortly after everyone was gone. Greg picked it up and reiterated to whoever was calling that I was just fine. Not to worry.

The phone made it into my almost comatose hand and Greg lifted it to my ear. The drugs were working wonderfully at that point.

"'ello," I mumbled, getting quite excited for a long nap.

His gruff voice brought me out of my fog. "Get out of there, Charlie."

"Who is this?"

"You're not safe. Go. Take the girl and your friend and just go."

"Who are you?"

"Take them to Greece. You'll be safe there."

"And if I don't?" I sat up, feeling a rush of adrenaline flood my veins.

It was silent for a heartbeat or two. My heart thumped loudly against my ribcage.

A gush of breath was followed by a more serious plea. "Then the girl will go without you." And then there was a click and the phone went dead.

I stared at Greg for a moment before speaking. "Who the hell was that? What did he say to you?"

He stuttered and shifted his feet. "Said he was an old friend. Just wanted to make sure you were okay. That you'd recognize his voice." His coloring changed slightly. "Said you were in the Army together."

I was bamboozled, but the thought of Bella going somewhere without me scared me to death. "Call Roald. Tell him you are coming for a visit."

He sat down hard on the seat beside me. "What was that call about? What's going on?"

"Nothing," I bit my lip and narrowed my eyes. "Just do it."

~~~

The next day, I phoned Russo from the limo on the way home, asked him nicely to meet me in Athens. I instructed Bella to pack and then got some serious lip from Greg. He had finally conceded and called Roald, informing him that we were coming for a visit and we were bringing the dogs!

"I still don't understand why we couldn't just leave them in a kennel." I shouted over the hum of the engine and Greg's horrible taste in Country music. "They're just dogs."

He looked at me as if I'd just cursed the Lord Almighty. "They're just dogs? How can you say that? They've been like family to you."

Bella was snuggled in the backseat, waiting for us to stop bickering so she could complain about missing the last few days of spring break with her friends.

"You should be counting your lucky stars, Miss Bella. When I was a kid, the biggest trip we took was to the Grand Canyon. You get to see Greece...again," I groaned loudly, not at all happy that I'd been coerced by a stranger to take Bella out of the country. But what was worse was the thought of someone else taking Bella out of the country.

~~~

Athens was warm and sticky even at dusk. Roald showed up right on time, just as our bags appeared on the roundabout, and took Bella and the dogs. Gregory stayed behind, insisting that leaving me alone was the stupidest idea on the planet.

"I'll be fine." I said grouchily, still waiting for food so I could take my pain medication. I'd survived with just a hell of a concussion, a black eye and quite a few bumps and serious bruises. "Just go with Roald. I don't want you anymore involved than you already are."

"Sheesh," he grabbed my bag to lessen my load and gave me a warm hug. "When your friend gets here I will vamoose, but not a minute before."

I smiled, appreciating his company and leaning against him for support in more ways than one. "There he is." I was almost giddy. I waved and held back the tears, but only until Russo gave me a warm hug and did that cute French kissy thing on both my cheeks.

"You don't look so good," he said with a disapproving shake of his head.

Greg cleared his throat.

I made a quick introduction and then kissed Greg goodbye and watched him get into a cab en route to Roald's luxury hotel overlooking the Mediterranean Sea. A sense of extreme loneliness enveloped me fully once I got into Russo's tiny European car.

He didn't speak.

I did.

I stammered with my first attempt and then started my inquisition. "Did you find Potter?"

"Non," he said.

"Did they finally ID The Rat? Is he dead or what?" I had a sneaking suspicion that he was not.

"Non," he replied. "But I still believe him dead, Charlie."

"Look," I fidgeted with the seat lever, pushing myself back into a more comfortable position. "Someone wants me dead. Or at least scared to death."

For the first time since the incident, something became clear. The car blew up when I was a good twenty-five feet away. All I did was remote the alarm off and unlock the door. If someone wanted me dead, they would have rigged it so that it blew when I started the ignition. Maybe this was just a scare tactic.

I reiterated that to Russo, who was impressed by my logic. "Good point." He scratched his balding head and removed his bifocals, gently wiping them dry with his ivory handkerchief. "If he vanted you dead, you'd be dead, right?"

I rolled my eyes, having heard that before. I thought of Joey and his cute smile, his warm hands on my feet and that super-spy jaw-clenching thing that Jack used to do. Then I just started thinking about Jack. I got solemn, sad and very quiet. I remained that way until we pulled into a driveway and a garage door opened wide. We drove in. It closed behind us.

The bed in the corner was just a wobbly cot. There was a computer on a folding table and a ragged chair set up in front of a window. Dust covered the tattered hardwood floors. Cameras were aimed out that same window at a row house along the river. A pair of binoculars sat atop the rusty windowsill.

"What..." I motioned to the camera.

"Stakeout. I think that is what you Americans call it."

I nodded and then got comfortable on the cot. It smelled of cigars and mildew, but it was soft and I was in need of sleep.

I felt someone nudge me slightly, but it was very dark in the room. Whoever it was smelled divine, so I didn't bother putting up a fight until it dawned on me that he was lifting me off the cot and into his arms. Then, and only then, did I scream out and flail with blind fury.

A hand wrapped around my mouth, and I was told to shush.

"Shut-up and listen."

At least he was American. I felt a sting in my ass, like a wasp had bitten through my jeans.

"Joey?" I half shouted, half panted, still in his arms, being carried through the room.

"How's your head?" He asked, taking me straight out and into a waiting SUV in the garage. "I'm really sorry about that."

My mind began to race.

I felt the vomit surge in the back of my throat when I realized that something was terribly wrong. I could breathe, speak and blink my eyes, but my body went numb. Limp. Like I was paralyzed yet still awake. It was by far the most horrifying experience I had ever had and, let me just say, I've had plenty of terrifying experiences in my life.

Our trip seemed excruciatingly long. I watched the sun rise through the back window, but all I could do was lie there on the leather and cry. My vocal chords wore out after my incessant pleas. I thought I could trust Russo. I thought I could trust the CIA.

I was dead wrong.

# Chapter Nine

My eye sockets actually ached from crying all day. They felt dry and scratchy and in desperate need of Visine. Our destination was a villa somewhere in Europe, yet I had no idea where exactly. This felt very real and very scary. I had no sign from God that I was going to survive this and no hope of getting out of a strange country in the shape I was in, so I resigned to die there -- on that very luxurious bed in that delightful room overlooking the most beautiful garden I have ever seen. It was as if I was already dead and in Heaven meeting My Maker.

Then my view was spoiled when he came into the room and removed my shoes. I heard my brain tell my leg to kick out and get him in the groin, but nothing happened. I just shut my eyes and prayed he wasn't a pervert on top of being a modern-day traitor.

"You'll feel normal soon. I'm so sorry, Charlie." He actually sounded sincere. The bastard.

"Go to hell!" I snarled through gnashing teeth, staring out the window at the roses in bloom. The sun was already setting beyond the veranda. Classical music filled my ears and the smell of braised pork had me inhaling deeply and clenching my teeth in anticipation. At least it seemed that he was going to feed me before hacking me into mincemeat and fertilizing the garden with my remains.

I could feel him staring at the side of my face, but I remained gazing out the window.

"Can I just explain?"

"Fuck off," I reiterated for the fifth time since he'd tried to explain to me. "What did you do to Russo...or is he a part of this too?"

He chuckled slightly. "I thought you didn't want an explanation."

I narrowed my eyes at him and felt my index finger flinch. Progress!

"I don't know how well you know Russo, but at this point, I don't trust anyone. I paralyzed you for your own good," he looked dangerously serious. "And mine."

"So, what's next? You kill me? Hand me over to The Rat? What?"

I felt my toes uncurl and that tingly sensation began climbing across my skin, starting at my fingers and toes and moving to my core. I remained extremely still, keeping the illusion that I was still under.

"It's not like that, Charlie." His tone softened and he moved toward me. When he reached out, I forced my fragile nerves to remain rigid and not give away that he was making my skin crawl. He brushed my cheek with his rugged fingers.

"I'm a good guy."

I didn't think I had enough strength to knock the wind out of him, so I stayed completely still, biding my time and not really paying any attention to what he was blabbering about.

"I'm sorry that I lost him in New Haven. I had him, right there in front of me and he just slipped away." He just kept explaining as he brushed the hair from my eyes.

One more minute. That's all I needed.

"If I could take it all back I would," he said toward the ceiling. "Lord knows, he's gonna be pissed that I let you get hurt." He got up and turned away from me, taking two steps away still muttering something about someone being really, really pissed that he dropped the ball, but that it wasn't his fault. That the guy was like a ghost and just disappeared in front of his eyes at a Starbucks of all places.

I sat up in one swift movement and grabbed the lamp off the table, swung as hard as I could and made a beautiful whooshing sound as I whipped it just inches from my target; his big head.

I fell flat on my face onto the hardwood floor and the lamp shattered beside me. All I could see was the side of his Nike cross trainers. An entire minute seemed to pass before I heard him let out a deep groan.

He turned me over and shook his head at me. "Damn it, Charlie, I said I was sorry."

"What?"

"Did you not hear me?"

He rambled on again about everything he had just said as he picked me up and laid me on the soft bed.

I was exhausted and could barely speak, but I managed to get out a few grunts.

"If you promise not to attempt to brain me again, I'll go get your dinner."

"Who?" I muttered, confusing myself with my own question.

"Who, What?" he replied.

"Who? Who were you following? Who did this? Why am I here? Why did you trank me? I hate getting tranked!" Sweat beaded on my brow.

He kissed my forehead and brushed the errant bangs from my eyes. "Let's eat and then I'll tell you all about it."

~~~

Did I trust Joey Potter? Sure, but only for about twenty minutes while we shared braised pork chops with mango chutney accompanied by butternut squash and steamed baby carrots. I ate, he talked, and by the time the Tiramisu arrived, I was starting to believe him. Still, it was hard to

believe Joey's theory that Russo is in cahoots
with The Rat.

"Hey, all I know is Russo calls me out of
nowhere, telling me there's a man sending you
dead rats and it might be in connection to a case
he's been working on. It's just too coincidental."

"It is not." I said, widening my eyes. "The
Rat basket arrived before I called Russo. Russo
had no idea I was in Orlando."

"Are you sure?" he took a bite of dessert
and offered me another bite off the tip of his fork.
I scowled and then used my own fork. "Didn't
you tell me in Orlando that you and Russo were
pen pals. Don't you think it might be possible you
may have told him your spring break plans at one
point."

I paused with the fork en route to my
mouth. Damn.

"But…" I replied lamely.

"But nothing. You know nothing about
this man."

"Well, how do you know him?"

"I don't." Joey said with a cocked brow.

"Then why…"

"Did he call me?" There went that serious
brow cock again. "No clue."

The plot thickens.

"I want a gun," I said.

"No freakin' way." He replied, getting to
his feet and brushing cake crumbs off his lap. His
jeans fit him perfectly. Even his dark brown t-
shirt looked like it was painted on. Everything
about him said, 'All American good boy,' but I

had once had that same thought about Jack
Sullivan and look where that landed me.
"What's next then?"
"We wait."
"For what?" I asked, kicking my foot out
of his grasp. Sure, a foot rub may have felt great,
but I'm no idiot. I knew that look in his eyes. And
how could he be thinking of sex at a time like
this. Is that what spies do in their spare time.
They wait…and have sex.
Wasn't going to happen. No sir!
He pulled harder on my foot. "How's your
head?" He carefully removed my sock with one
hand, while caressing my calf with his other
hand.
I think I moaned out loud. "Fine," I said,
feeling my eyelids droop. My hand dropped to
my chest and my breathing grew weaker. "Did
you just drug me again?" I was becoming very
weary. Tired. Downright sleepy.
Then it all faded to black.

~~~

I woke the next morning in my underwear
and nothing else. Joey was lazily peering outside
with a high-powered set of binoculars in his Levis
and nothing else.
"Mornin'." He grinned. "Sleep good?"
"Pig!" I shouted, kicking wildly to get out
from under the blankets. After my last fiasco

abroad, I wasn't as modest as I once was. I
suppose being in the Army for eight years,
trudging around for weeks at a time with a bunch
of guys may have contributed also.

"And no, I didn't drug you...not really. It
was just a common sleeping pill."

"Fucking PIG!" I shouted louder and then
struggled for breath on my way to the bathroom.
"Why?" I shouted through the white paneled
door.

"So you wouldn't kill me in my sleep," he
shouted back.

"Well, now I'm just going to have to kill
you when you're awake." I opened the bathroom
door with fire in my eyes and slowly walked to
the bed. "Why prolong the inevitable?"

He laughed at me, making his chest do a
little dance and, like I mentioned before, his chest
was to die for.

I rolled my eyes at myself in my moment
of weakness and climbed into my jeans and
sweatshirt. It was Jack's fuzzy blue sweatshirt
from our trip to Hawaii last year and it made me
sad for a fleeting moment. That moment passed
quickly when I realized what big trouble I was in.
Russo had sold me out. Joey had used the date
drug on me and I was still banged-up enough that
I couldn't fight back, even if I wanted to.

It's a good thing there was something
about Joey that made me feel peaceful. I felt
somewhat safe with him so I was willing to listen
to his other theories over pancakes and more pork
products.

"So, in Orlando you went for chopsticks and just happen to run into the guy?" I slathered my bite of sausage into the syrup before lifting it to my lips.

He shook his head, finishing his bite. "I'd seen him earlier that day and the day before. At first, I just figured he was a tourist, but there was something about him. He seemed off. Rattled, almost."

"What did he look like?"

"American. Six two, two twenty. Long blonde hair, pulled into a low ponytail. Blue eyes, five o'clock shadow and a scar above his left eyebrow."

I remember describing him in the exact same way. "DEA guy?" I muttered under my breath, feeling the flush of uncertainty jump around in my stomach.

"Excuse me?" he asked. "I thought you called him The Rat? What does the DEA have to do with this?"

Standing up, I planted my hands on my hips. "Are you really CIA?"

He nodded emphatically. "Yeah."

"The guy you described is not The Rat. He's DEA. I don't get this." I paced the floor. There was a lot I didn't get.

"I can't help you there," he said, apparently not ready to give me his side of the story. "All I know is what I saw. Russo said someone was after you and I thought it was that guy, so I took off after him and kept on him until he ditched me in New Haven."

"I still don't get why Russo called you."
With narrowed eyes and a special feeling in my
stomach, I so wanted to torture him with electric
shock therapy and make him sing.

"Maybe we know a mutual
acquaintance?"

"Maybe you are lying to me." I cocked a
serious brow that time.

"Want to play chess?"

"I'm black."

Hours went by when neither of us spoke
of The Rat or the DEA or the fact that I knew he
was holding something back. I hated that he was
beating me at chess, so I opened a bottle of wine
and had half a glass before passing out.

~~~

"You have to stop doing that to me." I
groaned the next morning, rolling over to hide
myself from the early morning sun that was
peering into the window. "I really am going to
kill you one of these days."

"And I look forward to the fight." He
grinned and slid off the couch. At least I knew I
was sleeping alone. "How's your head?" He
crossed the room with small strides. His modesty
was lacking to say the least and I think I preferred
him in the black boxers that he wore in Orlando,
as opposed to these striped blue ones.

"Why do you keep asking me that?"

"Because." His hand was warm on mine. "I really, truly am sorry for letting that guy out of my sight in New Haven. If I had been on him, your accident would have been avoided and he'd be dead right now."

"He's DEA. There's no way he tried to kill me, right?"

He shrugged his naked shoulders.

I have to admit that despite the fact that he drugged me two nights in a row, he was sort of growing on me.

We had breakfast on the veranda. To my surprise a lovely lady, who I presumed was the caretaker, brought us fresh fruit, biscuits and tea. It was refreshing to see someone other than Joey around because it gave me hope that I'd escape and figure out what was really going on.

"Can we go for a walk or something today?"

"Can't chance it," he winked.

"What could happen? We're in the middle of nowhere, in…" I glanced with wide eyes at his now-scruffy face. "What country exactly are we in?"

"Bulgaria."

"And who again is after me now?"

"We don't know," he retorted with a frown. "That's why you aren't leaving my sight."

"Under whose orders?"

He just stared at me with a blank expression and then winked and left me alone.

All I could do was sleep and watch TV. I swear he was either drugging me at lunchtime too, or I was just that exhausted from my accident. When I woke from my catnap it was nearly four P.M. and Joey was tossing things into his bag. His gun was out on the dresser. I looked at it for a moment too long. Probably with a yearning, desperate look in my eye.

"Don't even think about it." He gave me a serious headshake. "We gotta go."

"Now? Where?"

"Just get your shoes on. I'll tell you on the way."

I hurriedly got my shoes on and pressed a hand against my skull. The pain was agonizing and I knew I shouldn't be moving so damn fast. I sat back down and he grabbed my hand and tugged hard.

"Now!" he shouted as we ran out the back French doors.

About fifteen seconds after we left the villa parking lot, I turned and saw the entire left wing burst into bright orange flames. Joey slammed his foot down on the pedal, cursed several times and placed his hand on the back of my neck tugging me toward his lap. He kept his grip on my head until it was squished between the steering wheel and his torso.

I struggled because I thought he was being perverted, but when he growled and told me to stay the fuck down, I relaxed and looked up at him as he drove us into the west, never looking back and never slowing down. He kept stuttering

some fairly unique obscenities, all the while
muttering that he was a dead man -- A dead man
if anything should happen to me.

~~~

That night around a warm fire in our new
contemporary villa somewhere west of Bulgaria,
Joey took a chance and didn't drug me during
dessert. I thanked him by letting him share the
bed while we watched a good wholesome show in
a language that I didn't understand.
"Why are we here?" I mumbled sleepily
into my pillow before rolling over to look him in
the eye. "Was it you that called me at the hospital
and told me to come to Greece?"
He nodded and slid his arm under my
pillow, pulling me closer to his side. "Sorry, I
didn't mean to scare you, but I was told to get
you here no matter what. It's all I could think of. I
know how much you love Bella."
I smiled, thinking of Bella and hoping she
was having a good time with her father and his
entourage. "It worked. I'm here." I shifted
slightly, getting comfortable next to him. "Who
told you to get me here? What's this all about?"
His gaze moved down to my chest. I think
my breasts were heaving and I know I was
speaking in a slow sultry voice. I had planned it
that way. Actually, ever since he grabbed my

head and made me get up-close-and-personal with his package, I vowed to get answers.

I licked my lips. He then mimicked my action and scooted closer. "I can't tell you that."

"Whhh-yyy not?" I asked, tickling my finger along his jaw line.

He growled and leaned back on his pillow. I moved toward him and traced the contours of his tight red t-shirt, up and down his chest.

"You can tell me. I promise to keep it a secret."

His eyes widened, then narrowed with a flicker of something that curled my toes. We stared at each other for a couple of very tense, long minutes. Neither of us blinking or interrupting the sensual stare down.

"Just give me a minute." I slid off the bed and into the bathroom. When I shut the door, I wiped my sweaty palms down my thighs and slid out of my sweatshirt and jeans, wrapping myself in a white towel. I was ready. I was able and I knew I would feel much better when I got what I wanted.

After yanking the scrunchie from my hair and fluffing it a few times in the mirror, I stepped from the bathroom and noticed the lights were dimmed.

Joey was rolled onto his side facing me, playing with his gun.

I froze in shock and horror and then said fuck about twelve times.

"I thought so," he grinned and waved it in front of me playfully. "Would you really shoot a nice guy like me?"

"Yes!" I said, straightening up, doing a classic about face and then locking myself in the bathroom for the rest of the night.

~~~

I woke with a crick in my back, but I slept well in the bathtub. I had plenty of towels for bedding and had pulled the cloth curtain down to use for a blanket. I was becoming quite accustomed to sleeping in tubs.

"Can I please use the bathroom?"

"Sure." I said. "Just tell me the truth, slide the gun under the door and then I'll let you pee."

"Not a chance in Hell, sweetheart."

I leaned my ear against the door and heard the outer door shut. Being on the second floor and all, I knew it would take him at least three minutes to get down to the lobby, do his deed and get back up. Not much time, but it was enough for me to get dressed, grab my shoes and open the door.

He pressed solidly on my chest with his index finger and eased me back into the room. "Where do you think you are going?"

My right arm still hurt like Hell, so punching him in the gut would have hurt me more than him so I conceded and fell backward onto the bed.

He was quick in leaning over me, licking his lips and brushing them against mine in a sultry move that took my breath away. "Behave, please. This is my life we are talking about."

Then he moved off me and tucked his nine-millimeter back into his jeans.

~~~

We took a walk around the pond after lunch and drank Ouzo straight from the bottle. The grass was tall, the flowers were in bloom and it was rather romantic. We talked about our families, our favorite movies and what we wanted to do when we got home.

"When is that, by the way?" I asked, skipping a stone into the pond, thinking of my future. A future I hoped to have with Jack, but since he was MIA or dead, the FBI seemed like the right choice for me. "I sort of have a decision to make about my life and I'd like to get home...tomorrow if possible." Tears welled in my eyes, thinking of Jack again.

He scoffed and picked a daisy, placing it in my hair. He tucked it behind my ear and kissed my forehead. "You look sad."

"What makes you say that?" I let a single tear trickle out before wiping it away and gulping down another swig of alcohol.

He took my face in his palms and lightly kissed my lips. It was nice and I was damn attracted to him, but I pulled away, knowing it was the booze talking.

His wink made me smile and we continued on our walk.

Joey disappeared for nearly an hour that afternoon. He came back into our room around dinnertime and handed me his gun. He stepped back, looking rather grave. "There's something you should know."

"I'm listening." I said, thrilled that I had a gun in my hand. I always think better with a gun in my hand.

"I wasn't completely honest with you."

"And this surprises me, how?" I said, staring at the ceiling and then looking down at the gun I had suddenly pointed at his chest. "Why would you give me a gun and then say that?" I waved it at him in a menacing fashion. "Are you stupid?"

"It's not loaded." He shoved it aside and sat down on the bed. "It was just a test."

My heart jumped in disappointment. "Boy, I'm sick and tired of your shit!" I yelled, feeling my spiritedness come back in full force. I was somewhat feeling back to normal. "You're not CIA?" I began. "No... let me guess." I started to laugh insanely. "Your name really isn't Joey Potter. You're name is Rick Scorpio and you're the leader of a band of brothers ridding the world of extra terrestrials."

"That's funny, but no!"

He was wiping his hands on his jeans and muttering to himself again. "I think I know why they want you."

"Who?" I stammered, practically crawling into his lap.

"The ones who are following us."

"DEA guy?" It was if my whole life flashed in front of my eyes. DEA guy? Why?

With a grimace, he raked one hand through his dark, thick hair. "Grady Sanchez was the DEA's top inside man. He's spent years in the cartel earning trust and respect and when I say years, I mean like almost ten years. He was protected by the Cali Cartel's top dog. No one could touch him and they loved him. He was it. He was the man. The DEA had devoted a decade to getting him planted."

"So, why me? What did I do?"

"You helped Eddie Malone kill him."

I gasped and so wanted to slap him for saying that.

I had no part...okay, a small part in his death. But give me a break. I did not pull the trigger. Hell, I wasn't even on the same island when it happened.

I felt panicked, but then not so much. Drug Enforcement Agents don't just go around executing ordinary citizens. I think Joey'd been sampling the drugs he'd been giving me. "How long have you been in his unit?"

I shook my head. "I'm not. I swear to God!" I crossed my heart and hoped I wouldn't die. "Someone's really following us. Now?"

He nodded. "I torched our room at the villa hoping to slow them down." Joey stood up and held me close when my first tear fell. His body was warm against mine. "They've been on you since you got off the plane in Athens."

The sun had dipped back down into the horizon and it felt good to be where I was. Too good. The kiss came next. Hot and demanding. I felt somewhat compelled to shove against his chest and scream at him for taking advantage of me in my fragile state, but then again, his warm hands on my breasts felt pretty damn fine at that moment. He kissed me again and I felt all hot and gooey and protected. Very safe in his arms, like if it came down to a duel and it was CIA against DEA, Joey would win. I didn't know what it was that made me felt that way. I suppose I was just freaked out by what he had told me and I, for once, was giving in to what my body said was a natural thing. My brain usually wins in these battles, so I partially blamed the Ouzo too. I went limp in his arms and let him drag me toward the bed. Soon I was smashed under him, breathing hard and trying to make my brain behave and just let me have some uncomplicated sex for once in my damn life. I'm a grown up. What's so wrong with wanting a man I hardly knew…He's not Jack, that's why. I rolled my eyes at my conscience, letting them stay rolled back in that position while I helped Joey lift my tee shirt and unclasp my unflattering bra.

I had my head lifted slightly to keep our lips smashed together and when we broke to breathe, I saw a figure on the far side of the room, climbing through my window. "Holy Christ!" I shouted and scooted up the bed away from Joey's hot roving hands.

The dark figure crossed the poorly lit room with deliberate strides and stopped near the armoire just feet from the edge of the bed. "Damn, Potter! When I said keep her happy I didn't mean for you to use seduction." Jack's voice was tainted with both spite and amusement.

I was still scrambling to pull down my shirt as Joey grinned and slid off the bed.

"Well, if it's not dead-man walking. What the hell are you doing here, man?" Joey moved toward Jack with his hand outstretched and his jeans partially unbuttoned.

Jack smirked, extended his own hand and slammed his other fist hard into Joey's gut. Joey let out a loud woof and buckled over. Jack slapped his hand around Joey's neck and brought him to a standing position. For a minute I thought they would rumble, but then Jack's face softened and he looked more at ease. They did that manly-hug-thing and slapped backs. Joey kissed Jack hard on the cheek and gave him another big hug. "Glad you're back." He managed to get out with a breathless groan.

I still didn't know what to say. I wanted to cry. I wanted to scream, but I had a bad feeling that I mostly wanted to slap the crap out of him for doing this to me and what the hell was that, "keeping her happy" crap all about? How the hell does Jack know Joey?

"Uh," I mumbled when Jack stepped even closer to the bed.

"You okay? You look pale." He extended his hand and lightly brushed my bruised cheek with his warm fingers. It felt great for about two seconds.

I slapped his hand away and glared hard at this man I didn't know. He looked much different too. I hadn't seen his face that hairy since our time in Africa last summer.

"Get out!" I shouted. "Get out of here right now! I hate you!"

That's not really what I wanted to say just then, but it's what came out when I finally opened my mouth. "Go! Get the hell out of my life. I'm over you. We're through. I hate the sight of you." I screamed again and then broke down into long drawn-out sobs. Hyperventilating would be an understatement. I buried my face in my hands to hide my tears and then screamed into them when I heard the door shut. My face popped up from out of my hands, mortified that I thought he had left. I hadn't really wanted him to go. I was just mad and having a very emotional moment. I'm a woman. We do that from time of time, but it never means what men think it means. Men usually think it means what we say, but that's not true. Did I want him to go? Hell no. I wanted answers. I wanted a hug for God's sake.

When I refocused my damp eyes, Jack was standing in front of the door and Joey was gone.

"Baby," he said with arms outstretched like he was trying to tame a wild animal. "Babe, don't be mad. I had no choice."

I sucked in a breath and ran for the bathroom, slamming the door closed behind me. I shouldn't have looked in the mirror, but I did and then I was horrified by my reflection. The little bit of mascara that I had applied that morning was smudged under my eyes. They were puffy and red and I had my shirt on backwards. I'm a slut!

There was a light rap on the door. "Babe, come on, Charlie. Let me explain."

"I don't want to hear it. I thought you were dead. I thought I'd never see you again. Damn you, Jack." I opened the door and stuck my head out with murderous intentions in my glare. "If that's even your real name." I slammed the door hard and leaned back against it.

"It's my real name damn it. Just ask Joey! You two seem pretty close."

Guilt tore at my insides. I didn't know what to say. I was mad as all hell, but I felt like I had somehow betrayed his memory. Then suddenly I wasn't all that mad anymore, damn him. I opened the door and looked out at him. "Jack, I…"

He swiftly grabbed my arm and tugged me toward him. I sobbed again and laid my head on his shoulder to let it all out. It had been a very emotional five minutes.

"I missed you too," he said.

While keeping my head buried against him, I wrapped my arms around his waist and took a couple of deep breaths. We stayed huddled together for a long, long time before I broke away again and sat down on the bed. "What the hell is going on? Why are you here?"

"I need you, Charlie." He sat down beside me and smiled warmly. "I need your help."

"What can I do? I don't even know what the hell is going on."

"I need you to go see Blackman. Can you do that for me?"

"Why, why me?"

"Because he'll trust you. You did a good thing at the hotel in Connecticut -- Not selling me out. He'll trust that you're there to help."

"Wait," I narrowed my eyes. "What does that have anything to do with it? Why is the DEA after me? If I'm going to help you, then I need all the answers. I need to know everything." Okay, so not everything, but damn close. Like I didn't want to know where he's been living...or with whom? My imagination was still running rampant about my harem theory. "Everything, Jack. Don't lie to me, don't hold back on me. I've just about had it with this mysterious bullshit routine. I want a normal life, a normal job. I want..."

He kissed me then. A soft, serious kiss as his hand stretched out into my hair and held me tight. Our tongues touched, sending a shiver up my spine. A very familiar feeling of desire and need had me gasping and clutching the slick leather of his jacket. The kiss deepened, he leaned over me, pressing me down onto the bed before coming up for air and sighing against my parted lips. "You want me, I hope."

I nodded and kissed him again, feeling the hot skin of his neck against my lips. I suckled. He moaned. I bit, he growled. He was burrowed in between my thighs, hot and hard and feeling so good. Then the clothes began to fly. Too bad the door swung open and Joey appeared with a sour expression.

"Dude, why do you always get the hot ones?" Joey groaned.

Jack laughed against my lips and held me down so Joey couldn't see my naked breasts. "Because I'm the big brother. Big brothers always get the babes." Jack winked at me when I squirmed and whimpered beneath him.

"You're kidding, right?" I gasped.

Joey laughed.

Jack shot him a long look of warning and the door slammed behind him.

"Oh my God!" I shouted. "You are sick. You sent your baby brother to seduce me? You're a pig!"

"Half brother," he replied. "And I never told him to seduce you. I told him to keep you safe and happy. He just takes his job a little too seriously." He smiled and kissed me again with lots of tongue. "That and you are pretty hot. I don't blame the guy."

No wonder I was attracted to Joey. They come from the same gene pool. Still, I wanted to spit and brush my teeth three times. I'm such a slut. "I can't do this now." I felt myself retreat from his arms. "Sorry, but it's just too weird."

"Wait." He grabbed the back of my jeans when I tried to run. "You can't leave me like this. I miss you, Charlie. I need you. I want you. Come here and sit on my lap."

I couldn't help the laughter. Jack has a way with words. He can be quite the suave seducer when he wants to be. Right then, wasn't one of those moments, but he was pretty cute, looking all engorged and desperate. I straddled him and kissed his nose. "You're so pathetic."

"And horny." He nuzzled into my neck and sighed. "Come on, I said I was sorry. I swear, Joey will never kiss you again. If he does, I'll knock his block off."

"That was somewhat cool, watching you punch him in my honor. Maybe you are an honorable man after all." I laughed and leaned back so his lips had better access to my naked breasts. "Oh God, Jack," I whimpered. "Don't stop."

He didn't stop, in fact it just got better after that. During the following two minutes of foreplay I was reminded just how much I love Jack's hands on my body, his arms around my waist, and the ripple effect of his kisses that melt my insides to goo. I was in a euphoric state of well-being. Bliss. Comfort. That is until Joey banged on the door.

Jack tensed and retreated from the fun we were having.

"Leaving so soon?" I asked, brushing the damp hair from my eyes and brushing my hand against his naked chest, really, really annoyed that he was about to leave me alone. I was trembling at the thought of watching him walk out that door one more time. It scared me that I felt that way.

"Need to talk to Joe. Stay put." He gave me a hard, swift kiss and sashayed out the door a very frustrated man.

I was on my feet scurrying to the door to eavesdrop and hopefully get some answers. Their voices were soft. I could make out their words just barely so I cracked open the door and slid to the floor. I could scarcely make out Jack's jean clad knee.

"So," Joey planted his hands on hips and stepped toward Jack. I could clearly see the tight set to his jaw when he came fully into view. "You sent me to baby-sit your fucking girlfriend." He slammed his fist into Jack's shoulder. "Fuck! I thought this was a case of national security. You've got a lot of explaining to do."

Jack punched him right back, sending him stumbling back a few steps and out of my sightline again. "Fuck you," Jack retorted. "Who the fuck else was I supposed to send. This shit is real and if you haven't noticed, I'm up to my fucking eyeballs in Hell right now." His lips pursed together. He looked exhausted.

Joey stepped forward again and I saw concern in his expression but he didn't speak, he only grabbed his brother and pulled him into a brotherly embrace.

Jack wrapped his arms around his brother and held on tight. That's when I noticed Jack's tear. It was only one little sparkling drop, but it still took my breath away.

"You're the only one I trust with my life," Jack moved away and sniffled in a manly fashion, quickly reining in his emotions. "And that in there…" He motioned to the door I was crouched behind. "Is my fucking life."

My hand surreptitiously moved up to clutch my aching heart. I wept like a baby. So maybe I was wrong about Jack Sullivan just wanting me for sex. I just heard it. With my own two ears, I heard him say something completely out of character for him. Perhaps I didn't know my Secret Agent Man as well as I thought.

The tone turned grave after Jack was done showing off his emotional side. Which, quite frankly, I was delighted he had!

Joey leaned against the far wall. All I could see were his shoes. Jack began pacing, walking in and out of my line of visual capability. "Tell me what happened," Joey said sternly. "What's this shit all about? And why is someone trying to kill Charlie?"

Jack shook his head. "I don't know; that's why I'm here."

"You must have an idea," Joey replied harshly.

"Not now," he groaned.

"Why the fuck not?"

Jack shook his head with a snarl, took two steps down the hall and then turned and looked at Joey with a serious gaze. "You didn't kill Russo did you?" Jack's brow cocked upward.

"No. You said no casualties."

"Has she tried to kill you yet?" Jack's tone was both playful and serious. He knew what I was capable of and it then made sense as to why I had been drugged so many times.

"Only twice."

And then they both let out a little chuckle before walking down the narrow hall and out of sight.

Jack came back into the room ten minutes later with a big sandwich in one hand and his gun in the other.

"What happened, Jack? Please tell me what this is all about."

He couldn't look at me, or didn't want to look at me, I couldn't tell. He finished the last bite of his sandwich, tossed his jacket onto the chair beside the bed and climbed in beside me.

I didn't speak. I could hardly breathe because he was hugging me so tight. Words or no words, his actions spoke to me. He just hugged me and wrapped his entire body around mine before inhaling deeply and falling fast asleep.

# Chapter Ten

A new day dawned in which I was grateful to be alive, safe and comfortably snuggled in bed with a sexy spy.

That moment of harmony lasted about two and a half minutes. "I have to disappear again. Will you be okay?"

Throwing a temper tantrum came to mind. "Fine!"

"And you'll do what Joey says."

"Maybe."

His disappointment in my blatant honesty showed on his scruffy jaw. "Charlie."

"Jack," I said right back in the same patronizing tone.

His hand slammed down on the bed, making the mattress bounce a couple of times. "Dammit!"

I closed my eyes, rolled over and played dead just to make him that much madder. I figured if he got any angrier, he'd feel the need to cuff me and drag me with him. Being with Jack was ten times safer than being with Joey. Joey was an amateur compared to Jack. Besides, after my little accident in New Haven I was suddenly very paranoid that the Grim Reaper was the one following me. Add in the fact that Joey admitted he had screwed up and wasn't able to save me from getting blown across a parking lot and you have, me, – a bit skeptical that Joey could save my life. I, on the other hand, could save my own life. I have done it before, numerous times. I just need a couple more days to recuperate and a lot more firepower.

"Fine." Jack said with spite as he tossed a business card onto the bed beside me. "Get yourself killed. Why the hell should I care? You always do whatever the hell you want anyway. Lord knows how you ever got along in the fuckin' Army?"

Ouch!

But he was not going to make me cry. I knew this was just Jack getting pissy because I refused to bow down to the almighty Spy-Man and allow him to think that I was a scared little woman who should stay home and raise babies.

It was no secret to me that Jack hated that I refused to obey him. I had this thing about obeying the men I loved. I frequently disobeyed my father when I was young, always striving for his attention. Then in the Army, I obeyed my superiors, only because I didn't love them. But once I fell helplessly in love with Master Chief, Brick Miller, that all changed. We broke up. I had a broken heart. I quit. End of story, and all that just because I refused to obey him.

I have a disease, or at least a syndrome of some sort. I'm sure Dr. Freud would've had a field day with me.

Jack huffed a couple of times, refused to look at me and then got out of bed, grabbed his jacket and started for the door.

"Okay!" I turned over and shouted at him. "Fine. What do want from me?" I grabbed the card off the bed and read the inscription. All it read was D. Blackman, Kingdom Insurance and a phone number with a New York area code.

He paused for a moment, his hand on the doorknob. "Trust no one."

I saw his head shake slightly and he muttered something to the ceiling, having his own personal conversation with the Lord. He then looked at me over his shoulder, pain in his eyes. He left. Not even slamming the door in his wake. It just sort of flapped shut. And who would have thought that would make me so darn mad that I wanted to spit flaming balls of fire.

~~~

The Rocky theme was the only thing that kept me moving. I had visions of Stallone running through my head. Then I pictured punching out Mr. T and that cute Russian guy who quickly turned into DEA guy in my imagination. I knew that once my body was used to the pain and agony of lactic acid emission, I would feel much better. Stronger. Ready to take on The Rat, The DEA and Jack Sullivan all at once.

Who was I kidding? After one hundred and twelve sit-ups I was ready for a nap.

The villa had remained eerily quiet. Joey was stationed outside my room. I presume Jack had already disappeared, and my only shot at making a go of it alone was to drug Joey, grab his gun and slip out unnoticed.

I took a break to have a glass of water and paced the room to figure out my next move. I'd already rummaged through Joey's belongings and unfortunately there were no signs of the drugs he was slipping me. I was terrified to brain him with a lamp, now that I had knowledge he was family. Damn my luck, anyway. And as long as I was thinking about Joey as family, I got very perturbed that Jack lied to me. He told me in Hawaii that he had two sisters; Robin and Kristina. I then wondered if that was a big fat lie. I bet he lied about his parents too. Probably hired actors to portray them at last Christmas dinner. I thought I'd seen his mother before. She probably does Kotex commercials or something. Ohhh. My blood was boiling then. Especially since I had made his parents that very nice photo album of Jack and I with my very own hands. Damn him!

"Ouch!" I shouted out in pain, looking down at the broken glass in my hand. Guess I got my superhuman strength back. Just in time too!

Joey came hurrying into the room, narrowly shattering the windows with the flapping of door. "You okay?" He looked into my eyes, then directly down at my hand.

I just plain refused to look because I have an aversion to the sight of blood. Especially when it's my own. My hand felt hot. Gooey. Sticky...bloody.

I felt my eyes roll back, the white dots danced in my peripherals and I was a goner.

Joey was cleaning up my hand when I came to. I looked around. His gun was on the edge of the bed, just inches from my foot. He finished wrapping some white tape around my wrist.

"You scared me," he said, clearly enthralled with my perspiring chest. I was just in my sports bra and a pair of his boxer shorts because I really hadn't prepared to be kidnapped and I was running out of clean underwear. "You okay?"

"Sure," I groaned and with a swift kick toward my ass, I had the gun in my opposite hand. I'm very bendy!

I leveled it on his chest and politely asked him to step away.

"You wouldn't shoot me, Charlie."

"Not to kill," I said sternly, letting him know I was in no mood to play. "But I might just need to maim you."

"What about Jack?"

"What about Jack?"

"He's gonna kill me!"

"He won't kill his own baby brother. Don't be so dramatic." I said, keeping the gun steadied while I yanked the lamp from the wall and ripped the chord off with my teeth.

"Please put it down. I'll do whatever you want. You want to find out what's going on...I'll help you. I have connections!"

His desperate attempt didn't faze me one iota. I needed to do more than just figure out what was going on. I needed it to stop. I had a career decision to make. I had laundry to do, a hair appointment with Gigi, and I had to get back to Bella. My to-do list was growing increasingly long and I didn't have time for this bullshit. If the DEA wanted me dead, I'd be DEAD! I'm sure they don't mess around when it comes to government-sanctioned revenge.

I was fed up with playing the prey. It was time for me to become the hunter.

I knew I couldn't tie Joey up without putting down the gun, so I dropped the lamp chord and looked around the room for something to help me.

I found my only best choice. Sitting on top of the armoire was a full bottle of Irish Whiskey. Jameson's I believe it was.

I narrowed my eyes and kept a steady hand on the gun. He followed my sightline right to the bottle.

I think he assumed I was going to bash him over the head with it, so he looked mildly surprised when I told him to drink.

"You're kidding?" he scoffed.

"Down it, pal."

I handed him the bottle and stepped back. He'd be stinking ass drunk soon and I'd not only get a good head start, I'd also get some answers. There's nothing like Irish whiskey to break the spirit of a super spy.

~~~

I waited patiently for half of that bottle to disappear down Joey's gullet. It took him quite awhile to get it down. After about six giant gulps, I was afraid he was going to hurl it back up, so I told him it was okay to slow down. We had plenty of time and plenty to talk about.

"Just pretend you're back in college," I said, sitting down on the bed. I had him on the floor in the corner with nothing around him just in case he got any ideas or became an angry drunk.

"Didn't go," he said with a bit of a slur. "I was a Marine!" He thrust the bottle into the air with much pride about that fact.

Jack was a Marine too.

I got very curious.

"So, how come Jack never told me about you. He told me he had two sisters."

"We don't talk much about me at family get-togethers. I'm just sort of there...like the furniture. Everyone walks around me like I'm not even fuckin' there."

"Affair?" I asked, my heart sinking.

He nodded heavily. "Daddy was a bad boy!" Then he hiccupped quite loudly and took another swig.

It was somewhat amusing seeing him in that state, while I was stone cold sober.

"Tell me about him."

"Edward," he began. "Edward Joseph Sullivan. Great American Hero who couldn't keep it in his pants."

I could barely make out his slurs, but I was really starting to enjoy the show. I was also happy that Jack had been honest about his parents. I was sure then that I had met the real ones.

Joey became more animated at that point. "Mom didn't see him coming. Those big bwown doe eyes. Dat smoove silver tongue. Sonnabitch secuced her right outta her unifoam."

"Mom was a Marine too?" I was both shocked and intrigued.

He looked at me sideways. His eyes somewhat crossed. Eyelids drooping.

"Hell no! She was a volunteer nurse at the hoppital in Nam!"

"Oh. Dad was a Marine." I said, slipping my feet under the covers and getting comfortable.

"Damn tootin, toots!" He hiccupped again and tried to stand up.

"Down boy!" I shouted and reminded him that I had a gun.

"You know, Charlie. You're probabwy the sexiest woman who as ever pointed a gun at me."

206

"Thanks," I smiled, enjoying his compliment. "Now go on. What happened with your parents?"

"Dad was hurt. Spent a couple weeks in the hospital, thought he was a goner...said he never meant to hurt his family, but Mom was there. She was beautiful and loving and he didn't think he'd ever see his wife and son again."

There was a loud sob. I thought for a minute it was me, but then I looked closer at Joey and he was in tears too.

"Never did know who Dad was until Mom died when I was seventeen. Right before she died, she agreed to sign the paper to let me join the Marines. Been there ever since."

"Wow!" I swiped the tears from my own eyes. "When did you meet your dad...and Jack?"

"Tracked down Dad afta I turned twenty one. I was so full a pissin' vinegar. Wanted to have it out with the ol' man, but when I met him, all I could do was..."

He stared at his lap and wept hard. Took that damn bottle and sucked down another ounce or two. When he finished, he threw it hard against the opposite wall and broke into another round of loud sobs.

I was stunned. I was also pissed that he broke that bottle, but I think I had him drunk enough.

"Cry?" I said. I know that's how I would have felt and I'm not all that weepy. I don't usually cry at movies, or sad country western songs, but man, I was bawling right along with that poor guy.

I got myself together in an attempt to get back to business. "You're not CIA, are you?"

He shook his head with a frown. "Didn't want me."

"Do you work for Jack?"

He nodded again, with more of a scowl. "Wasn't good enough."

I wasn't quite sure I understood why Jack would send his incompetent, CIA-impersonating brother to save my life. That's not what Jack would normally do. Something was terribly amiss. More so than I had suspected before Joey started talking.

"Are you and Jack close?" I asked.

"Wike bro-ders." He smiled and held up his hands in surrender. After that, he sort of grew quiet. "Please don't go, Charlie." He begged. "Jack'll never forgive me."

A twinge of remorse washed over me, but it didn't deter my plan. "I have to. I know you don't understand, but I just have to."

I got up and grabbed my tennis shoes, laced them up and looked down at him all slouched over and drooling. "Joey," I said. I took a step toward him.

He grabbed my leg with a very shaky hand.

I instinctively kicked out and got him in the stomach.

He let out a groan and toppled over, looking up at me; trying to focus on my face.

"Charlie," he slurred. "Were you really a Sec 72?"

My Army Ranger unit was called Sector 72G. Badass soldiers with attitude and enough brains and brawns to kick some serious ass. I was one of them. Top ten percent of Army snipers; that was my specialty. The Marines were usually our transport. "Yeah, Joey. I was."

"Bitchin'," he smiled. His eyes glazed over. "Marry me!"

I laughed hard, and then tied him up.

~~~

The only glitch in my plan to escape was that I had no clue as to where I was or where I was going. Joey was drunk. I was free and I had a gun. But the rest was simply going to have to be made up as I went along.

The villa that we stayed in was off the main highway just north of a little city on the outskirts of Sofiya. I learned that from the nice lady in the café who spoke very little English. She pointed me in the direction of Sofiya, gave me a couple of scones and I was on my way.

The car that Joey stole from Russo was not quite was I was accustomed to driving and it took me a good mile or two to realize I was driving on the wrong side of the road. It took some getting used to, but soon I had the hang of it.

My own super-spy sense told me that I
was being followed. In layman's terms that meant
that I looked in my rear-view mirror and a black
Mercedes had been behind me for more than
three miles straight. That usually wouldn't cause
alarm, but since I knew someone was after me,
their tinted windows and the over-all weirdness of
being the only two cars on the road, had me
unnerved.

I turned into a small diner off the side of
the road. By now the sun was setting and I was
getting scared. I wished they'd just open fire on
me so I knew their intentions. Unless, of course,
their intentions were to kidnap me and torture me
within an inch of my life. I'd rather just be shot in
the head and that would be that. Slow painful
death terrified me more than anything.

After I saw them park along the highway
just outside the small parking lot, I walked
straight to the bathroom hoping I could actually
get them inside the diner for a closer look. There
was a small window in the corner, just above the
toilet. It would have been big enough for me to fit
through, if it hadn't been painted shut. It was an
emergency and I felt bad for doing it, but it
needed to be broken. I smashed my elbow against
it and winced at the loud noise the shattering
glass made.

With my sweatshirt pulled down around
my hands for protection, I crawled through.
Looking around, I made my way around a couple
of overgrown bushes and peered through the

leaves at the Mercedes. That's when a warm hand wrapped around my mouth.

"Shhh," the man whispered in my ear. He smelled of sausage and gravy. "Don't bite."

I snarled under his hand, but didn't move. I was afraid the gun pointed at the small of my back might accidentally go off and end my life.

"Walk."

I walked.

"Get in,"

I got in.

His car had been upgraded to a large sedan with leather seats and a retractable sunroof. His gun remained on me until we pulled out onto the highway. The sun had already set. My stomach grumbled loudly and he handed me a bag of jerky. My favorite.

"Do you know how much trouble you are in?"

I shrugged and yanked on that jerky as if my life depended on it. It was heavenly.

He mumbled some very cute French obscenities and rubbed the sweat from his bald spot. "If you my daughter, I'd be dead from a heart attack! I feared you were killed," he said, popping a few antacids into his mouth. "What did you do this time?"

"Me?" I shouted at Russo. "I didn't do anything. I'm innocent and I have no idea what you are talking about!"

"My friend," he said a bit calmer. "I'm only trying to help you."

"Then tell me what you know. How did you find me?"

He remained tip-lipped as we made our way through the Bulgarian back country. Sofiya became the past and all I could do was stare out the window at the beautiful surroundings that were whizzing by me.

When we finally pulled off the road and down a country dirt lane, I knew that I was in big trouble. Or rather, that Jack was in big trouble. Then my mind raced and wondered why Jack wanted me to see Blackman. He never did tell me why. He just said that he needed me to go see him. And that Blackman would know that I was there to help. It's a darn good thing Jack gave me that card because I highly doubt that Blackman's listed in the yellow pages under National Security Expert.

I sighed in relief when we pulled up to a villa just off the main highway. Russo got out, walked to the rear then opened my door for me.

I sheepishly got out and followed him through the lobby. The entire room was in dire need of some updating. The wood floor creaked, the cobwebs hung low and it smelled like sauerkraut. Russo spoke a different language to the portly woman behind the counter. She handed him two keys, one of which he handed directly to me.

"Get cleaned up and then I will change that bandage for you," he said with the same expression my father used to give me back when I was a juvenile delinquent.

I looked down at my hand and noticed the decimated half-ass bandage that Joey had given me. "Thanks," I said, brushing the sweaty hair from my eyes.

~~~

Hot Chamomile tea was consumed after I had a new wrap on my hand. It did wonders for Russo's mood.

He hesitantly told me what I needed to know after I began with my interrogation once again. "Jack called me two days before you did. Told me that you might call and if you did, I was to send Mr. Potter to find you. That's all I know."

"So, Jack knew The Rat was stalking me after all. Why else would he have called you?" I asked sipping tea and kicking my feet onto the table. My adrenaline was beginning to kick in again and I felt as if I could run a marathon.

The fax machine spit out the papers we were waiting for, while Russo shook his round face at me. "Non!" he said, pulling the paper from the tray. "I believe you have it all wrong. The Rat is dead and these are the men who were following you at the airport."

With a tremble in my gut, I accepted the information and studied the faces on the page. "I met these two guys in the hospital in New Haven." I looked wide-eyed, ready for an explanation.

"National Security. They are legit, Charlie. I think someone else is pulling the strings here."

"Why would the NSA be following me?" I said, then felt the blood run from my flushed cheeks. "They think I know something. They were convinced I was holding something back about the explosion. Wow!" I groaned and planted my feet on the floor. "So, let me get this straight." Saying it out loud was hopefully going to jog my mind into putting all the pieces together. "Jack calls you. I get a basket of rats at my hotel and call you. You call Joey. Joey comes to Orlando and then up and runs off after DEA guy," I stopped for air. "DEA guy is in New Haven when my car explodes and so is Joey. National Security interviews me at hospital. Joey calls and tells me to bring Bella to Greece and NSA guys follow me…" I stopped for a long sip of tea. "That's where I get utterly confused. Who told Joey to get me to Greece? And why Greece?"

"Jack, of course," Russo said confidently. "Where else would you be comfortable leaving Bella? He knows of your love for the girl. He knew what he was doing."

"Good point!" I said with a smirk. "So Jack tells Joey to get me to Greece. So why then did Joey abduct me from you and tie you up? Aren't we all on the same side here?"

"That's where I get confused also," Russo said, scratching his head. "I thought Jack trusted me."

"Jack said, 'trust no one,'" I reiterated again, thinking that maybe I should not be having this discussion with Russo. Then I dismissed that because I know that Jack trusts Russo. Why else would Jack contact Russo? Unless, of course, Jack knew that's the only person I would have called to help me because he knows I trust Russo. The fog was thickening again in my head. "That makes perfect sense!" I stood up and beamed at my balding friend. "Jack knew that I would contact you once I got to Greece. He knew I would be with you, so he told Joey to intercept me from you. But why?"

"Because," Russo said with a smile. "This is where experience comes in. You never, ever under any circumstances tell anyone the entire story. This way, Jack tells Joey only what Joey needs to know in case Joey gets into trouble. Same with me, and, it seems, you too. Jack is probably the only one with the entire story. The rest of us are getting small pieces of intelligence on a need-to-know basis only. It makes much sense to me," he said with a pat to my upper back. "Agent Sullivan knows exactly how to play."

Play. That's not exactly how I would describe what I had been doing the last couple of days. The worst part was that I was still at square one and had lost my tail. My tail was my only connection to finding the truth and getting out of this mess before the week was up and I was forced to make a decision about my life and hustle home with a potential bad dude on my ass. It was time for some action.

"I need a favor," I said to Russo and then finished my sleepy-time tea.


The following morning, I took a long run. Long meaning, around the tennis courts, up the hill and back again. I was still feeling the after-effects of my near death experience and didn't want to overdo it on my first day out. I showered after a couple sets of crunches and some deep lunges. My legs burned, but I thrived on feeling the burn.

I had a scone and some tea and then I waited for Russo to get back from his errand. He knocked twice before letting himself into my room.

"It's done," he said, slapping his hands together. "Should be here within the hour. Are you sure about this?"

"It's our only chance, right?"

"Right," he said. "But I will miss you."

"I'll miss you too. Don't worry about me. I can take care of myself." I had to believe that to be true and, if in fact, someone was trying to kill me, I didn't want Russo around. He had no stake in what was going on and it was time to let him go. I hugged him tightly and thanked him again for leaking my whereabouts to a friend at Interpol. I'm sure the NSA agents were already receiving that intel and were scurrying to get back into their Mercedes to come find me. I hoped for the best and got into a car that Russo had arranged for me.

Ten miles down the road, it dawned on me
that I was all alone for once and I had trusted
Russo. I glanced back and saw a sinister looking
van pull up behind me. I almost lost bladder
control and I most certainly forgot how to
breathe.

The side door slid wide open and I
careened off the side of the highway kicking up
dust in my wake. I quickly got it together, pressed
my foot to the gas and did a fast u-turn that also
turned my stomach. Adrenaline surged, my pulse
raced, sweat beaded in between my boobs and I
finally took a deep breath.

I repeated some heavy pants down the
highway with the van on my tail. Its lights were
flashing; the horn honking wildly as it tried to get
along side me again. But I was having no part of
it. I swerved, narrowly running them into the
trees, but they recovered and came after me even
more determined than before. With my hands
clutching the wheel and my jaw clenched tight, I
swerved again and bashed in their front fender,
just enough to create friction on the front tire,
slowing them down enough for me to escape.

Another five miles down the road, I pulled
off onto a dirt road and stopped. I hadn't even
realized that I had been crying. My shirt was
damp. My nose was all dripping with gunk and I
just wanted to click my heels together and go
home. There's no place like home! There's no
place like home.
I opened my eyes, mortified that my little
daydream had not come true. What was even

more terrifying is that my car was steaming pretty heavily and then made a loud kachunking noise before finally fizzling to a dead quiet.

"Well, fuck!" I shouted out the window and then calmed my inner-ranting self and thought about my idiot plan again. I thought by putting my whereabouts out there for everyone to get, I'd feel somewhat safe, but the funny thing is that I had asked Russo to inform Interpol that I was in Sofiya. Sofiya was another hour away, meaning someone was still on my ass and had probably been watching me since Russo took me to the diner. Or was Russo not completely honest with me. Was this another set-up? The ridiculous part was that I still didn't know who was doing what. I knew someone was trying to kill me, someone was trying to scare me, someone was trying to spy on me and someone was trying to rescue me.

NSA, DEA, Joey, The Rat. In no particular order. But in no way did I feel secure that I'd be rescued before someone kidnapped me, or worse, put a bullet in my brain. I had to think. I had to pee and I had to get a new car. In no particular order.

I didn't know if I could trust Russo anymore and since Jack warned me to trust 'no one' I was out of options. I walked four miles up the highway, under the cover of overgrown trees and I called Greg once I could get a clear signal.

# Chapter Eleven

With the help of some very nice elderly people in a tiny European car, I was on my way to seeing a friendly face. Greg had immediately coerced Roald's chauffeur into picking me up at a café in Petrich, a small town, near the Bulgarian border. It took him a little over six hours to get there, but I had curled up into a ball in a corner booth and taken a catnap.

When the black shiny limo pulled into the lot, I grabbed the cell phone that Russo had given me and paused before heading for the door. I was too late for my own good. My last thought before seeing them was that I couldn't believe I had done something that incredibly stupid. I had used that phone to call Greg.

Three men converged on me, pulled me up by my armpits and shuffled me into the awaiting limo. I didn't bother to squirm and fight. Resistance was futile.

"I'm so sorry," Greg shouted and held me tight once the doors slammed shut. He was crying. Clearly distraught that he was now caught up in my own personal hell. "They weren't going to take no for an answer." He sobbed between well-needed breaths. "Oh, God, Charlie."

He was so darn dramatic.

I sighed and patted his arm. "Where's Bella?" I wasn't as concerned as Greg was because I knew two of the three men who had just man-handled me. They were the same suits from the hospital in New Haven; National Security agents.

"She's fine. Roald took her to Crete for the day. They're on George Clooney's yacht." He fanned his face. I'm sure he was thinking of Mr. Clooney without a shirt.

"Good," I said and then closed my eyes with a sigh.

Greg was dropped off in Greece along with the limo and the driver. I got to hug him goodbye and write Bella a cute little note telling her that I would see her at home soon…or so I hoped.

~~~

We hitched a ride back to the states on a military plane. It was filled with bad-ass soldiers, some suits, me and the three National Security Agents. I had not said one word to any of them other than to let them know when I had to use the facilities. I figured it was best to shut up and just do as they said. I knew I was in deep shit, but the wonderful thing about it was that I was safe. Kind of cool, huh?

We arrived at Andrew's Air Force Base at almost two P.M. Eastern Standard Time. Then took a short helicopter ride to the pad at the Pentagon. It was my first time in Washington D.C., let alone the Pentagon. I was ushered inside and then asked to please sit down by the taller of the two agents. "Would you like some lunch? You didn't eat anything on the plane."

I shook my head. I was starved, but I was playing cool. "Let's just get this interrogation over with so I can go home," I said with a confident, yet snotty tone. Then I swallowed the lump in my throat and said, "Please."

The lights dimmed when one agent pressed a remote control device in his hand. "This is the man who we think may be following you."

A picture of DEA guy flashed on the screen. It was an older photo of him, in a Marine uniform and a buzzed scalp. He looked much younger.

I just stared at the screen on the wall as more pictures flickered into view.

So, DEA guy is not DEA. That was my first thought.

"And, Miss Ford, we think you may have somehow drawn the attention of this man also."

A picture of a man I didn't recognize showed up next. The agent flipped through some photos and I shook my head. "Who is he?"

"Salvadore Aurturro. Does that ring a bell?"

"No," I said, very self assuredly. "Should it?"

"He was in the Bahamas the same time you were. On the same island. Staying in the same resort. You sure you've never seen him before?" His tone turned quite nasty.

I turned my head to the side and glared. "What is all this about? Why don't you just tell me why I'm here."

He held up the remote and punched the button again.

"How about him?"

I looked at the wall again and shook my head. "Nope, never seen him before in my life." He looked oddly familiar, but I couldn't place him. He looked European. Tall, blonde hair, skinny, with little beady eyes...like a rat.

I sucked in a breath and then flushed.

Another agent swiftly entered the room and flipped on the light. "Ferdinand Rchevicha."

That name sounded awfully familiar too. "Any relation to..."

"Son." The agent handed me a file. "Doug Lyons sent this over to me. Want to tell me what's been going on?"

Oh boy, howdy! My hands began to tremble. There were just too many balls in the air. Jack needing my help. The Rat's offspring trying to get revenge. A DEA guy who isn't who he seems. Russo who might have sold me out. My head was swimming. "I need to sit down," I mumbled breathlessly, feeling that all familiar panic rise in my chest making it hard to think, let alone breathe.

"You are sitting, Charlie." He put his hand on my shoulder and reminded me to breathe. "We can help you, but we need you to tell us what you know first."

"I know...I know nothing," I said a little too quickly. "I mean, I...I have no clue why these guys are after me. I'm not that cute, am I?" I chuckled lightly and wiped my sweaty palms against my jeans. "I need to go home. What day is it?" I stammered, feeling the air electrify around me. I stood up and felt a stinging pain in my ass. The room spun. The agent who was closest to me started looking all deformed and funky. Suddenly it all faded to black.

When I woke up, I was in a different room. The reclined chair I was in was quite comfortable. I focused my eyes on the eye chart on the wall. A nurse was seated in the corner, reading a People magazine. Nicole Harrison's picture was on the front with an announcement of her engagement to the ex-lead guitar player of Bruiser, a popular rock band. That woke me up! I wondered if Bella knew yet, and if she did, how she was handling it. I needed to get out of there. I needed to be with Bella in her darkest hour. The tension between the mother and daughter was already too much for any normal person to bear and now with the news of the engagement - I was sure that Bella would be livid...and depressed and disappointed that I was not there with her.

I struggled to speak. "'Scuse me." I said to the nurse. "What happened to me?"

She looked up from her gossip rag and then pressed an intercom. Her voice was distorted quite a bit. My hands felt like Play Doh and my tongue was huge. It felt as if it was taking up the space of my entire mouth.

I rolled my eyeballs around to see another set of g-men enter the area. I'd seen Conspiracy Theory a few times and let me just say that I was surprised that the evil Patrick Stewart didn't enter my tiny room. I was drugged. I knew it because I'd been drugged before. A lot. And the funny thing is that when I was a teenager, I was truly against doing drugs. I was the poster child for D.A.R.E.! Now, I seem to be making up for it.

"What?" I slurred at the agent who got in my face first. "Your breath is hideous. Get a mint."

He glared hard and moved away from my nose. "Let's start at the beginning," he said, flipping on a little recording device.

I had heard once or twice that if you believe something to be the truth, that you can actually beat a lie detector. I never personally tried, but I wondered if the same were true for Sodium Pentothal. It mattered not. I was so relaxed and dizzy that I would have sold out my own mother just to enter dreamland.

"What was your objective in the Bahamas?"

I started crying. I couldn't help it. That happens to me when I get overwhelmed, or too drunk. I tried to concentrate on anything and everything that did NOT have to do with Jack Sullivan...or shall I say, Eddie Malone? Oh hell. I was screwed.

The nurse handed me a moist towelette and then monitored my blood pressure again. It must have been way too low, because she cursed a couple of times and shoved the g-men out of her way while she checked the dilation of my eyes. "Hurry up, she's not going to last long." She shook her head. "When was the last time she ate anything?"

Agent number one shifted his weight and then glared at me, clearly blaming me for not taking up his many offers of food. "Charlie, just tell us what you wanted with Grady Sanchez."

"Grady is dead," I said with a slur. I think drool trickled from my lips. "He was a really nice man. Kind and gentle. He had a horse ranch in Miami and another in Texas and I'm positive that he was NOT a hitman. I think he was just a lonely man who liked to look at babes in bikinis. I don't see anything wrong with looking at babes in bikinis. Really I don't! I don't know why they killed him" I wept again and closed my eyes. "I'm starving."

"Not now."

"You're an asshole," I said between hiccups. "Trust no-one."

I shut my eyes and took a deep breath. "The Rat is dead. His son wants me dead. What does that have to do with Grady Sanchez?"

"You help us out and we'll help you out."

"So…what?" I lifted my head slightly. "I give you Duane and you get rid of my problem."

They exchanged glances. "What do you know about Duane?"

Duane, Vince, Ryan. I tried to think of the name that most fit Jack; the name that my utmost subconscious still referred to him as. I was even surprised when that name popped out. Then I just repeated those names over and over in my head until I forgot who I was talking about.

"Vince is my best friend. He's a spy. He saved me from some bad South African's in Kenya. I saw a giraffe. Bella was there. She saw him too. He's really real. I did not make him up, I swear! He made me burnt peacock and then he looked at my boobs. He's very sexy and he makes the cutest grunting noises when we're doing it."

Oops. Had I said too much?

The nurse looked at me with an apologetic smile. "I think we over did it." She turned to the agents and shrugged. "She's loopy. Sorry guys, maybe you can try again in the morning." And then she shuffled them out the door.

Two hours later, I was jostled awake by a different nurse. "Charlie."

"What?" I groaned and flailed my arms at her. It was dark in the room. All I could see was a penlight that she was using as a flashlight. "Charlie, wake up."

"Huh," I opened my eyes all the way. I could barely make out her tall figure in the room.

"Charlie, it's me. Liza." She snapped her fingers in front of my face and then continued with the chore of unraveling my restraints.

I grabbed her hand and got somber. "Liza," I said. "What the hell are you doing here? You have to go. They're after Jack."

"I know. Shut up and listen," she replied, and to my surprise, her Australian accent was gone. I guess that was part of being a spy. "We have to get you out of here."

"I don't think I can walk. My legs feel funny."

"It's the Sodium Pentothal. I made sure that she gave you enough for a horse. Sorry, the effects will wear off soon. I didn't want to take any chances that you would let something slip." She smiled at me. "You did great. Jack would be proud." Then she lifted a sheet over my head and began pushing me down the corridor.

I heard her stop once and say something in a very sultry voice, yet I could not make it out. Then I heard a thud. When we rolled past, I turned my head and could see part of a man's limp body on the floor. I hoped she hadn't killed him. I would have felt very bad about a good guy getting killed on account of me. He probably had a wife and three kids at home. I said a little prayer and held on tight as she hurried down the hall.

"This might hurt," she said and then I heard a hollow pang, I felt my toes come off the gurney and then I was sliding down a long, narrow, very cold tube. Down, down, all the way down to a pile of dirty laundry. I think I may have screamed once or twice, but I just prayed that it was muffled.

As soon as I hit the bottom of the laundry basket, it began rolling. I made my way through the nasty towels as best I could and then saw a big bay door open and I was pushed into an awaiting truck. Sirens were blazing. Lights were flickering above and then there was an explosion that sounded far off. The sirens kept getting farther and farther away, until they stopped all together and I finally took a breath and thanked God for teamwork!

"You okay?" Gilbert asked me quite a few miles down the road. "You can get out now."

"I can't," I mumbled. "My legs are Jell-O."

"Here," he grabbed me by the arms and pulled me into a precarious position. One leg was functioning at fifty percent. The other one still felt as if it were detached from my body. "Give me a hand," he yelled to Serena.

I smiled when they had finally pulled me free and I was laying on the floor of that dirty truck, leaned up against the wall. "Thanks."

"No. Thank you." Gilbert grinned. "I heard you did well."

~~~

I wasn't filled in on details. I was just driven to a dark farmhouse in the middle of the

country. The truck pulled up to the red barn just
as the sun was coming up and the roosters were
doing their thing. I yawned and pulled the blanket
off my legs. Without the weight of the heavy
wool, I thought for sure I was going to be able to
walk. Not taking any chances, I crawled to the
ledge of the truck and waited for Gilbert.

Serena and Kaia had been up front. That
left me, Liza and Gilbert in back.

"Where's Mia?" I asked with wide eyes.
The mood was already somber, but I seemed to
have made it worse with my little question.

Gil and Liza looked at one another, then at
me. "She doesn't know, does she?" Gil said
quietly.

"Know what?" My voice quivered. My
guts tied in knots and I thought for that little
moment of silence that I might vomit. I felt my
world implode again and I was sure that was
impossible, as I had already felt my lowest of
lows when I thought Jack was dead for the first
time. "What?" I shouted again, clenching my
muscles in anticipation of horrendous news.

"Randy's dead." Serena spoke softly from
behind me. "He was Mia's brother. She's off the
radar."

"Dead?" I sucked in a breath and was
happy that it wasn't Jack's name she had just
said. Then I got sad. Randy seemed nice. I barely
knew him though. "How?"

The posse of super spies all looked around
and then helped me inside. No one said anything

until I was planted on the couch and a bottle of whiskey was making the rounds.

Liza was the first to chime in. "We aren't sure what happened to Randy. He was killed in the Bahamas. Right after...well, after Grady. No one knows what happened. He was just gone."

"Maybe he's not dead then." I said with a yawn. I didn't mean to be rude, but I was spent.

"No," Gil shook his head at me. "Gone as in..." he put his finger to his head like a gun. "Dead. One shot. Professional."

"Cartel?" I asked.

They all shrugged and passed the bottle around for one more shot. "Eddie's missing too. No one's heard from him. His place was torched. His communications are out. We haven't been able to locate him or the secondary team members. It's like we're all alone."

"Hhm." I said quietly. Trust no one was running through my head, but I knew that Jack worked with these people and trusted them with his life on more than one occasion.

Liza was the first to engage me with her stare. "Have you seen him?"

Then the others got antsy and began staring at me too. "Yeah, and why was the NSA all up in your ass? What's going on? You didn't say anything, did you?"

Russo once taught me a little thing that I thought I would try out. Not giving them the entire story. It seemed like the right thing to do since they had all just risked their lives for little old me.

"Someone blew up my car in New Haven."

A sudden chill stole into the room, but I continued as they watched with wide eyes.

"At the hospital, two NSA guys showed up with the FBI and wanted to know who I thought did it. They asked me lots of questions about Grady Sanchez." I shrugged my shoulders and kicked my feet out when I felt them tingling wildly. "Then I got scared and jumped on a plane for Greece. I have friends there, but those agents followed me and then nabbed me at the airport." I paused after my little fib. "Remember that guy who confronted me at the café at the resort?" I looked at Liza. "He's been following me too. Why?"

The others looked to Liza for an explanation.

She pressed her lips together and stood up. "He's a rogue DEA agent. Went nutso about a year ago."

"Are you sure?" I asked. That wasn't the story I got from Jack.

No one said anything. Perhaps none of us completely knew the truth about anything.

~~~

I think I slept most of the day. My legs were somewhat back to normal. Gilbert makes a damn good peanut butter and jelly, so I was ready

for some action. "What's next?" I said between
bites. I had a cup of coffee in front of me, and I
was surrounded by some fairly glum people.
Glum and lazy. No one was plotting our revenge.
No one was standing up to be the hero. That
someone had to be me. I wanted my life back. I
needed to get home and comfort Bella, but mostly
I needed to see Jack.

"What would Eddie do?" I was still
calling him that because with the exception of
Liza, everyone else still referred to him as Eddie.
Not sure if Eddie was his nickname or not, I
played it cool and only called him Jack in my
dreams. "We have to do something. I need my
life back."

"We all need our lives back." Serena said.
"But that's impossible. Blackman's off the radar
too, that means none of us..."she motioned
between the four of them. "Exist."

"I get that," I groaned. "But something
has to be done. What do you do when a mission
goes sour?"

"We get drunk." Kaia smirked.

"That's very funny," I said more
seriously. "Don't you have like, a back up
contingency...like in Mission Impossible? They
were all supposed to meet back at the hotel at a
certain time. Did you do that?"

"You watch too many movies. There's no
contingency plan. A mission goes to shit and
we're fucked. So far, in seven years, this has
never happened before." Gil replied. "It's not like
we can just go back to our apartments and think

we're safe. I think Eddie had the right idea. He's a ghost and he's probably the only one of us who will survive. Someone is after us, Charlie. All of us."

"So, I'm not the only one with a near death experience?" I gulped and held my hand to my chest.

"Serena's apartment just happened to catch on fire. My brother's house was invaded and Gil's sister-in-law was tied up, gagged and tortured. None of us are safe. Someone wants us all dead and we can help each other," Liza said, staring at me with her big green eyes. "If we trust each other."

My pulse rocketed. Who can I trust? I wandered away from the table, knowing that I was surrounded by trained professionals and I did not have a foolproof poker face. I show my emotions on my sleeves. That's why up close and personal is no good for me. I need to be out of sight.

Liza followed me into the family room. It was musty and smelled like skunk and dust. I took a seat and stared out the dingy window at the cows and goats in the pasture.

"Look," she began. "I know this is difficult for you, but someone is after us. We need your help, Charlie. We need to find Jack."

"I haven't seen Jack," I said quietly, still staring out into the field. "But what about Blackman. Can't we pay him a visit? Ask him to help out?"

"It wouldn't do any good," she said solemnly. "We need Jack. Can you think of anyone who would know where he is?"

I shook my head. "No. And why is it that you call him Jack and everyone else knows him as Eddie?"

"I've known Jack longer. Before he became Eddie Malone," her tone was soft. I could tell she was going through a very hard time. "And I know about you too, Charlie."

My head snapped around to face her. "What do you mean?"

"Jack told me how much he loves you. He asked me to make sure nothing happened to you if things got ugly."

"Really?" I replied. "Why didn't he just tell me that?"

"I don't know," she said with a shake of her head. "That's why I think you can help us. It makes me nervous that Blackman just flew the coop. That's not like him. I can't help but wonder if he's involved."

"No!" I said a bit too loud. "Seriously."

"That's why I don't think we should pursue him. I think it might be a trap."

I thought long and hard about that. It made sense to me. After all, Blackman knows all.

An hour or so later, after a lot of moping around, I confronted Kaia and Gilbert out back. They were unloading the van. They had explosives, weapons and an entire arsenal of super-spy gear, ropes, harnesses, gas masks. It must have been my Army special forces training because seeing that equipment gave me an idea.

"Who do you think is behind all this?" I asked Gilbert. He was the one I trusted the most.

With a headshake, he frowned. "If I had to guess, I would say an internal leak. DEA maybe, Blackman, but one thing I do know, it's cartel related. Someone's got inside information and knows things they shouldn't."

"Where would you go to find Blackman?"

"He has a card. A blank business card with a phone number on it. Without that card, he's a ghost. We'll never find him and even if we did, he'd deny knowing us. It's just part of our lifestyle, Charlie. When things are great, we've got the United States and about thirty other countries behind us, but when shit hits the fan, even our own leaders don't want to know us. It's sad, but it's just the way it is."

I dug around in my mind and wondered where that card was. Then I remembered stuffing it into the toe of my tennis shoe. I wiggled my toes to make sure I could still feel it. Yep. Still there. Only, I wasn't really sure I was ready to divulge that I had it. If Jack trusted these people, then why wouldn't he just come back and hook up with them. Why the Cloak and Dagger shit?

Trust no one. Shit, I couldn't turn off my damn brain.

"What do we do now?"

"Pray." Gil quipped.

"I think we confront Blackman."

"I'm game, but I don't happen to have a get out of jail free card."

"Who has one?"

"As far as I know, Eddie and only Eddie."

"Let's just see about that." I winked and wandered back inside to find Liza on the telephone. She quickly and abruptly hung up.

"Just checking on my brother. Did you think of anything else?" she said, cradling the receiver back to its position on the wall.

"Actually, yeah." I took her by the elbow and sat her down at the kitchen table. "Gil tells me that the only way to find Blackman is through a card, a very special card," I said, bluffing my way along. "I think you have one."

She stared at me with a blank, confused expression, but for one flittering moment, I swear I saw her squirm. "I don't know what to say to that."

Just then the others came in, staring at Liza. "Is it true?"

"No, I mean…we can't. We can't see Blackman. What if Blackman is the leak? What if?"

"Then we take him out, but we have to try, don't we?" Kaia said, clearly rattled. "You know where he is, don't you? He always had a special thing for you, I knew it! Where is he?"

Liza stood up and got fidgety. "You guys are all I have left. No! We are not falling into his trap. We need to find Eddie. Screw Blackman. He'll be waiting. He'll be ready. I'm not going to risk anyone else dying. It's over. Let's just move on and work on finding Eddie."

"I think we should find Blackman." I put in my two cents. Gilbert and Serena chimed in too. "Then let's do this. You guys have experience with this. You know what to do."

"Liza," Serena said with a calm tone. "Charlie's right. You've been watching Eddie for years. You can do this. We can do this."
It was like a damn pep rally.

"All we need is an address." I said. "Eddie said you were the best of the best. Let me see you prove it."

Whoops and hollers resounded in my ears and we all got straight to work.

~~~

The next morning, Liza had drawn a fairly good map of Blackman's vacation home outside of Mexico City. It was like a damn castle. With large rock walls and a waterfall on one side. A cliff on the other. Logistical nightmare, but I had seen worse. Much worse. In fact, I had once been on an extraction mission in Haiti where our mark lived in a Cliffside resort much like the one we were preparing to sneak into.

"We need more men," I said after a bite of my ham and Swiss sandwich. "We can't possibly take the north side and cover the west with the four of us. "Why don't we just tranq him and drag him down the back stairs?"

"Nice," Serena said. "And what if he's not the bad guy? How do you apologize for that one?"

"Good point."

"Are we really doing this?" Kaia asked. "Blackman was the best. I'm sure he lives in fear and has the best security known to man. How do we even know he's going to be there?"

"We'll watch. We'll do our research and we'll wait. It's our only chance." I said. "Now, tell me how we should get him and his wheelchair from point A," I circled his bedroom on the map and continued. "…to point B." I drew another circle around the awaiting SUV; preferably stolen. The plan was drawn out, but every once in awhile Liza would waffle and asked us repeatedly if we really wanted to do this. The mantra became the same.     "Yes, damn it!"

~~~

We slept one more night in the farmhouse and then all headed to different airports with different identities and plenty of cash in our pockets. I used to wonder how spies funded their ops and it was just as I suspected. They had a safe with cash from just about every single country. They also had about four to five passports each. Credit cards with even more identities and even some very cool disguises. I got to be a man; a man named Drake Cloutier. I looked rather handsome if I do say so myself. I took a flight from West Virginia to Houston, Texas. When I landed in Houston, I got off the plane, bypassed the luggage carousel and went directly to the first mall I could find. There, in a dressing room in Macy's I changed back into a woman.

I bought a pair of jeans, three new shirts and a pair of tennis shoes that were perfect for running. Paid cash for all of it. It was almost like spending Monopoly money.

After having a taco and a raspberry smoothie in the food court, I walked up to the top level and plugged a couple of dollars into the pay phone. I dialed Greg's cell phone and got him on the third ring.

"Don't say my name." I stuttered, still thinking I was in hot water with the NSA. Which I probably was and since they had Greg by the short hairs once, I was sure I had about twenty-eight seconds before I was made. "I'm okay." I stammered as he tried to say something. "Don't talk. I only have a minute. I just wanted to make sure Bella is okay. I read about her mom and that horrible sleaze-ball. Is she okay?"

He didn't answer. It was just silent. "Gregory!" I shouted.

"What?" he yelled back. "You just told me not to talk."

"Sorry," I giggled. "So is she okay?" I had about ten seconds.

"She's a complete wreck, but we're keeping her busy. She misses you."

"Tell her I love her." Then I hung up and wiped my clammy palms against my jeans.

It took me another seven hours to get to my next destination of Mexico City. I was Wanda Bayley by the time I landed at the airport. I had blonde curly hair down to my ass, a good look on me, and I had the cutest southern drawl. Okay, so the drawl was completely amateur, so I tried not to talk too much.

We all met up at a rundown Hotel just south of our final destination.

I knocked three times, made a belching sound and was let in by Serena.

"That was by far the longest and weirdest damn day of my life." I groaned and landed face first on the bed. Then I realized how skuzzy the room was. Filled with cooties. I had probably just planted my face in dried up semen.

I went into the bathroom and washed up. When I came back out, Liza had finally arrived.

"Well, has anyone decided against this yet?"

"No!" We all shouted together.

I laid down and went over my job in my head. I had the easy part. Steal a car and drive. Just drive. My job was to drop each of them off at their various points and then when security went down, my job was to pull into the garage, get

Blackman and drive to the airstrip on the other
side of town. Piece of cake.

I hadn't slept well that night. I woke about
every hour and just stared at the LED readout on
the clock. Gil snored. Kaia was grinding her teeth
and Liza was up pacing most of the night and
making phone calls. I wasn't awake enough to
actually get out of bed and listen, but I could hear
her speaking Spanish to whoever was on the end
of the line.

When the sun finally graced the sky, and
the crack in the curtain, I stretched and went over
my objective in my head again. I was fairly
scared. Okay, so I was terrified. But I also wanted
my life back and knew this was my only shot.

"Good morning," I muttered to Gil with a
smile. "You ready for this?"

"As I'll ever be," he muttered sleepily.
"Did she even sleep at all?" He motioned toward
Liza. "I'm worried that she's fried. Might not be
on top of her game."

I glanced over at her, watching her smoke
a Virginia Slim with unwavering poise. She
seemed almost eerily calm; unlike the rest of us
who couldn't seem to sip coffee without spilling
it on our laps. Kaia had chewed her beautiful
nails to the nubs and I was close behind.
Watching her nibble made me think of Bella and I
wondered if her bad habit had come back.
Probably ten-fold since the news of her mother's
impending marriage.
I felt so bad that I couldn't be with her. I felt
responsible for the decimation of every single one

of Bella's nails. As I'm sure there would be nothing left once I saw her again. Then I swallowed hard and hoped that I would see her again. If this was in fact a horrible setup and Liza was right, what if I didn't make it? What if I never saw her again? Or my parents. Or my brothers. My nieces and nephews. Jack.

I swiped the single tear from my eye and stared out the window.

Liza brought me a cup of coffee.

"Thanks," I said, sipping carefully.

It was quiet for a heartbeat. "Jack really loves you. You know that, right?"

Another stream of tears trickled as I shook my head. I think I agreed with her. Even if she was just buttering me up, it was a nice comforting thought.

She continued. "He would do anything for the ones he loves."

I remained quiet.

"Are you sure you don't have any idea where he could be," she asked, grabbing my hand and giving it a gentle squeeze. "We could call this whole thing off and just meet up with Jack…think about it. He'd want us to come to him. He really would." She sounded almost impatient. "Jack wouldn't want us to do any of this. He feels a certain amount of love for all of us." Her eyes glazed over as if in deep thought, or perhaps jaunting down memory lane.

For one alarming moment, I almost felt resentful. I most certainly felt a jolt of envy run through my veins because she looked like a

Goddess and she was speaking about Jack like she knew him intimately.

"You're sure you haven't heard from him?" She asked again as she stood up.

I simply shook my head.

~~~

My day of reconnaissance started early. I was in the parking lot of a busy shopping center by nine A.M.. I took out my sunglasses and simultaneously pulled my sweaty tank top off away from my boobs, hoping for a bit of a breeze. No such luck.

I watched children screaming. I saw a couple of deadbeat bums begging for change and then I saw a very nice SUV being vacated by a nice elderly gentleman who looked older than death. I somewhat hoped that in his harried state, he would forget to remote the locks, but when he got about twenty feet away, the car chirped.

I knew I had no time or patience for alarms. The only problem with that was that most nice posh SUVs had alarms and their drivers were very diligent about using them. That made my job that much harder. I gave up and went and had a churro.

I met up with Gilbert and Kaia for lunch. No Liza to be found.

"You don't suppose?" I said, checking my burrito for errant onions. "Nah." I licked the tip of my thumb and then the burrito grazed my lips. I stilled before taking a bite because for a fleeting moment, I felt the hair on the back of my head standing on end.

I had felt that same feeling many times in my life and usually my hunch was right. I was being watched.

"Suppose what?" Kaia said, forking her boring, low-cal salad. I guess to look that good, one had to make sacrifices; like food that you can actually taste.

I looked around casually while taking my first delicate bite. It was beyond heavenly. Who knew that my fear of death would make food taste that much better?

I saw nothing out of place. No strange G-Men in long overcoats staring at me through cheesy sunglasses. Every person in the little Taqueria looked as if they belonged there.

"Nothing," I moaned after swallowing. "I'm just a bit paranoid."

Gil had a map laid out and we were going over our method of entry once again. It was not going to be easy. He'd spent the entire day before looking over the security around the compound. State of the art. Blackman was either one paranoid spook, or Liza was right and we were all about to fall right into his trap.

I knew I needed a big monster SUV. Everywhere I looked, I was preoccupied with finding the perfect vehicle. That's all I had to do.

Get the getaway car...that and drive. And I knew I could drive. Stealing a car is another matter entirely.

A minute or two passed in which I was no longer convinced that I was being watched. Liza arrived looking like she always did. Gorgeous. I couldn't help the open- mouth gawk. The idea of Jack in bed with that, made my heart ache. How could I ever compare to someone like Liza. She was perfection. Classy. Smart. Gorgeous. Even her toes were fucking perfect!

"Does everyone know what they are doing?"

I nervously laughed and spewed burrito from my lips. Sure, I knew what I was doing. I was getting myself in way over my head, but with a damn good reason.

# Chapter Twelve

The next morning, I rose with the sun. I had a bottle of water. Took some vitamin C for good luck and steady nerves, then I laced up my running shoes and headed for the door.

"Take this," Liza said, handing me a Glock. "I don't want anyone taking any chances."

I looked down at the weapon and then back up to her eyes. "I'm just going for a run."

"Just in case. Please. Keep it on you all the time."

She was starting to sound like Jack. Jack had told me time and time again to always be on guard. Never ever let my surroundings be my demise. Well, Liza was a disciple of Jack, so I should have expected it. I took the gun and tucked it in the waistband of my sweats.

I went down the crickety steps and hit the pavement running. I needed to clear my head before things got seriously underway. I got no more than thirty feet in front of the hotel when a bomb blast rocked the earth out from under me. My hands and knees were the first things to feel the impact of my fall to the asphalt. It took a good few seconds for me to get a grip and look back at the toppled mass of bricks and mortar behind me. Then it took another minute for the panic to set in and I ran. I ran as fast as my feet could carry me, down the hill with sweat and tears dripping from my face.

I was out of breath and freaked beyond a doubt when a car pulled along beside me.

"Get in." Gil shouted. "Charlie, get the fuck in."

I got in. I had forgotten that he had left before I decided to go running.

I reached for my gun, but he was quicker.

His gun rammed against my ribs. "What the fuck is going on?"

I put my hands in the air, dropping my gun onto the floor of the SUV. It was posh and roomy. Very nice.

"I don't fucking know!" I shouted right back. "Liza was in there! Kaia? Serena?"

Gil shook his head and swore, yet kept driving.

It seemed like an eternity later when he spoke again. He did pull his gun away from my body, but kept it pointed straight at me. "So, they're all gone? Dead?"

I nodded. What more could I say. His entire unit. His family. Boom. Gone in one blast that could have easily taken us all. Then I wondered why it hadn't. Could it have been on a timer and whoever had set it off didn't know that Gil and I were early morning joggers? Or was it remoted and the bomb was meant to just kill the gorgeous girls? I shook my head at myself. Who the hell kills beautiful women?

Sick people. Maybe even insanely jealous ugly people.

"Could Blackman be onto us?"

"I suppose." Gil shook his head with a scowl.

I supposed at that moment when he pulled into a tiny garage in the ghetto that he could have been the bomber! Either way, I figured I was dead soon, so grabbing the wheel and biting his arm seemed like a good place to start. I bit hard too and we clipped the side of the garage, narrowly taking down the entire structure.

He howled in pain, dropped the gun and yanked hard on the back of my head. My hair was knotted around his knuckles. It hurt!

"What the fuck did you do that for?" he snapped viciously.

"How do I know you didn't do it?" I shouted in pain and wiggled from his grasp. We were both breathing extra heavy.

"How do I know you didn't do it?" He shouted right back, nursing the bite marks and blood on his forearm. "Fuck, that hurt!"

I rubbed the back of my head and frowned. "So, you didn't do it?"

"If I had done it, you'd be dead too." He growled. "I've very good at my job."

"Well…" I didn't quite have a comeback for that one. Then the ground began to quiver beneath us. "Shit!" I screamed and the garage toppled in around us. A giant dust cloud muddled my vision. I heard glass breaking and the earth shook as the cement blocks crashed around us.

When we emerged, the SUV was piled under rubble and I was dusty from head to toe. Worst part was, we were somewhere in the Mexico City ghetto with no car.

"Did you steal that?" I asked, while dusting off my sweats.

He nodded with pride.

"Excellent!"

We walked in silence. Clearly we both had a lot to work out. I had a gun. He had a gun, but neither of us raised them again. The streets were fairly quiet except for kids playing in the dirt and screaming. It reminded me of Bosnia. The ghetto. War-torn. Kids playing in dirt without proper shoes or clothes, yet had no idea of the horrible things around them. They seemed so innocent. My gun was hidden beneath my shirt, but with my hand gripping it tightly. I wasn't taking any chances and if Gil hadn't blown up the hotel, I wondered who did and, then of course, my mind reeled at the idea that we were being followed. Someone was just biding their time before attempting to kill us too.

"What should we do?"

"Get to Blackman," Gil said adamantly. "The plan is still in effect. Only this time, we go in with a bang, grab the old man and get the hell out."

"I can do that," I said. I'd done it in the past. Sometimes ops went down quietly, sometimes not so much. This would just be one of those times.

"I'll need something bigger than an SUV." I grinned and felt comfortable tucking my gun back into my waistband.

I found that something ten minutes later when we ran past a hospital entrance. I don't really know when it was that we started actually running, but it seemed that the more we talked about our plan, the faster we ran. I was out of breath, but not as insane as Gil seemed to think I was.

"You're going to jack an ambulance." His head shook with laughter. "When I suggested something bigger, I was thinking a tank. Maybe a chopper."

"Ambulance!" I glared. "It's perfect. The lights and sirens on. No one will suspect a thing seeing that barrel down the streets! Goddamn, I'm a genius!"

~~~

Our new plan was set. My ingenious idea to steal an ambulance was perfect, so after a satisfying meal of microwave burritos from a convenience store, Gil and I made our way back toward that hospital. We were traveling light with just the clothes on our backs. For the first time in my life, I felt like a common criminal. Stealing food and coffee. With no money and no government to back us up, I felt alone. Abandoned. A woman without a country.

The cover of night came quickly. We loitered around the entrance of the hospital long enough to know that when ambulances pulled up, the driver usually left the vehicles running. That was a good thing because I was sure my hands would be shaking too much to actually hot-wire an ambulance.

Gil gave me a signal from the other side of the driveway and I ran my hands across my sweats a couple of times. I breathed in and breathed out. This was going to be the easy part. The hard part would be later when we would have to hold up a local merchant to steal guns, ammo and more food. I just can't work on an empty stomach.

An ambulance rambled by, lights blazing, but no siren. The driver got out first, followed by the passenger EMT. They were both around back, unlocking the doors and being met by a couple of orderlies and triage nurses. As soon as the gurney was clear of the back, I swiftly walked toward the driver side. I looked around and behind me. Everyone was still engrossed in conversation. My heart was beating wildly; like it was getting ready to jump right out of my chest. I hoped the ambulance drivers in Mexico City were not armed, and then I made sure there were no policia cars hanging around nearby. Then I gave the signal to Gil, opened the door, jumped in and pressed my foot to the pedal as I slammed the transmission into drive.

It took a few minutes to figure out the siren, and once I got it on, I sped through the parking lot, turned east onto the parkway and headed toward our rendezvous in a remote part of the ghetto that I knew all too well.

It took Gil quite awhile to meet me, so I had time to park the monstrosity, stumble into the back and hook myself up to the oxygen tank.

~~~

The garage I had parked the ambulance in was abandoned on the outskirts of what I called the ghetto, yet I'm sure in Mexico City, it was the suburbs. The door rattled a couple of times. I raised my gun and then lowered it when Gil's bright smile appeared.

"Nice work."

"Thanks," I said with a smile. "Did you bring me anything?" He was carrying a duffel bag and a grocery bag. I hoped for more firepower and some hot tamales.

He smiled and handed me the grocery bag. Junk food. Yum.

I got to nibbling, while he pulled out a tourist map and did some creative doodling. "Tomorrow night, this will all be over. We'll either have our lives back or we'll be dead." His dark brow cocked in my direction. "Either way, it's closure."

"I'm not too hip on the dying part." I gulped down a couple of gigantic bites of Ding Dong. "Are you sure about this?" I asked, because I sure as hell wasn't. I knew that my objective was to get to Blackman. Jack had said I had to get to Blackman. I knew then that I was going about it completely ass backwards. I chewed another bite and felt a tightening in my chest. The girls were dead. Gil was here with me. Jack was nowhere to be found. With one swift explosion, three more of Jack's unit were taken away. That meant three less people for me to be suspicious of. I was sure that Blackman was not involved. Or was I?

"Ah hell," I said under my breath. My stomach clenched, but it seemed like the right thing to do. "I have a card."

Gil dropped what he was doing and looked directly into my eyes, with a narrowed gaze. "A card?"

"Blackman's card." I gulped. "I have one."

He was quick. His hand wrapped around my throat so tightly that I couldn't breathe, let alone answer his question. "What kind of shit is this?"

I grunted. My face felt flushed. Then I swiftly brought my knee up to his groin. He countered my action with his knee and then tightened his grip on my larynx.

His eyes narrowed. He looked possessed. Like a man hanging by a thread. I felt the tears well in my eyes and was powerless to stop them.

He dropped his hand and stepped back. "You better get straight with me right fucking now."

With a quick maneuver, I sidestepped him and sat down before taking a few deep breaths and wiping the moisture from my eyes. "Jack gave it to me."

"Jack?"

"I mean Eddie," I said. "Eddie Malone." I continued to stutter.

He sat down, still keeping his dark eyes narrowed at me. "When did this happen?"

"About a week ago, I guess." My days had blurred together into one horrific nightmare. It all seemed like the same damn day to me. Just one bad thing after another.

I could see that he was working something out in his head. It took a few minutes for him to speak again, and when he did it was like the man was speaking in tongues. Every other word was an obscenity. Some very colorful ones, I might add.

"Holy fuck!" He ended with a knee slap. "I should have known something was fishy."

"What?" I got closer to him. I don't know why, but I trusted Gil. Probably it will turn out to be my horrible life-ending mistake, but I trusted him just the same. "What do you mean by that?"

"We've got a call to make."

~~~

The phone was ringing non-stop. Gil grabbed it from me and lifted it to his ear.

"He's not answering."

"Yeah," I said, "So what does that mean?"

"Something's not right," Gil answered and hung up. Then he put in a couple more coins. They clinked into the machine while he redialed. Again, he waited with eyes wide.

He slammed down the receiver and hurried me back into the ambulance. "Drive."

I drove. I didn't say much. Actually all I did was stutter a few times while he barked directions and had me turning up the hill toward Blackman's place. My eyes got wider as we got closer. The hill got steeper. The landscaping got nicer. It wasn't anywhere near dark outside. I was scared out of my mind, but I drove just the same.

Gil flipped on the lights and sirens as we approached the gate. "Ram it."

Again, my eyeballs protruded. "You got it." My foot slammed down all the way, pressing the gas pedal to the floor. We lurched forward, slammed the gate and I think I screamed like a girl when it buckled and then popped from the hinges. I reversed. With skidding tires I did it again. This time the gate broke free completely. The ambulance bounced a couple of times as we drove over the curb to miss the brunt of the collapse.

"What now?" I said still speeding down his long narrow driveway, trying to get my gun free from under the seat. I knew something was not right. Like in some secret code, Blackman not answering his phone was a desperate call for help.

When we approached the house, I turned off the siren. Nothing looked out of place. Not that I had ever seen his house before, but it looked fine. No one had used an ouzi to get in the front door.

"Stay here," Gil said, gripping his gun tight. "If I'm not back in ten minutes, head to the airport. A chopper is waiting."

I grabbed his arm as he slid out. "Wait!" I yelled. "How will I...?"

A blast halted the rest of my question. Glass shattered around me. I felt a sting of pain in my ear. Again, the timing was impeccable. Another minute and Gil would have been inside when the house got blown to smithereens. I felt lucky to be alive.

Needless to say, we didn't take a minute to breathe. He jumped in and we hauled ass out of there. I didn't even take the time to turn around; I drove that ambulance straight down that long driveway – in reverse.

"Holy shit, holy shit, holy shit!" I sucked some wind and did an impressive one-eighty at the end of the driveway. "What the hell?"

Gil was silent. He was bleeding. But then again, so was I.

I remember crying. I probably screamed out in agony when Gil pulled a shard of glass from my thigh, but I don't remember much due to the fact that I passed out. I woke up on the floor, and my thigh was already bandaged.

It was getting dark and the funny thing was it only seemed like we stopped for ten minutes to get bandaged up. It was a good thing we were in an ambulance because we had plenty of ground to cover. I had tiny nicks and scratches all over my face and shoulders.

"I want to go home," I said, my voice shaky and nearly an octave above normal. "I just want to go home."

Gil comforted me for a few minutes and placed his hand on my shoulder. I appreciated the comfort and his warm embrace. His smile was warm too. "That chopper is still waiting for us."

"Can we be on it?"

"Can you walk?"

I brushed the tears from my eyes and let out a nervous chuckle. "Are you kidding, I can run if it means I can just go home."

"Let's do this then." He hopped up front, only he didn't seem excited to be going home. Probably because he had nothing to go home to. No unit. No Blackman. No Jack. Somehow I was the lucky one. At least I had a wonderful family and Bella and Greg.

"I'm sorry," I said as I climbed in beside him. "I really wanted to help you. I guess I wasn't much of a help after all."

"Are you kidding," he said with a smile. "You're all I've got, Charlie. And if it weren't for your early morning pep talk and insane idea to get up and go for a run, I would be dead right now."

"Yeah," I scoffed, "But if I hadn't insisted on coming to get Blackman, everyone would still be alive."

"No," Gil said. "You can't take blame for any of this. This shit goes way deeper than even I imagined."

I didn't say anything to that, but I did wonder about it. I wondered about it all.

~~~

The drive took another twenty minutes. When we got to the airstrip, it was deserted. Gil pulled the ambulance behind a tanker and waited. He watched.

I watched him watch. "What is it?" I said with wide eyes.

"Something's not right."

"Boy, you say that a lot," I growled. "Please include me in your theories. I'm a big girl."

"Okay." He blew out his breath. "I think we're about to be ambushed."

I gulped loudly and looked around with even wider eyes.

"That, or our chopper is about to blow up."

I looked at the chopper and cringed. "Can't we just drive home?"

He took out his gun. I did the same.

"Stay right behind me."

"Yes, sir," I said with a little salute.

Then we got out into the cool air and took a minute to get familiar with our new surroundings. There were no people milling around. I could see the chopper clearly, but no pilot. The air smelled of humidity and dust. The wind had picked up and the only sounds I could hear were that of nature. It was eerie, like in scary movies when the big bad bloody guy is about to jump out with a chainsaw.

I shivered and placed my hand on Gil's shoulder.

I guess he was as anxious as I was because he jumped and turned. "Shhhhhh."

"I didn't say anything," I whispered.

"Yeah, but you're breathing too loud. I can't think."

Sheesh!

I heard the roar of a semi truck behind me, so I turned to see where it was coming from. An entire fleet of trucks was headed our way, so we ducked down behind the tanker and waited for the cloud of dust to clear.

What looked like an entire Army of Latin types emerged from the second truck. The first semi was still parked in our view, but no one was getting out. Then a tall dark- skinned man unlatched the back of the truck and my stomach not only rolled, it quivered and jumped to a higher position in my body.

They rolled Blackman down the ramp first. Another band of Latinos followed him down. All holding more gun power than I could imagine.

Gil and I looked down at our pathetic weapons and then glanced at each other with the same, 'oh shit' expression.

We turned and watched again. They were all speaking Spanish which I appreciated because that was actually a language that I understood. Yet, they were yelling and speaking so darn fast that I only caught a couple of words that made no sense.

I shrugged my shoulders at Gil and sent him a smile of ignorance. I was at a loss.

"No comprende?" He mouthed.

I shook my head, and then we got back to watching the show. A stretch limo showed up next, followed by another truck of Latinos.

Before the limo had time to come to a complete stop, all hell broke loose. Two big ass combat choppers whooped into view and began laying down a layer of suppressive fire. Men were shouting and running and all I could do was sit and stare. The limo backtracked behind a small modular building, kicking up dust and gravel in its wake.

Then we realized we were sitting under a tanker filled with fuel and we ran. Back toward the ambulance and then down between two other trucks toward a smaller hanger.

Explosives went off. Our chopper did get blown up. It jumped in the air, howled and hissed, then landed upside down. The blast sent shrapnel in every direction. In fear of our lives, we backtracked away from any large objects that might have been the next target. That pretty much made us sitting ducks.

"Get to the fence." Gil shouted among the chaos. It was like a war zone. Fortunately, I had been in a war zone before, so the noise and mayhem didn't seem to bother me like it bothered Gil. He even closed his eyes and wrapped his arms around his head a couple of times.

We reached the fence and then turned and watched from our new position. "What now?"

"You got me," Gil said, clearly shaken. "I can't figure out who's who?"

"This is only a guess," I said, watching the men usher Blackman to a safer area. "Cartel."

"Yeah, I figured that, but who's Blackman with?"

I stared harder through the dust and weapon blasts. The limo that had emerged just before the choppers, pulled to the other side of the hanger and then I saw the long legs of Liza; except she was supposed to be dead. The world seemed to tip to the side. I was bamboozled. "LOOK!" I shouted and pointed. Gil watched where I had pointed and then slapped it down and grabbed me, covering my mouth with his hand.

"Shit, Charlie!"

"What does this mean?" I gasped in both horror and surprise.

"There's only one way to find out." And he was up, running back toward the ambulance;

trying to get a closer view of something we were both curious about. Liza.

I followed Gil, cussing up a storm at him for running out in the open like a damn fool. I only had one gun. A very little gun at that, and I still didn't know who I would shoot at if given the chance. Blackman appeared to be with the Latinos. Liza appeared to be with the Latinos, but someone up above was trying even harder to blow the Latinos away. Boy, my mind was exhausted from pondering the various scenarios.

I tripped over my own feet a couple of times, but made it safely to Gil's side, back in our precarious position under the fuel tanker.

"Shit!" I shouted. "I thought we decided this was a bad hiding spot."

"We have to get closer. I don't want to take any chances."

"And your theory is..." I asked.

"I do have a theory, but it's not a nice one, and to be honest, I'm not sure who to kill first."

"So, you think one of them is bad...or both."

"One," Gil said. Then he blankly looked at me and ran off without another word.

"Fine!" I shouted, and then slammed my hand against the tanker. I looked up and that damn helicopter had it's light on and it was getting too close to me. I didn't want to get mistaken for a Latino, so I ran to the next row of trucks and hunkered down near the back end; far from the fuel tank. Men were still shouting and running around, shooting toward the sky.

I made one more decisive move and got into earshot just as Liza pulled a gun from her side and pointed it at the man in the wheelchair.

# Chapter Thirteen

The sounds of gunfire and my grumbling stomach made it hard for me to decipher the words that were said. Blackman was still quite calm for someone who had a gun rammed into his back. I had no idea what Liza was saying to him, but I was sure it wasn't pleasant. I had felt the growing frustrations of the team since I had come to stay with them. And then there was the sinister hotel blast to consider. Who knew that it would end up like this? Does this mean that Kaia and Serena were alive too?

A gunshot ricocheted off the semi truck behind me. I jumped, said the 'f' word a number of times and then hunched down even further. These guys were dead serious.

"Charlie," Gil yelled and tossed me another gun; a semi-automatic. "Try not to get killed." He chuckled and then left me alone with my two guns and three men closing in fast.

I hunkered down below the truck and made my way under the jacked up undercarriage. I envisioned what it would feel like to drive such a beast and then wondered if I still remembered

how to hot-wire a car. I learned that trick in the
Army. In Bosnia to be exact. Cory Welch taught
me when our unit had gotten shanghaied in the
urban jungle. We had survived that horrific day in
the middle of Hell, so I was quite sure that I
would survive this day in an airstrip parking lot in
the middle of Mexico City. Hell, from where I
was crouched, I could see Taco Bell. I felt like I
was in Greenwich except that I had a gun in my
hand and I was aiming to shoot a Columbian
cartel member in the head.

I took the shot and he lifelessly dropped to
the ground. That gave me just enough time to
crawl under the large tanker and creep around to
the other side. Another bullet whizzed past me
and I ducked. Then I got down on my knees and
began praying.

I was cornered. I lifted my hands in the air
and dropped my gun. It clamored around by my
knees and the man in front of me said something
mean and nasty in Spanish. I thought I was a
goner. Destined to die in the gravel in Mexico
City with a bullet in my brain. Thankfully my
enemy felt the need to continue to insult me
before pulling the trigger and ending my life.

Just a short distance from his left
shoulder, I saw a tall figure. He looked very
familiar. Like if he had a ponytail, he might be
DEA guy. He had his gun drawn. At first it was
aimed toward me and then he quickly whipped it
around. He took the shot and the man in front of
me dropped to the dirt.

"Stay out of sight!" He yelled. He then
tossed me another gun, winked and was gone. He
was like an angel. There to save me one minute
and before I had time to blink, he was gone again.
I grabbed my guns, crept back under the tanker
and got even closer to Liza and Blackman. I still
couldn't hear their words, but I clearly saw her
shake her head in anger and then step backward a
few paces before pulling the trigger and shooting
him directly in the chest at close range.

I gasped, completely horrified. I stood up
and screamed. It was like I wasn't really there.
Like it wasn't happening. It was a bad, bad
dream.

Liza glanced over at me and then leveled
her gun on me. "I'm sorry you had to see that."
She yelled out into the noise. The wind was still
howling. Her hair flapping around like it did that
day on the beach. She looked amazing. Scary, but
amazing.

I lifted my arms in the air and dropped my
guns. They bounced around on the hot asphalt.
Her gaze seemed to miss me, like she was staring
at someone else in the distance.

I stilled. The tiny hairs on the back of my
neck did a little dance then stood at attention,
sending a frightening shiver down my spinal
cord. And then I turned slowly. Jack was just
twenty feet away, gun drawn. Looking like he
needed a shave and a haircut. I was relieved for a
moment until it dawned on me that Liza was
pointing her gun at Jack and not me anymore.

"No," I shouted and jumped between them. "It's Jack. He's on our side."

"No," she growled. "Jack isn't on anyone's side. Jack thinks about Jack and Jack alone."

I noted the grim look in her eyes and turned to see Jack, getting into a more serious stance.

"Charlie," he yelled.

I turned all the way around, with my back toward super babe, carefully keeping my body between the two of them. "Jack!" My voice cracked.

"What did I tell you at the villa?" His tone was even-keeled. Unfretted. Incredibly steely. "Huh?" I yelled over the whooping of the chopper blades. Another helicopter had landed nearby. That meant we either had back up or more Columbians to shoot. My brain pounded against my skull.

He just stared at me as the seconds ticked by. The air was thick. Humid. I could barely breathe because of the moisture and he was trying to get me to remember shit that happened last week. I was flustered. Nervous. Nauseous. My mind racing about what had just transpired.

The look in his eyes was something I was sure I would never ever forget. His muscular, bushy jaw clenched. I could clearly see the tension in his entire body. He didn't flinch or hesitate as he spoke. "Trust no one."

I barely comprehended what happened next. I saw a flash of light, like a camera flash going off. A split second later, I felt a horrendous pain. Like someone ripped open my flesh with a white-hot barb, then rammed a fireplace poker into my shoulder. I didn't even feel it when my body hit the asphalt. All I felt was the life running from my body. I was cold. In shock maybe. And definitely pissed off that Jack had shot me.

~~~

I woke in a hospital. My eyes darted around the room looking for any sign that I was back in my homeland. Everything I saw was written in English. I was thankful for that because I had heard about Mexican hospitals. Trust me, you don't want to get shot in Mexico.

"Morning, sleepyhead," my brother, Dave, said from beside me. He wasn't in his usual white coat and Dockers, but a pair of sweats and a faded University of Oregon t-shirt. His five o'clock shadow was painted on. On the other side of him were my mom and dad. I choked back the tears.

"What?" I tried to speak, but ended up busting into sobs. I didn't think I would ever see any of them again. I had wild dreams of a chocolate covered heaven, with apple martini rivers and Eskimo bars being handed out at the pearly gates. "What're you doing here? Where am I?"

I struggled to sit up but failed miserably. Dave kissed my forehead and handed me

a Dixie cup full of ice chips. "San Diego," he
said. "How are you feeling? Numb anywhere?"
He grabbed my hand. "Squeeze hard."
Dave. Always playing doctor.

"What happened?"

"You were shot, honey," my mom said.
Duh.

Oh, God! Did my parents know that my
boyfriend shot me? Actually, they thought we had
broken up, so this probably wasn't all that
unexpected. Jilted lovers, dueling it out in a
Mexico City parking lot; perhaps fighting over
CDs and houseplants.

"But how…" I started to ask, but then the
door creaked open and I paused. Jack walked into
the room with a bouquet of long-stem red roses. I
didn't know if I wanted to cry or scream for the
police.

"Hey, you," he swiftly walked toward me
and then planted a kiss on my forehead. His face
was clean-shaven, except for his usual goatee. His
black hair back in its usual extra-short style. "I
called your parents. I figured you would want
them here," he said against my lips before kissing
them lightly.

This action induced bile to rise in my
throat. Not only did I not know what was going
on, I was being kissed in front of my dad! My
face flushed and I know my heart rate went
berserk. I could hear the monitor beeping like
crazy.

Dave stepped away to look at the EKG
print out. He whistled loudly.

"I was just about to tell your parents how
it happened." Jack said quickly, sensing my angst
and terror.

Oh goody. I couldn't wait to hear him spin
his web of deceit.

"Oh," I said suspiciously. "Go ahead
then."
I kept a meager smile on my face as to not alarm
my family members. After all, they thought Jack
was in insurance. Dave knew of my Army
training and my summer spent abroad last year,
but he, just like my parents, didn't know about
Jack's involvement with a top-secret government
agency.

"Well, as I was saying," he started as he
pulled up a stool and took my hand. I glared hard,
but didn't wiggle from his grasp.

"I had to go to Mexico City our yearly
'adjustor of the year' conference. Charlie came
with me and we were having dinner at a local
hotspot before the awards ceremony back at the
hotel. I had heard they had the best authentic
Mexican food around..." he chuckled lightly.
"Believe it or not, it's difficult to get good
Mexican food in Mexico."

My father chuckled too and my mom put
on her best fake smile, probably still worried to
death that I had been shot! She didn't look too
thrilled and by the way she kept glaring at Jack, I
was sure she was suspicious of something. She's
very keen.

"Anyway, we were just getting out of the
car and I heard a hollow bang. I thought a car had

backfired. Next thing I know, Charlie's on the ground." He held my hand tighter and looked at me with those big brown eyes. "Totally random. The Mexico City Police says it happens quite often. It's really hurting tourism, but they just don't have the man power to fight the gang wars." He winked at me.

I looked at him and glared. My jaw clenched tight.

"We'd better get some dinner," my dad said. The tension in the air was even bothering me. "Dave," he prodded my brother in the back. "We'll be back soon."

My mom planted a kiss on my forehead and gave me a smile. "I love you, sweetie. I'm glad you're okay." Then she tussled my hair. "And to think, you survived eight years in the Army, just to get shot on vacation in Mexico."

Dave chuckled loudly, and then snapped his mouth shut. I'm sure he was on pins and needles waiting to hear the real reason why I was lying in the hospital.

The room cleared out except for Jack who got up and pulled the curtains. "Don't be scared, Charlie."

"I'm not scared."

Big fat, stubborn lie.

"I had to do it. If I wouldn't have shot you, Liza would have, only she would have aimed higher."

I digested that tidbit of information and although it made sense to me it still hurt. Both physically and emotionally. As soon as I had seen

Liza shoot Blackman with that look of cold
cruelty, I was suspicious of her agenda. I just
hadn't been fast enough of the uptake. That's
probably why I was lying in a hospital bed
instead of receiving some sort of Congressional
medal.

"So, she's dead?"

He nodded. "I'm sorry you got caught up
in all this."

"And Randy?" I held out my hand. "Is he
really…?" He took it, gave it a gentle squeeze
and winked with a solemn expression.

"I'm okay," he said sadly. "I'll rebuild."

"And Blackman." I shook my head. "I feel
like this is all my fault."

He bent and kissed me softly. "This was
not your fault. It was mine. I should have been
more careful. I should have hid you better. I
shouldn't have trusted anyone."

"You have to trust someone sometime,
don't you?" I inquired. I needed to know that he
trusted me.

"There will never be a doubt in my mind
about you, Charlie Ford. You're special." He
kissed me again, and then backed off when we
heard the door creak open. Much to my surprise,
Jack's parents entered the room with an
impressive bouquet of flowers that was even
bigger than the one Jack brought.

I looked at Jack and I think a tear trickled
out.

He winked. "They were worried about
you."

His mother was the first one to come around the bed and hold my hand. She's a petite woman, probably sixty-two years old. With silver short hair and big brown eyes like Jack's. "Jack told me we almost lost you."

I gulped down the lump in my throat. "Thank you for the flowers."

Jack's father gave me a warm smile. He was a larger, taller version of Jack with blue eyes like Joey. He was very handsome and in great physical shape. Jack had never told me what his father does for a living, but it made sense to me that he too was in some sort of government work.

We chatted for a couple of minutes and then, thankfully, my parents came back just as Jack's dad began questioning our plans for the future. I think his father's exact words were, 'when are you going to get your asses in gear and give us some grandbabies'.

"Mom, Dad," I said. "This is Edward and Megan Sullivan. Jack's parents."

Edward was not giving up easy and shook my father's hand whilst saying, "I was just bugging these two to hurry up with the grandbabies. We're not getting any younger." Then he jabbed my poor dad in the ribs. "Am I right, or am I right?"

My father, God bless his heart, chuckled while sending me a sympathetic smile.

Jack laughed and took a seat beside me. I loved his scent. He never wore cologne. He just smelled like a man. My man.

My mom and Jack's mom got busy talking about decorating and retirement and next thing I knew, they were planning coordinating vacations, even trying to get Jack and I to agree to come along on an Alaskan cruise in the fall.

"I'm not sure where I will be next fall, Dad." Jack replied after the tension got thick and our parents were staring us down, probably trying to envision what the fore-mentioned grandbabies would look like. Jack's father nodded in a fashion that told me he completely understood what that meant.

I could barely comprehend anything in the room. My head was killing me and I kept finding myself glaring at Jack for shooting me and putting me in that hospital room where our parents had suddenly decided to plan our next vacation...and our course for the future. I'm surprised the moms didn't suggest wedding venues in the area. I thought it was wonderful that they were getting along so well, but it was scary. They liked each other. Any normal person would be happy about that, right?

A nurse came in, took my blood pressure and then told everyone to let me rest.

"Thank you," I whispered to the elderly woman in white who was taking my temperature. "It was getting hot in here." I closed my eyes.

Everyone left me alone after more hugs, kisses and well wishes for my fast recovery. "We'll be out here. Yell if you need me," Dave said with a wave and a serious look of desperation. I knew I would have to tell him the truth, and soon.

My mom was the last one to leave the room. She stopped smiling when the door closed. "Is there something you aren't telling me about Jack?" Her shoes made a clattering sound as she hurriedly stepped toward my bed.

I felt my stomach flop around a bit and I know my cheeks burned. "No," I said with a slightly higher voice than normal. "Why do you ask?"

"Mother's intuition maybe," she replied seriously. "You looked frightened when he came in earlier. I just want to make sure that you're okay. You're okay, right? You wouldn't lie to your mom, now would you?"

What could I say to that? I hated lying to my parents, but some things just can't be explained. Like why Jack shot me. She'd never understand.
I didn't have a chance to reply because Jack came back in the room, against the nurse's order.

My mom left after giving Jack a kiss on the cheek, followed by a curt look. "You better take good care of my baby."

She left and I was too exhausted to put up a fight when Jack nudged me. I had so many more questions, but he pressed his finger to my lips, crawled in beside me and lulled me to sleep with his deep breathing.

It was probably two or three hours later when I heard a rustling and then a loud thud, followed by several booming obscenities. Startled, I opened my eyes and saw Joey at the foot of the bed, grappling with a bedpan while trying not to drop the flowers he was holding. They were daisies. My favorite.

Jack grunted and rolled over. "Joe?"

"Hi," I said, somewhat surprised that Joey would actually come visit me after I ditched him; drunk and depressed in Bulgaria. "What are you doing here?"

"Trying to wake up the whole damn hospital?" Jack's gaze narrowed on his brother. "Dad know you're here?"

Joe shook his head and moved around the bed. "Can I talk to Charlie, alone?"

"Hell, no!" Jack chuckled. "Last time I left you alone with her…"

I caught Jack in the ribs with my elbow, warning him to lay off with my glare.

He grudgingly got up and stepped from the room. It wasn't until the door shut that Joey smiled and handed me the flowers.

"My favorite!" I grinned. "Joey, I'm really so…"

He cut me off with a shushing sound and a warm smile. "Don't worry about it. You did what you had to do. I'm sure Jack will forgive me, someday."

"So," I said, clearing my throat. "Who are you, really?"

"I'm a marine."

"And you just happened to know all about the inner workings of the DEA?" I had so many questions and I knew it would take me a lifetime to get answers from Jack. Joey seemed more at ease and relaxed. Besides, we had a special bond.

"I'm on a special task force that works along side the DEA somewhere south of the border and that's all you ever need to know."

He leaned closer. So close that I smelled cinnamon gum. I know I flushed, remembering the last time his lips were that close to mine. The seconds ticked by slowly and then he leaned closer and caught my lips, brushing them with a soft lingering kiss.

Jack, with his super-spy sense, bolted into the room. "That's enough!"

I blinked a couple of times and Jack was by my side, glaring at Joey in a matter of seconds.

I'd never witnessed such bullshit in my life.

They were toe to toe, glaring. Nearly snarling at each other like wild dogs. I didn't know why I liked it so much. I'm so ashamed!

Joey backed off with a smirk and sunk down on the tiny sofa.

That caused Jack to relax and climb back onto the bed.

"So," Joey began. "Who was it?"

"Liza," Jack said.

"Told you." Joey laughed and looked over at me. "His downfall is beautiful women. I tried to warn him."

"Bullshit," Jack quipped. "You said she wanted in my pants, not that she wanted me dead."

"Same thing." Joey laughed. "I said you shouldn't trust her motives. You should have listened to me."

"And what makes you the expert on women?" Jack replied with spite.

Joey didn't say anything; he just winked at me and sent Jack an all-knowing smile. I felt the air chill around me and could feel Jack tense beside me. They had some serious sibling rivalry going on and my guess was, I had become a sick little part of it.

Joey got up and stretched. "I'd love to stay and chat, but I have a flight to catch." He moved around the bed and gave my nose a little tweak. "If you ever get sick of Jack disappearing for months at a time or if he shoots you again, give me a call."

That earned him a hard smack to the shoulder.

He grabbed at his charley horse and laughed. "See ya, Jack."

"Take it easy," Jack muttered and then got up and followed Joey to the door. "Thanks again for everything. I really mean it."

Joey pulled him into an embrace. "Anytime."

Ten minutes later, Dave walked in with coffee. It smelled divine. His beeper was in his hand. "I have to go."

"Thanks for coming." I said, wondering why he was looking at Jack the way he was. "Jack, can you give us a minute?"

Dave looked relieved to see Jack leave the room. He took a stool beside me and narrowed his eyes. "Jack's not an insurance adjuster is he?"

"No," I said. Why would I lie now? Dave was smart and he'd just keep pushing and pushing anyway. Plus, I liked that we had become closer. It was nice to have my brother to talk to. I was still trying to make amends with my other brother, Josh, but since he's an egomaniac and an NFL superstar, I rarely get the chance to sit down and chat with him. Dave, on the other hand, had become my ally. The one person in my family that I could really talk to. Tell my secrets to. It mattered not that we never really got along in the past. What mattered now was that I had become the Godmother of his new baby and a friend to his wife. I even stopped using the annoying nickname that he hated; Doctor Dave.

I spilled the beans about everything that happened in the past month. He knew about last summer, so I just let him know that Jack was that secret agent man and that I had been caught up in the mole hunt of the century.

He was baffled once again. His cheeks flushed like I'd never seen before. "So, he shot you?"

I was just about to explain why when Jack came back in the room.

The metal stool clanked to the floor when Dave stood up abruptly. He was just about the same height as Jack, but Jack out-muscled him. That didn't stop him though. Dave hauled back and punched Jack right in the jaw. And Dave never fights. He's a surgeon for Christ sake!

Jack stumbled back, grappling for the bed to steady himself. "Shit!"

He got himself upright and I gasped in horror. "Dave!" I shouted. "He did it to save my life."

"Oh!" Dave said with a sheepish tone. Then he pulled Jack into a hug and held him tight for a few long seconds. "Thanks for saving my sis." He backed off and ran a hand through his thick hair. "You understand, right?"

"Completely," Jack replied, still trying to straighten his jaw. "Nice jab."

I laughed because what else could I do. I was out of tears and I had never seen Dave so mad in my life. Cool. It is good to have a big brother after all.

~~~

Three days later, I was well enough to take a private flight from San Diego to Bethesda Naval Hospital. Jack, unfortunately, was not with me. He had important things to do. If I had a nickel for every time he left me with that lame excuse that it was a case of national security, I'd be a very rich woman.

It was nice that I was chaperoned by a couple of naval officers and a very nice nurse.

My new home was in the rehabilitation wing on the eighth floor. I got settled in. Jack had sent me some pajamas and sweatpants and a note saying he'd see me soon. I changed into my favorite pair of blue sweats and a white tank top and then hobbled to the window, wondering how long they were going to make me stay. I sighed and stared out at the parking lot below.

I felt a cool breeze and turned around to see the door open. A few seconds later, I was stunned to see Blackman being rolled in. I sucked in a breath and clutched my chest. My heart was thumping rapidly against my ribs.

"Hello, Charlie," he said quietly.

"Uhhh," I muttered. I had to sit down on the bed. I wish Jack had warned me. Said something. Or maybe Jack didn't know?

"I didn't mean to startle you." He waved the orderly out of the room, swiveled around and closed the door, then rolled over to my bedside.

"Does Jack know?" I asked, keeping my voice from quivering.

He nodded. "Sure, he knows. It was his idea."

"So you knew about Liza? How?"

"We figured out it was her because she was the only person who knew things. Knew things about you. You and Jack."

"How?" I was surprised by that. Jack told me that no one knew. I was positive that even Randy hadn't known about us, and they were friends. It did make sense though, because she's the only one who ever referred to him as Jack.

"Liza and Jack were the first ones I recruited. Almost twelve years ago, I guess it was. They were on the original Blacklist."

"Your unit?"

"Yep. It was Jack and Liza. We were like family."

I wondered how close Jack and Liza actually were. From what Jack and Joey had talked about, I was certain I was about to hear some horrific details that I didn't want to know about.

He began again, after staring off into space. He seemed saddened by her betrayal. "They were like my own kids. Brother and sister."

Okay, so I was wrong. "So what happened?"

"I lost my legs in a mission gone bad and had to give up the team ten years ago. I told Jack to dismantle it, but he wanted to keep Liza. They worked well together, but I warned him that it's just not done. You don't move on with the same family when shit goes down. You rebuild. You start over. Everyone knows this."

"And Jack didn't listen," I said. No surprise there. He was as stubborn as they came.

"Nope. He insisted on keeping her on his team. Time and time again. I think she started to resent him because she'd given her life to him and he didn't feel the same...if you know what I mean." He cocked a brow.

I swallowed hard, catching his meaning and squashing my urge to purge. "She was in love with him?"

"That seems to be the general consensus, although we will never know her motives for sure. I'm sure it was that and the fact that she never got her own unit. She began to resent him. Jack kept her under his wing and denied her last request to branch off. From what the girls told me, she began hating Jack. Hating that he had a girlfriend. Hating that she was never the one calling the shots. It was eating away at her, so when the opportunity came up to get ahead, she took it."

"So, it wasn't about money? I'm sure the cartel was paying her, right?"

"I'm sure her compensation was in the millions, but I think her motivation was personal. Jack told me that he confided in her when he got back from Armenia last year. She was the only one who knew him as Jack Sullivan and she was the only one who knew about you."

"Wow." What else could I say to that? I had some psycho woman so jealous of me that she used me to flush out the man she apparently loved so she could either kill me in front of his face, or kill us both. A tight knot formed in my stomach. "So the cartel was paying her to kill the man that was hired to take them down…only she was using their money and their connections for her own sick agenda." I just shook my head with a deep scowl. "That's twisted. She was sick in the head."

"It happens," he replied sadly. "This business can do that to you. Especially to the women. It's hard to keep emotions out of the job and even more so for a woman. It just starts to eat at you after awhile."

Blackman got real serious and told me what I already feared. "We're going to need a statement from you, Charlie."

"And..." I said, clearly scared out of my mind. "What should I say? I don't know anything. I don't even know who Jack is. I don't know who you are. I'm just a nanny!" I crunched my jaw together to hold back the tears. I was happy Blackman was not dead, but right then I was not particularly happy to see him.

"That's right, Charlie! You're just a nanny." He did something weird with his eyes. They opened and then narrowed slightly when he said the word nanny. "Just answer as honestly as you can and you won't be in any trouble. It's just a formality," he said and I felt a ripple of nausea in my gut. "Just answer the questions."

The way he said it made my toes curl. I had a feeling that he was trying to tell me something, but I wasn't sure. Then I remembered what Russo had told me. No one needs to know the whole story. So, what Blackman probably meant was that I should only answer what they ask and no more! I clasped my sweaty palms together and nodded to him with a weak smile.

~~~

I was taken to Fort Meade via a serious looking SUV with tinted windows and US flags waving from the top. Blackman sat across from me along with two other suits, one of which was the same one that followed me to Greece and more recently had been instrumental in injecting me with truth serum. Needless to say, I pretty much glared at him the entire way to NSA headquarters.

When we arrived, Blackman got situated in his electric wheelchair and I followed him into the building with two giant thugs on my ass.

The corridor was long. Everything was automated. Once we reached the conference room, we were greeted by two other male agents in dark suits and a nice elderly woman with a big gray bun atop her head. She wore a gray suit and some ugly black utilitarian looking shoes. A transcription machine was set on the table in front of her.

"This is Special Agent Chris Harbinger and Special Agent Mike Jeffries," Blackman made the introductions and I smiled as best I could. I was having a fairly serious moment of alarm, but I trusted Blackman. I also realized that even though Jack was not with the NSA, I had a feeling that Blackman was. Jack's unit was somewhat like a general contractor, working for those who needed them, but not on any specific payroll. Or that was my theory.

"Have a seat, Charlie," he said and then once I was seated, he left me alone in that room with the strangers.

"Miss Ford. How are you feeling?" Mike passed me a glass of water and then poured one for himself.

"Good." I said. "My shoulder still hurts, but the pain gets better every day." My arm was still snuggled in a white sling because my collarbone had been shattered by the bullet. I was still waiting to undergo one or two more surgeries to fix it properly.

"We're just going to ask you a few questions."

"Shoot," I said and then chuckled. "Just kidding. I've already been shot!"

The mood was somber. I didn't even get anyone to crack a smile. "Sorry," I sat back and lifted the glass of water to my lips. I stilled and looked down at the swirling liquid. I really needed a sip. "You wouldn't dare drug me again, would you?"

"No," he said without a hint of emotion.

Not taking any chances, I set down the glass and sat back with my arms folded at the chest. "What do you want to know?"

Harbinger cleared his throat. "First off, let's talk about Eddie Malone."

"Eddie Malone?"

"Yes." Harbinger snapped. "The man standing next to you in this photo."

He slid an 8x10 over to me. It was Jack and I on the beach in the Bahamas. I was talking to him while he sat in his director's chair and stared out at the photo shoot.

"What do you want to know?"

"Who else knew you were sleeping with Eddie Malone?"

My cheeks flushed. Since when had my sex life become a topic of national security? I didn't see the relevance of the question, so I remained quiet.

"Someone knew, Charlie. Someone knew every detail of your life with him They knew where you lived. They knew about last summer. They knew about 'The Rat'. Someone knew and we need to know who that person was."

I remained silent, not knowing what I should say.

"Tell us about your conversations with Grady Sanchez. Is there anything you can tell us that might be of help?"

"Grady and I had breakfast one morning and shared a walk on the beach. We talked about his ranch in Miami and I made up some stupid story about my life, so it was pretty much small talk."

"Is it possible that Eddie could have mentioned something about your relationship to Randy Sutter?"

Back to that. I shrugged. "I dunno. I doubt it." Then I finally sipped some water. Feeling my throat close up in memory of those dead agents. I knew I wasn't going to get any answers from these men and they knew they weren't going to make me slip up either. Liza was dead. Case closed, right? "Look. As far as I know, Eddie had told no one about us. Besides, I'm just a nanny. What would I know about all this?"

They asked me several more questions about the Bahamas and how I ended up in that parking lot in Mexico City. I answered the best I could and was honest about Liza and the team abducting me and taking me to a secret farmhouse where they were plotting their revenge against whoever had sold them all out. I didn't divulge anything other than what they asked and I think that made them proud.

Harbinger was the first to shake my hand, followed by the cute one, Mike Jeffries. "It was nice meeting you, Charlie. Take care and let's hope we never have to see each other again."

I nodded and smiled. "That would be very nice!"

They left and Blackman came back in looking rather grim. "Sit down, Charlie."

I sat.

I stared at him, awaiting his next word, with bated breath and sweaty palms.

"I know that things have been very difficult for you lately and I want to tell you how proud I am to have met you. I know that Eddie would have liked to see you as part of the unit, but I think we both know after what transpired that you just aren't what we need. There are just too many risks and too much history. Do you know what I'm trying to say?"

I nodded and felt saddened. I had been waiting to make a decision about what I wanted to do and working with Jack seemed like the best option for me. Just because I took a bullet and had been caught up in something sinister, didn't deter me from wanting to join the unit. If anything, it made me realize that I'd be good at it. I'm good at what I do and I'm not talking about being a nanny. I'm a hell of a soldier and I have what it takes. But now? It was hard to digest that one of my options was being pulled out from under me like a used carpet.

"I'd like to extend my deepest, heartfelt gratitude for your help in this matter and I wish you well with the FBI or whatever else you decide to do. You'll be a success, Charlie." He extended his hand and I took it. Then he looked directly into my eyes and squeezed my hand a little harder. "I have some more grim news."

My heart jumped around. What else could he possibly say that could make me feel any worse?

"Eddie Malone was killed this morning."

That would do it. I felt the blood rush from my face and go straight to my toes. Fainting came to mind, as did screaming out in horror, but I remained calm. Docile. Now was not the time for me to lose it and start shrieking like a girl.

I cried. Hard. Then he patted my hand and continued.

"He was killed in a car accident, burned beyond recognition. He'll be buried at sea in a private ceremony this week."

I was still weeping into the hand that he wasn't holding onto. He cleared his throat. "Charlie, did you hear me? Eddie is gone."

I lifted my chin and sucked back my last tear. It was the way he said Eddie that made me narrow my eyes.

He casually winked.

I casually wiped my nose with my sleeve.

He handed me a plane ticket. First class all the way back to LaGuardia International airport. "Have a safe trip home."

I smiled and thanked him again.

The next thing I knew, I was being taken back to the hospital where I remained for another week. I underwent two minor surgeries and when I couldn't stand it another day, I begged to be let go. The government was doing a wonderful job doting on me, and putting me all back together but I was bored to tears and missing the hell out of Bella and Greg. All I could think about was going home and getting on with my life.

A Lincoln town car picked me up outside the hospital and took me to the airport. Dulles was a chaotic mess. I had only one carry on with me, so security was easy and I had three hours to catch up on my reading and world events, so I found a cozy, overly crowded coffee shop and sat down to read the paper.

I got through the New York Times and had just grabbed a People magazine when a familiar scent wafted around me. My toes curled and I inhaled to breathe him in.

"I heard you died...again." I said, flipping open the People magazine and reading the inside cover to see what page Nicole's engagement announcement was on.

He slipped his finger under the magazine and tried to pull it from my grasp. "I want to show you something."

"I bet." I said irritably. "Bella's probably catatonic by now." I held up the photo of her mother and that skanky rocker she was about to marry.

Jack shook his head. "I'm sure she's going to be fine. You'll see her in a couple of days."

"Days?" I said with a snarl, noting that sexually explicit look in his gaze. "The doctor said no physical strain for at least a couple of weeks."

"I'll be gentle." His smile was lazy. Sexy. And making me painfully aware of the feelings I had for him.

"No!" I said adamantly. "I want to go home to Bella."

"No!" he said just as stringently. "Two days. Please?"

His smile was so endearing and I was exhausted and nauseous from my pain medication. I stared into his eyes and struggled with my inner-demons. A very small part of me wanted to tell him off in a way that would cement my independence from him forever. But the other bigger parts of me, like my heart, wanted to jump into his arms and never let go. That part eventually won. Why not? He had a lot to make up for. I was in a piss poor mood and didn't mean to take it out on him. On the other hand, he did shoot me!

I took the hand that he generously offered me and then he picked up my bag and carried it out to his awaiting SUV.

~~~

I was fairly sure that my bad attitude and pre-disposition of growling at Jack came from a place deep in my heart that I wasn't quite ready to visit. And I'm not talking about my Jack-inflicted-gunshot-wound. I came to this realization when we finally pulled into the long driveway that leads to the house that Jack actually lived in. Twenty-two miles from downtown Bethesda, down a winding tree-lined lane. The wind blowing in my hair and Jack's hand entwined in mine. It was almost too good to be true and I guess that's why it was so scary for me. We'd been through a horrible ordeal, in which, I thought he was dead…not once, but twice. Not good for my fragile heart and what's even scarier is that when it was made clear to me that Jack loves me and thinks of me as 'his life' I felt a tugging sensation in my womb.

"This is home," he said pulling up to the impressive country house. The front porch even had a rocking swing. Tall willows were swaying above the roof. The sunset was something out of a classic western movie. "Charlie?"

I was in tears.

"Baby," he said, gripping my hand tighter. "What is it?"

God, my heart ached like it never had before. Even more so than the wound in my upper chest. My arm was still wrapped tightly in its sling. I looked at him and didn't know what to say. This all seemed so real and I knew if he said anything else, I'd be a goner. I'd become a blubbering woman with nothing more than marriage and children on her mind. I was too young to be having the thoughts I was having. Coming that close to death made me think hard and I realized that I hadn't lived yet. I wanted to experience things and make decisions based on my dreams. Besides, loving Jack meant that he might have to shoot me again sometime.

It was much easier on my heart when I thought I was this super spy's sex toy.

He brought my hand up to his lips and kissed it softly.

I retracted, both emotionally and physically.

"Damn it," he groaned and slid out from behind the steering wheel. "I said I was sorry." He was the first one out of the SUV and inside the front door.

I followed slowly, but took my time so that I could rein in my uncontrolled emotions and get a friggin grip!

The house was light. Bright. With plenty of windows and oak woodwork. It was immaculate. The dust covers were still draped over much of the furniture, but it was still incredibly beautiful. Almost like my own dream home. The one I promised I would buy for my dog, Ruger. With acres and acres of jackrabbits to chase and a big shade tree in the back that I could lie under and daydream. It was perfect.

Who would have thought that would drive me into a fit of confusion?

"Jesus," Jack retorted at my obvious scowl. "How can I make it up to you? Oral sex? Money?" He grabbed me and pulled me close in a menacing fashion. He felt good. Too good. "How about this one." The kiss was soft at first, and then it became demanding and incredible. I felt his hands hot across my back. One moving down to cup my butt, the other moving into my hair. I moaned into his open mouth, I clutched his shoulders and then he slowed and the kiss became sweet and loving. I'd never had Jack kiss me like that before. It was endearing. Intimate. Unnerving.

He grinned at me and took my hand in his, placing it on his left pectoral. Covering his heart. "Charlie," he began.

"Jack," I said in extreme discomfort. My heart battling with my mind and slowly losing. "Umm." I looked around, wondering where I was going to run and hide.

"Charlie," he said again, "I know I don't always say the right things and Lord knows I'm not the most sensitive guy, but I have something…"

I ripped my hand from his clutch and stepped back. "Where's your bathroom?"

"Now?" He tried to grab me again. "Can it wait?"

"No!" I shouted, doing a good impression of a toddler doing the pee pee dance. "It was a long drive."

He pointed to the hallway that was past the kitchen.

I slammed the door behind me and grasped the sink with my one good hand. There is no going back once those three little words are out in the open and what if it was more than just those three little words. What if it was more like those three little words followed by two even-more important words. I glared at my own wide-eyed expression in the mirror.

I knew I couldn't stay shacked up in the bathroom all day and night for the next two days. Shit!

My hands began to sweat profusely. I flushed the toilet for effect and then opened the door. Jack was leaning sexily against the wall, staring at me with fire in his eyes.

"What's up, Chuck?"

"Nothing." I lied and stepped past him, quickening my steps into the kitchen. I got busy with grabbing sandwich ingredients out of his stainless steel fridge.

His heavy footsteps seemed to resonate through the entire house.

I inhaled sharply when I felt his hand wrap around my stomach and his lips graze my neck.

I jumped from his grasp.

"Still mad at me, huh?" he grabbed a piece of sharp cheddar and took a big bite, making his way past me to the fridge. He pulled out a beer and slammed it under the counter and pulled. The lid popped off and did a little dance on the hardwood floor. "You'll get over it soon enough."

"I'll get over what soon enough?" I asked, clearly confused.

"Blackman."

"What about him?" I glared hard. Something in my gut told me that Jack knew about my meeting with Blackman. And all this time I thought he was being extra nice to me to make up for the fact that he shot me. He actually pulled the trigger and shot me. And, yeah, it hurt!

He slammed down his entire beer and wiped his lips with the back of his hand before engaging me with his chocolate brown eyes. "I just don't think you'd be right for the position, that's all."

I felt my hair begin to stand on end. It all became so clear. "That was your doing?"

He shrugged shamelessly. "Don't get me wrong. I don't want you running off and joining the FBI, I just don't think you and I would work well together. You seem to have this little problem with following my orders." He actually seemed somewhat cavalier. "Trust no one."

"Damn you!" I shouted and threw a tomato at his big pig head. It missed and landed with a splat on the table behind him. "I wanted to make that decision for my damn self! How dare you go and change your mind after months and months of convincing me to come aboard. You'd be damn lucky to have me!"

I held back the tears. Suddenly, I was not good enough either. I suppose that's how Joey felt too. It stung deep and I ran for the bedroom.

He grabbed the door, but I was quicker and madder. I heard him grunt and groan and then rap lightly on the door. "Okay. That's not the entire truth."

"Go to hell!"

"Come on, Charlie, open the damn door." He yelled, slamming a hand against the frame. "I can't lose you again and I'm not strong enough to keep it professional. You're always going to be my number one priority and that can get us both killed. Don't you get that?"

"Get lost!"

"Haven't you learned anything from what we just went through? Someone is always going to be after the ones I lo…"

"Go AWAY!" I shouted again, louder and with more shrill to my voice. "You shot me!"

"Damn it, Charlie. I'm trying to tell you that I lo…"

I whipped that damn door open so fast; the gust of air took my breath away.

Jack was stunned and stepped back from the doorway. He looked wide-eyed at me with a pained look of surprise on his face.

"Don't!" I screamed. "Don't you dare say that to me." My heart clunked a number of times in my chest and I felt completely flushed, from head to toe.

"Don't tell you that I lo…"

I slammed the door again. "Get out!"

"It's my house!" He chuckled. "You get out!"

I was silent for a minute, while I contemplated jumping from his bedroom window. When I turned to judge how long it would take to escape, I noticed I was in the master bedroom. There was a real wood fireplace on the wall opposite the bed and a big cozy chair in the corner. A deep purple comforter was draped over the bed and something on the nightstand caught my eye. I walked to it, still somewhat perturbed by Jack's incessant pounding on the door. To the right of his bed, on the oak nightstand, sat the same picture that I kept of Jack at my place in Connecticut. The one of us at the Bills game last year, in our matching snowcaps - a big sappy smile on my face.

I hurried back to the door and yelled through it. "Don't do it, please, Jack."

"Why not?" I could hear the laughter in his tone. Most likely because he thinks I'm somewhat crazy and he loves to laugh at me.

That's when the tears began again. "Because," I said, leaning against the wood and drawing little hearts against the grains with my finger. "I won't be able to make a sane decision and I might resent you forever because now is the time in my life when I have choices. I want to do something more. I want to be a part of the team and I want to work for you, with you…maybe not up front, but behind the scenes. I'd be good on the secondary team. I know I would."

"And you can't do that if I tell you I lo…"

I opened the door before he could finish, shaking my head and begging him with my eyes. "No!" I explained. "I'll want to stay home and have your babies."

I was in no way fast enough to evade his hands that time and, I suppose I, really in all honesty, didn't want to.

He pulled me into his arms and held me tightly. "You don't want to have my babies?"

I chuckled through my tears and leaned my head on his broad shoulder. "Not yet!"

## Epilogue

After my third orgasm, Jack told me of his plan to rebuild his unit with his new identity. He had months of work to catch up on, and an entire unit to build from the ground up, which meant that he'd be in the states for a long spell. I liked that idea. I also liked his suggestion that we take another long Hawaiian vacation before I figure out what I want to do with my life.

I asked about Serena, Kaia and Gilbert.

"Just Gil," he said after suckling my collarbone. "The rest have either been killed, disavowed…"

I grabbed his hand off my naked boob. "That's really true?"

He looked at me funny. "What's true?"

"Disavowed, like in Mission Impossible. Ving Rhames was disavowed in the first movie, remember?"

I felt his laughter even before it erupted from his wide smile. "You watch too many movies, babe."

"Sorry," I kissed his neck and begged him to finish his story.

"Anyway, as I was saying, the rest have either been disavowed, or have voluntarily taken on new identities and moved on. It's something we all do from time to time anyway."

"And so who killed Grady? Where does he really fit into all this?"

"That would have been Liza." His jaw clenched. "Our objective was to keep Grady safe, get the information we needed and lure the Cartel to the island, where the DEA was waiting to pick up the hit-man. Liza took matters into her own hands once she found out about Grady's real identity."

"And who leaked that?"

"The cartel has ways."

I felt that familiar tingly sensation in the pit of my stomach that told me I was getting close to another fantastic, erotic moment of bliss. I gasped and sucked in a well-needed breath.

He paused and stopped rocking for a minute to look into my eyes. Perched above my chest supported by his elbows, he lifted his weight off my chest and burrowed his hands into my hair. "And I promise, not to have a bunch of gorgeous women in the unit this time, just you," he said with a long drawn out sigh. He then resumed his rhythmic lovemaking until I squealed.

"Really?" I whimpered.

He winked.

I moaned.

He groaned.

Then we slept.

~~~

I woke up after a couple hours of peaceful slumber, encompassed by his warm body. I shivered and sat straight up in bed, clutching the sheet to my chest.

"What is it?" he grumbled, sleepily and wrapped his arms around me, pulling me back against him in bed.

"What about The Rat's son? Is he still after me?"

"Can we talk about this in the morning?"

"No!" I said. "I had a bad dream. I hate rats! Tell me now."

"He's never going to bother you again."

"How can you be so sure?" I shuddered and surreptitiously rubbed my gunshot wound. Remembering how much I dislike near-death experiences.

"Because," he said, snuggling me closer. "He had a boating accident and is somewhere at the bottom of the Adriatic."

"Oh," I replied. "So, it was him all along. What did he want?"

"You," he said candidly. "Dead."

"Oh," I replied again. "I guess I owe you my life."

"No, you can thank Russo for that one."

"No!" I sat up. "But…"

He pulled me back down and kissed me softly. I felt his parts trying to connect with my parts. The man was insatiable. "Russo didn't want you to worry, but he had been notified that Ferdinand was on his way to the US just after The

Rat was killed in prison. Ferdinand sent your underwear back and then he sent you the rest of your things, but then he disappeared when you came to the Bahamas. Russo's men lost him, but he kept his eye on your place anyway. When you were in Orlando and got the basket of Rats, that wasn't Ferdinand's doing, that was Craig."

"DEA guy! Why?" I closed my eyes in appreciation of his subtle movements.

"Craig and I go way back. Back to Marine boot camp. We're still close. He knew all about your little adventure abroad last summer because I told him over beers one night in Los Angeles. He knew that you were receiving strange Rat gifts so when Grady and Randy were killed and I disappeared, he figured his best bet of finding me was to go through you. Craig went off the deep end when Grady was killed. They were pretty tight and he somewhat blamed me for his death. That's why Craig tried to get you to rat me out." He kissed me swiftly. "That's why you got the gift in Orlando and that's where Joey fucked up."

"Because Joey thought Craig was the bad guy when he saw him in Orlando."

"Precisely," he said with a moan. "It wasn't until you came to Greece that Ferdinand caught back up to you. It was his men that tried to run you off the road in Bulgaria."

"And so, who blew up my car?" I asked with wide eyes. "Craig?"

"Liza."

"Oh." My stomach tied in knots at the mere mention of her name.

His hand clutched my naked waist and he kissed my shoulder with a tender, featherlike kiss. "I'm so sorry."

"It's okay," I, in turn, melted against his soft lips. "I learned something."

"What's that?" I could tell he was amused by my tone.

"Trust no one."

He chuckled and we resumed our comfortable lovemaking.

Later as I dozed off to sleep, it dawned on me that I shouldn't have been so pre-occupied with Rats and kept my eyes wide open for a more dangerous rodent...The Mole.

Printed in the United States
140807LV00002B/55/P